RETURN TO
MCCALL

By the Author

McCall

London

Innis Harbor

Last First Kiss

Wild Wales

Laying of Hands

Return to McCall

Visit us at www.boldstrokesbooks.com

RETURN TO MCCALL

by

Patricia Evans

2023

RETURN TO McCALL

ISBN 13: 978-1-63679-386-3

This Trade Paperback Original Is Published By
Bold Strokes Books, Inc.
P.O. Box 249
Valley Falls, NY 12185

First Edition: March 2023

CREDITS
EDITOR: BARBARA ANN WRIGHT
PRODUCTION DESIGN: STACIA SEAMAN
COVER DESIGN BY TAMMY SEIDICK

Acknowledgments

A huge thank you to Brenda Trobaugh and LJ Hooper, who have helped me immeasurably on both *Return to McCall* and *Last First Kiss*. Your expertise and experience with law enforcement and firearms made these books what they are, and I treasure your friendship.

This book is dedicated to Michelle O'Keeffe,
who has no idea how beautiful she is, inside and out.

And Jennifer Pettijohn, who reflects the shimmering courage
of a thousand female warriors that came before her.

CHAPTER ONE

A spicy waft of cinnamon enveloped Sam Draper as she opened the door of Moxie Java, cradling the phone between her face and shoulder as she searched her jacket pocket for her wallet. "I'm here now, babe, and it smells like they have those amazing cinnamon rolls. Want me to drop one by the restaurant before I head back to the station?"

Sam pulled her wallet from her pocket as she said a quick good-bye to her wife, Sara, and dropped the phone back into her jacket. For once, there was no line at Moxie Java, the only coffee shop in the tiny mountain town of McCall, Idaho. Sam congratulated herself on her timing as she spied their famous cinnamon rolls dripping with cream cheese frosting on a cooling tray behind the counter.

"Good morning, Heather." Sam smiled at the teenager behind the counter, who stared back blankly, her face strangely pale and tense. "I'll take two of those beauties behind you and a large black coffee."

Heather bit her lip and stood stiffly in place, an unattended lock of bright teal hair falling across her face, her eyes locked over Sam's shoulder. The walls seemed to echo Sam's words, bouncing them across the café, then watching as they drifted slowly to the floor, reverberating in the hollow silence. The tension in the air settled onto Sam's shoulders as she instinctively shifted her focus. Her eyes flicked to Heather's hand, stiff and motionless by her side except for the single finger pointing to the left. Sam shifted her face into neutral and turned slowly where she stood, keeping her gaze soft and steady as it settled onto another thin teenage girl. This one held a Glock semiautomatic weapon, her hands shaking, her finger pulled tight against the trigger.

Sam studied the girl's red-rimmed eyes and uneven black hair haphazardly tucked behind one ear. She wore glasses with a crack down the center of the left lens and had a tense grip on the gun. Too tense.

"Hey there." Sam kept her voice soft and wished that she'd worn her service weapon while off duty for the first time in her career. "Take it easy. My name is Sam."

The girl shook her head slightly as if to discard Sam's words, then jerked her head toward the sound of a young boy coughing in one of the window seats. His mother pulled him closer and whispered in his ear, looking frantically out the window before wrapping him in her jacket.

Sam took a quick glance around at the situation. Moxie Java was at about half-capacity, about fifteen people in the building, including herself and the staff behind the counter. Everyone was staring, their eyes darting back and forth between her and the gun pointed in her direction, including a portly deputy in a beige Ada County Sheriff's Department uniform handcuffed to the back of his chair. His shiny bald head was slick with sweat, and his wrist strained against the metal rungs as he stared at the gun.

Sam turned back to the shooter and softened her gaze. "Look, why don't you tell me why you're doing this? There has to be a reason." She paused, watching the girl's eyes fill with tears that were quickly blinked back. "What's going on?"

"Stop talking!" Her words were sharp, staccato, and seemed to clatter and fall flat onto the floor in front of her. "I just need her—" The girl paused, then jerked her head toward Heather. "To go lock the damn door so no one else can get in."

Heather waited until Sam nodded, then walked with shaky steps around the counter to lock the door. She hesitated before she went back toward the counter, her eyes still locked on Sam.

"Why the hell is everyone watching *you*?" A touch of panic elevated the girl's voice, and her eyes spun wildly around the room. "I'm the one with the gun."

Silence settled between them. Out of the corner of her eye, Sam caught one of the employees starting to say something, so she jumped in first.

"The rumor is that I look like a tall Tom Cruise." Sam flashed her most charming smile, silently willing the McCall locals to take the hint and not reveal her status as law enforcement. "So that could be it."

"No." The girl studied her with the barest hint of a smile. "That's definitely not it."

One of the bussers behind the counter snorted, and she glared at him, the smile fading quickly from her face. The boy in the window seat started wheezing again as his mother dropped to her knees at the end of the booth, pulling him toward her.

Sam kept her eyes on the girl with the gun. "What's your name?"

"Why?" Her eyes snapped back to Sam. "So you can pretend to care?"

"Look, it sounds like that kid is having an asthma attack. And if he doesn't get out of here and get treatment, things could get real serious, real quick." Sam paused, locking eyes with the shooter. "And I can tell you don't want that to happen."

"Right, so they can go straight to the cops?" Her glance flitted to the ground, then back to the boy. "That's all I need. More police up in here." Her eyes flicked over to the handcuffed deputy, then back to Sam.

Another snort from the teenage busser, and this time, both Sam and the shooter turned to look at him.

"Um…" the busser said, trying not to look at the gun she now had pointed at his head. "Hate to burst your bubble here, but…" His voice trailed off as he nodded in Sam's direction.

"What?" The shooter haphazardly swung the gun back in Sam's direction. This time, it was close enough for Sam to see that the safety was off. "He's a cop?"

Sam was about to answer when several local voices behind them did it for her. In unison. "*She's* a cop."

The gun in her hand sagged slightly as she registered the information, then snapped back up.

"Listen," Sam said softly. "I'd love to return to this fascinating discussion on misgendering butch women, but I think something else is more important." She looked pointedly back to the boy struggling to breathe by the window. His breath had sunk to a low, audible scrape.

"Just go." The shooter's voice was low and soft as she caught his mother's pleading gaze. "Get him outside. But nobody else moves, and you…" She spun the gun toward Heather. "Lock the door behind her."

The mom scooped him up in her arms and carried him to the door, followed by a nauseated-looking Heather, who quickly unlocked the door to let them out, then locked it behind them. She walked back toward the counter, lifting her eyes to the girl only once. "She said to tell you thank you."

For just an instant, the girl's face softened before she pulled it back to stone.

"Look, unless you want me to start calling you Moxie, you need to tell me your name." Sam paused. "It's not too late to get out of this, but we're going to have to work together for that to happen."

The girl kept the gun trained on Sam but lowered one stiff hand and shook it out. The busser chose that moment to pick up one of the cinnamon rolls and leisurely fold half of it into his mouth, icing dripping onto the front of his apron.

"All right. Moxie it is." Sam turned her attention back to the girl and took a slow breath. "You need to let the rest of these guys go. Whatever you want, they don't have it. So let's simplify things here."

The last of Sam's words were drowned out by sudden shouting from the deputy, who'd decided now was a good time to get up, wave his one free hand around, and act a damn fool. "Goddammit! I've *had* it!" He attempted to drag the chair toward the front of the restaurant, his face fury red and spitting with every word. "All I had to do was get one lousy delinquent from point A to point B, and I'll be damned if I'm going to let that little thieving Mexican bitch make me look like a—"

Moxie's face was expressionless as she trained the red laser sight at the deputy's head with a look serious enough to make everyone but the deputy duck under the nearest table. Dust floated in the wide beam of silent sunlight between them, and everyone watched the next move in the deputy's master plan, which was to stand in the middle of the floor and wet himself, apparently.

It was all Sam could do not to roll her eyes as she turned back to the girl. "Listen, Moxie." Soft sounds of crying and true panic had started from every direction as Sam paused, choosing her words carefully. "We've got to get everybody out of here. I'm not going to be able to help you fix this and closer to what you want if that gun goes off."

"Why do you think I want something? Why does everybody always think that?" Moxie lowered her gun and swiped at a tear with the heel of her hand. "'Cause I don't. I just can't go to one more stupid house." She paused to draw in a shaky breath. "I can't. And I'm sure as hell not going to where that guy just tried to take me."

Sam looked out the expansive front windows of Moxie Java at the officers running up to the building in formation, guns in the low ready position. Her brother-in-law Murphy brought up the rear and signaled them to surround the building. Sam caught his eye through the glare of the window as he held his hand to his face in the phone sign.

"Listen, if you put that gun down long enough for me get these people to safety, it'll be just you and me. We can figure out how to get past this."

"Yeah, right." Moxie glanced up, suddenly looking very young and completely exhausted. "How do I know you're not trying to trick me?"

Sam shook her head, her voice soft. "I don't trick people, Moxie. That's just not my style."

"Yep, that's true." The same busser finished the last of his cinnamon roll and swiped at the icing of the next one with his finger. "Draper's good people. Everyone knows that."

Sam turned back to Moxie and lifted an eyebrow in a silent question. Moxie slowly lowered her gun and stepped back as Sam stepped into action, informing the officers outside of the plan with a quick call and making the exit process as smooth as possible. Everyone but the deputy was out the door in under sixty seconds until the busboy stopped to swipe one of the chocolate muffins out of the display box.

"Oh, for the love of God, man." Sam signaled him out the door, trying not to laugh despite herself. "Step on it!"

His hair flopped into his face, and he grinned as he passed her, tucking a sugar cookie into the chest pocket of his shirt.

Finding the keys and unlocking the fuming deputy's handcuffs took forever, and Sam walked him to the door to put as much distance as possible between him and Moxie. He jerked from her grasp and out the door, shouting more of the same tone-deaf obscenities. It was all she could do to not slam the door behind him.

When she got back to the front of the shop, Moxie was sitting on the floor, the gun still cocked, but it was now lying quietly in her lap. Sam got a takeaway cup of water from behind the counter and set it on the floor a few feet away. When she raised her head to speak, Sam noticed a smattering of caramel freckles across her nose.

"Why are you being so nice to me?"

"I've been in law enforcement a long time. Long enough to know this isn't what you want to be doing." Sam steeled herself against the smile she felt forming on her face. "So tell me, how did you get away from the Deputy of the Year over there?"

Moxie's face melted into her first smile, at least until she saw the officers with their guns pointed at the glass door.

Sam's phone buzzed, and she checked it, then held it up. "It's the officers outside. They need an update. Is that okay?"

"Whatever." Exhaustion softened the edges of her words as she dragged a hand through her hair. "Just tell them to back the hell up."

Sam phoned one of the officers. The second Murphy picked up, he asked her if anyone was hurt. Sam said no, feeling the burn of Moxie's stare as she glanced in her direction. Murphy paused, then asked if Sam wanted the officers to hold their position until otherwise instructed. Sam hesitated before she said yes. She was betting on her ability to get through to this girl, but she was very aware that that's exactly what it was. A bet, one she could lose in a split second.

Sam slipped the phone back into her pocket. Moxie traced the lines of the gun with her finger, then tipped her face to the ceiling. A tear slipped off her chin and onto the black barrel in a silent splash.

Sam looked around until she found what she knew would be there. A rumpled black trash bag stuffed to the top and slumped against the table leg where the deputy had been cuffed. "So," she said, waiting until Moxie met her eyes. "Foster kid, huh?"

"What?" Her eyes locked onto Sam's in a look of delayed shock. "How'd you know that?"

Sam nodded at the limp bag leaning against the side of one of the tables. "Your fancy luggage kinda gave that away."

She nodded, swiping at another tear with the heel of her hand. "Yeah. I feel like I live out of those."

Sam nodded, noting the bruise on her cheekbone that had faded to a greenish-yellow outline. "So the deputy was taking you to your next placement?"

Moxie nodded, then reached for the water and drank it greedily with a shaking hand, as if she'd just remembered she was thirsty. Afterward, she crushed the cup, sinking it into the corner trash like a pro.

"You play?"

"I did. I was at my last place for my first two years of high school." Moxie shook her head, still staring at the trash where the cup had disappeared. "I made the varsity team, but who knows now? I don't even know where they're sending me."

"So just a sudden shift, huh?"

Moxie nodded, her eyes fluttering closed for just a second before she tightened her grip on the gun in her lap.

Sam nodded toward her. "Something to do with that bruise on your cheek?"

Moxie's fingers rose slowly to the side of her face. "How could you possibly know that?"

"It doesn't take a genius to figure out a shiner like that and a new foster placement at the same time means trouble." She softened her voice and met Moxie's eyes. "You get in a fight?"

"Nah. Not really." Moxie shook her head. "My foster mom caught her new man picking the lock on my bedroom door a couple of nights ago and decided she needed to remind me who he belonged to."

"Yeah, she doesn't want to lose that one." Sam rolled her eyes to the ceiling. "He sounds like a straight-up prize."

That made Moxie laugh, and the tears had cleared from her eyes by the time she looked up. "Hey, didn't I hear you tell someone that you were bringing them a cinnamon roll?"

"Yep, my wife, Sara." Sam smiled. "She owns the restaurant across the street."

Moxie nodded, clicking the safety back into place. "Gus's Place or something, right? I saw it as we came into town."

"Exactly. Sara makes the most amazing food, but I've got to be honest, she'd trade me in a heartbeat for a Moxie Java cinnamon roll. And I'm not sure I blame her."

The girl glanced at the trash bag across the dining room. "What are they going to do with me out there? When we leave?"

Sam got up slowly, retrieved the bag, and set it down between them as she helped Moxie to her feet. "You're worried about your stuff, aren't you?"

She nodded. "Yeah, it's kinda everything I own."

Sam looked out the window at the officers, who lowered their guns slowly in response to her signal. "Listen, here's what's going to happen.

First, I'm going to wrap up a cinnamon roll for Sara. Frankly, I'm scared of what'll happen if I don't, and then we'll walk out there together. But no matter what, I won't let anyone touch your stuff, okay?"

Moxie looked up, worry fading from her eyes as she carefully handed Sam the gun. "Thanks for being so nice to me. You didn't have to be, especially with me threatening to shoot the place up and everything."

"So how old are you? Really?" Sam laid a ten-dollar bill on the counter and dropped the only cinnamon roll the busboy hadn't touched into a bag.

"Fifteen." She hesitated, starting to say something twice before it fell out in a rush. "And you're a real cop? No offense, but you don't seem like one."

"Well, you got me there, Moxie." Sam sent a quick text to the officers outside to let them know the suspect had been disarmed, and they were on the way out. "I'm not a cop. I'm McCall's Chief of Police."

CHAPTER TWO

L ily Larimar slammed the car door shut and leaned back against the headrest, kneading her forehead with tense fingertips as she fought back the memories of the book signing from the previous night.

A random woman grabbed my ass in public? Seriously? Lily rolled her eyes and wished for the tenth time that the water bottle in her console was vodka. *Who does that?*

Lily pulled swiftly into the sun-soaked LA traffic on the way to the airport and ignored her agent's frantic texts pinging the phone she'd just tossed into the passenger seat. She'd skipped out on the meet and greet after her book signing the previous night; everyone was expecting her to be there, smiling and charming the readers, but being grabbed by random strangers was where Lily drew the line. Her ninth novel, *Embers into Fire*, had dropped a few weeks ago, and she'd been doing nothing all month but signings and personal appearances at all the lesbian hot spots in Southern California.

The last few days had been a blur of gin-soaked conversations with overeager singletons and pitches from "industry insiders" who all seemed to want to break off a piece of her mind and take it home with them. Promotion was part of her job, but it was the part she hated. And it had gotten significantly worse after her agent booked her a couple of guest spots on *The L Word: Generation Q*; suddenly, she felt like she couldn't go anywhere without someone recognizing her.

Lily blew a lock of hair out of her face and focused her attention back on the road. She was due in Toronto tonight for the TIFF film festival to meet a director interested in turning one of her books into a movie, and her flight left in just a few hours from LAX. The glare of midmorning sun slid like liquid gold across her windshield as her phone buzzed again with another call from her agent. She turned to click it off and realized the next second that she'd missed her exit. Lily slowed, watching cars whiz past her on both sides before forcing herself to accelerate back into the crush of commuters. She'd take the next exit and circle back, but she needed to switch her phone off if she had a hope of making it to the airport alive in this traffic.

She had just reached for her phone again when a sky-blue Maserati slid like sudden water into her lane and cut her off as she tried to pull back into traffic. That's when she felt it starting. Again. Her seat belt was tightening across her chest with every breath, and a fine mist of chilled sweat broke out over her face and neck. She fumbled in her purse for the pills her doctor had given her after her last panic attack, then remembered she'd taken the last one stashed in her purse that morning and had packed the rest into her suitcase, which was impossible to reach now that she was in the middle of eight lanes of cutthroat traffic. She glanced behind at the densely packed cars and counted the minutes until the airport exit would appear on her right.

Just breathe in and out.

Lily whispered the words through the warm salt of tears on her lips. Everything about her life was overwhelming now, and as much as she tried to push that fact to the back of her mind, it seemed her body was hell-bent on reminding her. All the yoga, meditation, and green juice in LA weren't going to fix the fact that she hated being looked at and talked to and just…crowded every minute of the day. She'd become the product her publishers were selling just as much as her words on paper, and the harder they pushed, the more the real Lily Larimar shrank until even she couldn't picture who she was before. It was like she'd just disappeared.

The sign for LAX loomed with a sudden shout over a semi-truck to her right, and she swerved just in time to squeal into the exit on what felt like two tires. Her heart was still pounding in her throat as she followed the signs to the parking garage and circled up several floors to the open-air top level. It was almost deserted, just a single dented Buick LeSabre in the far corner slot surrounded by the late afternoon heat, shimmering like a desert mirage just above the concrete surface.

Lily threw off her seat belt and jumped out, gulping in the air and open space around her. The hot metal of the car door slid down her back as she sank to the stained concrete beside the car. Tears stung her eyes, and Lily felt the air being squeezed from her chest as if the life she'd never wanted was getting heavier by the second. She didn't have the breath to scream; the only option was to lean forward, cement and gravel cutting into her palms, and remind herself that she was safe, that no one was watching. For the moment, anyway.

It was twenty minutes before Lily finally stood and noticed her gold filigree bracelet still on the ground. She'd bought it four years ago, the day her first novel was released, and hadn't taken it off since. The gold felt heavy and too warm against her fingers as she picked it up. The sun was setting now, dripping past the concrete edge of the parking structure, and the last of the deep orange glow melted into the bracelet links as Lily closed her fist around it. She felt deliciously alone for the first time in forever and stared into the horizon as she walked to the edge of the parking deck.

There was no one there to watch as she leaned against the safety wall and uncurled her fist. No one else felt the liquid slip of the gold falling from her fingers or watched her close her eyes to listen for the metallic clink against the pavement below. The gold cage that had circled her wrist for the last few years had disappeared as silently as if it was never there.

The last of the molten sun slipped out of sight as Lily tilted her face up to the darkening violet sky and drew in the first cool, deep breath of her own air.

❖

Sara Draper swiped a floury hand across her forehead as she opened the door to the oven and was suddenly awash in a savory cloud of potpie-scented steam.

"Damn, girl. I'd have married you myself if Sam hadn't beat me to it." Mary winked at Sara as she popped the top on a cold beer bottle, staring with impatient longing at the golden crust of the chicken potpie Sara slid onto the prep counter in Gus's Place. "I said it at your wedding, and I'll say it again: I'm still not convinced she deserves you."

"Well, at least I'm good for something."

Sara shed her oven mitt and scooped up the flurry of blond waves that now reached to the middle of her back, twisting them into a hurried bun before she went for Mary's beer and took a long swig. It had been five years since she'd landed in McCall, still reeking of smoke from the fire that had burned down her riverfront restaurant in Savannah, Georgia. Mary was her first friend in McCall, and they'd grown even closer over the years, which was why Mary sat back on her stool and put down her fork when she saw Sara reach for her beer.

"Oh, honey. I'm so sorry—" Mary stopped abruptly when Sara held up her hand. After five years of friendship, she knew when to change tack. "On second thought." Mary reached into the prep fridge under the counter and popped the top on another beer. "Talking is overrated. I'm just going to dig into that pie and burn the tar out of my mouth as the good Lord intended."

Sara put the bottle down on the counter a little too hard and managed a weak smile. "I was only four weeks this time." Her voice cracked as she laid the palm of her hand over her belly. "It wasn't as bad."

"Wasn't that bad, my ass." Mary held out her arms. "That shit hurts. I know it does."

Sara smiled as she walked around the corner of the prep table and sank gratefully into the hug. She and Sam had been attempting in vitro fertilization since they'd gotten married three years prior, and every round had either failed or she'd suffered a miscarriage after the first few weeks. She'd never really thought about having children until she'd met Sam, but once they'd decided to start a family, she couldn't think of anything else.

"I'm getting past my prime anyway, age-wise." Sara stood and dried her eyes with the edge of her sleeve, selecting a knife out of her chef's roll to cut the perfectly cooled pie. "I'll be thirty-eight next month. I need to give it up."

"Well, I'm calling bullshit on that too." Mary held out a wide, shallow bowl. "I had my youngest at forty-three, and you know it. So don't you dare give up. Both of you have so much love to give." Mary winked at her and gave the steaming pie in front of her a loving look as she lifted the flaky crust and admired the creamy gravy and tender vegetables underneath.

Sara watched, finally cracking her bright, trademark smile. "What do you think? I'm thinking of doing five or six of these for the locals' dinner this Sunday." Mary held up her hand for silence and closed her eyes as she savored the first bite, making Sara laugh hard enough to reach for her napkin and dab at her eyes. "Mary, I swear, a fresh potpie is no less than a religious experience for you." Sara smiled as she dished up her bowl and climbed onto the stool she'd dragged over to the prep counter.

Gus's Place, her modern spin on a retro diner, had become the heart of the little town of McCall, Idaho, in the five years it had been open, and Sara fell more in love with it every day. She still closed every Sunday afternoon for family dinner, which was really just a big potluck for the tiny mountain town's colorful locals. Mary, who had become convinced cell phones would be the inevitable death of polite society, had started collecting them at the door at some point and holding them hostage, and it had only brought the town closer. Everyone from teenagers to seniors crowded into the diner right on time on Sunday afternoon, carrying foil-covered casseroles and side dishes. Sara always provided the main course, and the next few hours flew by in a familiar flurry of laughter, hugs, and local gossip. There had been a couple of marriage proposals over the years, one near fight over the last slice of Sara's French silk chocolate pie, and more than a few friendships started and deepened amid the warmth of Sunday afternoons at Gus's Place.

Mary broke off a piece of the hand-rolled piecrust and peered over her glasses. "How has the retreat been going this summer? The second session starts tomorrow at Lake Haven, right?" She popped the crust into her mouth and picked her fork back up to spear a tender piece of chicken from Sara's dish.

"Hey!" Sara's last sip of beer almost flew out of her mouth with laughter as she slid her plate out of Mary's grasp. "You've got your own!"

"Sara, I've told you this a thousand times." Mary savored the chicken and picked up her beer with a satisfied sigh. "What's yours is mine when it comes to your cooking."

Sara dished her up a second helping, then laid a warm hand on Mary's shoulder as she sat back down. "There. That should hold you off for a bit."

"Seriously, though, has it been easier than last summer? You guys hired a camp director for this season, right?"

"Yep, that's Charlotte. Once we got the property renovated with the waterfront cabins and main lodge, we were at a loss about what to actually do with people when they got there last summer, so she's been a big help. She could run a country if she had the chance." Sara paused, pushing a pea around on her plate with her fork. "Everyone loves her."

Mary glanced up, obviously avoiding asking the question that hung in the air between them, which Sara was thankful for. "Well, I think a retreat center for lesbian couples is genius. They get to be on that gorgeous property and just focus on each other for a while."

"And this year, on top of waterfront activities and tons of classes, we also have a chef who does family style meals, an on-site couples counselor, and a Latin dance instructor." Sara brightened and bumped Mary's shoulder. "Too bad you refuse to date anyone. I think our new dance instructor might sway you over to our side."

"Oh, I saw her, I think. She wandered into the drugstore the other day during *Days of Our Lives*. I'd forgotten to lock the damn door, as usual." Mary popped the last forkful of piecrust into her mouth and winked. "Tall, dark, and handsome, right? Let's just say I turned off the TV and showed her where the Band-Aids were."

"I knew it!" Sara laughed as she reached for her napkin and pushed her dish away. "I told Sam when we hired her that no one would be able to resist that charm, even—"

Sara's last words were drowned out by a loud pounding that sounded like it was about to shatter the front door. Sara jumped off her stool and ran out to the dining room, feeling the color drain from her face when she saw her sister, Jennifer, on the other side of the glass doors.

Mary swept her aside, then pulled Jennifer through the door with one swift movement, sitting her on a nearby chair before she could get a word out. "What is it? Is it the baby?" Mary's words tangled together in a rush of sudden panic as she laid a protective hand on Jennifer's pregnant belly. "How far apart are your contractions?"

Jennifer burst into laughter, pulling up a chair for Mary beside her, who, by this time, seemed completely out of breath. "Mary, you've got to relax! You've been thinking I'm going into labor every time I so much as sneeze."

"Actually, since the moment you and Murphy announced you were pregnant." Sara wrapped her arms around her sister's shoulders and hugged her. "Well, I'm on Mary's side with this one. You were banging on the door like the world was on fire, and your due date is getting close. What's up?"

Mary clasped a hand over her heart and took a deep breath. "I swear on everything holy, Jennifer. You're going to give me a heart attack before that little guy finally makes an appearance."

Jennifer squeezed Mary's hand with obvious affection before she went on. "I mean, I know the diner closes at three, and you two usually have a late lunch in the back, but have you seriously not seen what's going on down at the coffee shop?"

Mary and Sara got up and pressed their faces against the glass as they looked down the street toward Moxie Java. Mary finally opened the door and stuck out her head. "What the hell is going on down there? They've got everything roped off, and every officer in town is outside."

"Sam was supposed to be here ages ago with a cinnamon roll. I forgot all about it." Sara pulled out her cell phone and dialed Sam's number with shaky fingers. It rang only once before Sam picked up. Sara held her breath, fear settling heavy on her chest and preventing her from drawing another until she heard Sam's voice.

"Baby, I'm fine. We had a little situation at Moxie Java, but everything is handled."

Sara turned toward the kitchen and spoke closer into the phone. "Are you sure? You sound out of breath. I don't like this."

A gentle knock behind her made her turn to see Sam, tall and handsome in her uniform, holding up a Moxie Java bag outside the door. Sara ran to the door and fell into Sam's arms, hugging her a little harder than usual, only letting go when she thought to ask what the hell was going on. Sam didn't speak, just cradled her face in both hands and kissed her slowly, brushing Sara's lips with hers at the end as if she couldn't bear to let her go.

Mary rolled her eyes and took another look out the window. "Yeah, this is cute and all, but will someone tell me what the hell is going on before I have to go down there myself?"

That was enough to make everyone laugh, but Sam's phone started ringing as she opened her mouth to answer. Sam only had a moment to skim over the details before she clicked on her phone and raised it to her ear as she headed back toward Moxie Java with a quick promise to share more later. She blew a kiss to Sara and pointed at her watch before she turned and jogged back down the street where Murphy, Jennifer's husband, was taking up the traffic blockade.

"What did she mean by that?" Jennifer said, eyeing the Moxie Java bag in Sara's hand.

"It's our shorthand. She won't be home till late." Sara smiled and handed the bag to her sister. "Here, it's all yours. I can't even think about eating."

Mary squinted her disapproval. "You know I'm only allowing this handover because you're pregnant." She closed her eyes as she continued. "Otherwise, that sweet, sweet pastry of God would have been all mine."

Sara and Jennifer turned, already laughing. Sara had anticipated exactly that sentiment.

"What?" Mary said with a sniff. "What are all the kids saying these days? I'm just keeping it real."

Lily rolled the window down to take in the White River falling and crashing over boulders as she took the narrow, winding road beside it up the mountain from Boise to McCall. Afternoon was falling into evening as it did only in the mountains, and the air had cooled to a shimmering blue as she neared the summit. She opened the skylight of her bright green rental Jeep to take in the blaze of copper streaks and shades of melting sienna hovering just past the evergreens lining both sides of the road.

She glanced at her phone just as it lit up for the hundredth time in the passenger's seat. This time, she finally felt far enough from LA to pick it up.

"Lily, what the hell are you doing?" her agent screeched. "I've been trying to reach you all day! You can't just walk out of a meet and greet. Do you know how hard it was to spin that so everyone wasn't pissed off?"

"I did that because I had to." Lily paused for a long moment, choosing her words carefully. "Clyde, the next book will be on time. It will be good. Better, even, than the ones before it. But you have to give me some space. I need to go home for a while."

"Boise fucking Idaho? Are you kidding me with this?" A long sigh underscored his mounting irritation. "What could you possibly need in Idaho that you can't find in Cali-fucking-fornia?"

"No, Clyde, I'm not kidding."

He started to speak but seemed to think better of it, the silence settling heavy and sudden between them. Lily started to feel her chest tighten again before she remembered where she was and drew in a deep breath.

"Besides, I'm not going to Boise." She almost smiled as a white-tailed deer took off into the woods. "I'm going home. To McCall."

She hung up before he could reply and turned off her phone, tossing it back onto the seat beside her. Dropping everything to go back to McCall, even with her plan to rock up unannounced at her ex's new retreat center, made a lot more sense than talking to Clyde for one more second. She couldn't keep doing the same things she'd done for the last five years and expect things to change, even if she didn't know what the change would be.

She turned onto McCall's main street as the last of the twilight sank into darkness, and the streetlights clicked on. Everything looked exactly as it had the last time she'd seen it: Mary's drugstore with the handwritten Closed sign hanging slightly off-center against the glass door; Gus's Place, looking even homier now with its shiny newness sanded down along the edges with love scuffs; and of course, Moxie Java, her favorite spot in the world to sit and write. As she passed it, something new behind it caught her eye. She turned right at the corner and saw a log cabin with an expansive stone patio strung with tiny copper lanterns glowing with golden light. Tables lined the wood railing at the edges of the deck, each with a cast-iron cauldron in the middle and a glass jar of marshmallows to one side.

Lily got out, watching as a server with a turquoise ponytail and bright orange flannel shirt placed a handful of kindling and a couple of mini logs in each cauldron and carefully lit them before moving to the next table.

She looked up as Lily stepped onto the patio. "Aren't these the cutest? We just got them."

Lily glanced up at the split-log sign above the door. *The Other Place.* Clever. "How long has this place been here?"

"Less than a year." The server retrieved more tiny split cedar logs from the pile stacked against the wall and tucked them under her arm.

"The owner came here to ski last winter and fell in love with McCall." She looked around, her bright ponytail swishing across her back. "She said the only thing it needed was a bar. So she opened one."

"Well, she's a genius. I used to live here, and the only time everyone got together for a drink was Wine and Fire on Sunday nights at Moxie." Lily zipped her black puffer vest up over her faded denim shirt, looking back over her shoulder at the coffee shop behind them. "Do they still do that, by the way?"

"Oh yeah. This place closes Sunday afternoon so the staff can go to the locals' dinner at the diner, then most folks just wander over to Wine and Fire once Mary starts giving their phones back." She paused to brush some bark off her sleeve and roll it up. "It's a thing."

Lily started to ask what she meant, but people were beginning to fill the tables on the patio, and Candy, according to the name tag on her flannel, excused herself to get their orders before they started lighting their menus on fire. Lily hesitated, then clicked the lock on her rental Jeep and walked into the bar.

Glossy split-cedar walls glimmered under the lights of the enormous antler chandelier, with red buffalo plaid couches in muted shades of cranberry and black framing an expansive bar along the far wall. A few tables and chairs were scattered around, but other than that, Lily was reasonably sure she'd just walked into Ralph Lauren's living room.

The bartender, a younger guy with a Bieber swoosh of hair low on his forehead, placed a black leather coaster on the bar as she sat. "What can I get you?"

"Whiskey." Lily shrugged off her down vest and laid it over the stool to her left. "Neat."

He nodded and picked up a bottle off the top shelf, filled a rocks glass with a high pour, and placed it on the leather coaster. Lily brought it to her nose, drew a long, deep breath, and let her eyes flutter closed as she set it down. The muscles across her shoulders unfolded slowly, and she kneaded the back of her neck with her hand as she drew in the scent of the place.

The logs were new cedar oiled with linseed, which gave them a drier, deeper scent, like August wheat baking in the sun. The bar was antique, silent, and stately under layers of luminous mahogany lacquer, and the cut crystal of her tumbler pressed its shape into the tips of her fingers as she lifted the glass and took the first sip. Lily memorized its burn, like rising fire, as it slipped down her throat, the echo dry and languid into the back of her nose, leaving behind notes of silky caramel and forgotten smoke.

When she finally opened her eyes, someone was sitting on the stool next to her with an old-school, high-fade haircut. It was a few seconds before a slow smile reached her dark eyes, and she nodded at the bartender. "I'll have what she's having."

Lily smiled before she thought the better of it. "You sure you can handle it? This isn't exactly a piña colada."

The woman held her gaze for a moment, then picked up the glass the bartender placed in front of her. She rolled the whiskey along the sides and took a sip before turning back to Lily. "You don't know me yet, but there's not much I can't handle."

Lily picked up her glass and nodded, relaxing into the slow warmth as it warmed her from the inside out. "You don't exactly sound like a local. Where are you from?" She was usually good at placing accents, but this was one she hadn't heard before. It was smoky and intense, like dark silk sliding over her skin.

The woman flashed a smile and picked up her glass, touching her tongue to the rim before taking a sip and setting it back on the leather coaster. "I immigrated from Cuba when I was seventeen, but I've lived in the States for longer than I was in my home country. I got my citizenship when I was twenty-five."

As she spoke, Lily let her eyes drop to the hand still around the base of the stranger's glass. It was angular and graceful, with subtly masculine fingers. It was clear right away that she was a masculine-presenting woman, but to anyone else, she could easily be mistaken for a tall, intensely attractive guy. Lily made herself look away but realized as she did that for the first time, LA seemed like a million miles away, like an odd, forgotten feeling. She was starting to remember how to relax into the space around her.

"So where did you learn to appreciate good whiskey like that?"

Lily glanced over, but the woman was still examining her glass, and it was a long moment before she met Lily's gaze. Her eyes were a silent brown, like a dark handful of wet, overturned earth, with dense black lashes. Her skin was darker than Lily's by a few shades, and her gaze didn't waver.

"I've always loved whiskey. I even spent a month in Scotland last year taking an immersive course in regional scotch." Lily nodded when the bartender asked if she was ready for another, pushing the glass to the edge of the bar. "When I was younger, everyone around me was drinking endless cans of beer and those fruity wine coolers, but I never could figure out why." She paused. "I like the intensity, I guess."

"Do you work in the industry?"

It took Lily a moment to realize what she meant. "The whiskey industry? God, no." She paused, choosing her next words carefully. "I don't do anything nearly that cool. In fact, I'm not working at all at the moment." The bartender set a fresh drink in front of her, and Lily swirled the whiskey gently up the sides of the glass to let it warm and open up. "What do you do?"

The woman smiled, lifting a subtle finger when the bartender looked her way. The sleeves of her black button-up shirt were rolled to the elbow, revealing tattoos on her lower arms, graceful patterns of shaded, swirling smoke and script in Spanish that was too small to read. Lily watched her muscles flex as she ran a hand through her hair, then reminded herself to get a grip.

"I teach."

Lily snapped back to reality, confused. "What?"

The woman smiled, reaching for her drink as the bartender passed it in her direction. "You asked me what I do. I teach."

"Oh God. I could never do that."

For some reason, this seemed to amuse her. "And why is that?"

Lily ran her finger around the rim of the tumbler and tried to put the words together. "I don't know. I guess people are too much for me sometimes." She paused, an unfamiliar thought flashing across her mind. *Maybe I should just say it out loud. I'll never see her again.* "It feels like everyone wants something from me, I guess. It's... exhausting." The whiskey burned like slow fire as Lily met her eyes. "That's more than anyone gets out of me, and I don't even know your name."

"Alex." She smiled and turned toward her on the stool. "And I tend to have that effect on women."

"Noted." Lily flashed her a smile and reminded herself to breathe. "Nice to meet you, Alex."

"So, are you hungry?"

Lily shot her a look. "There'd better be food here. Otherwise, you're just teasing me, and I will retaliate."

Alex threw her head back and laughed. Everything about her was deep: her voice, her energy, her laugh, even the way she moved. She waved the bartender over and asked for something Lily didn't recognize, but the truth was, she didn't care. The place was starting to fill up for the evening, and a cluster of lit ivory candles appeared at each end of the bar. Sultry Creole Jazz clicked on in the background as Lily watched Alex joke with the bartender.

When was the last time I felt this relaxed?

The last time she remembered feeling that was here in McCall, listening to the rhythmic lap of the lake against the docks or the late-night crackle of the fireplace she used to have on the back porch of her home. Five years ago.

Alex turned back to her, eyes closed. "I love this music. I brought it in one day, and now they play it all the time, thank God. The stuff they used to play made me want to bring headphones."

Lily sipped the last of her whiskey. "You love Creole Jazz? That's random. I'm not sure I believe you."

Alex winked in her direction and downed the last of hers. "And you know what that even is? I'm not sure I believe you, either."

"Prove it." Lily narrowed her eyes. "Who's your favorite soloist?"

Alex laughed again; her eyes lit up like sudden stars in an inky night sky. "You first, Miss Creole Jazz."

They looked at each other, and Lily had the sudden feeling of being one of two warriors in a swordfight, circling. "King Oliver," they said in unison, and Alex brushed her knee lightly with warm fingertips as she laughed.

The bartender placed a cheeseboard, beautifully arranged atop a scarred oak plank, on the bar and asked if they were ready for more drinks.

Lily held up a hand. "I'd better not. I still have to drive at some point."

"Same." Alex nodded, plucking a grape off the silvery red bunch on the end of the board. "I'll stick with water." She folded a thin slice of pale cheese with a peppery edge onto a water cracker, topped it with tapenade, and handed it to Lily.

"What is this?"

"Just taste it. If you like it, I'll tell you."

Lily bit into the cracker and closed her eyes, savoring the nutty rush of flavor that seemed to melt instantly on her tongue. The mellow sweetness lasted only an instant, then disappeared under the briny bite of the olives. "God, I love it." Lily opened her eyes and picked up the other half of the cracker. "What is that?"

"I lied. I'm not telling you."

Lily smacked Alex's knee lightly and rolled her eyes. "Fine. Tell me what you love about the music, then."

Alex thought for a moment, picked up her water glass, then set it down without drinking. There was something faraway in her eyes, like the memory of a place she'd never see again. "It reminds me of Cuban street music, I think. Although, stylistically, that and Creole Jazz are almost nothing alike. Cuban music is all about voice and the strings and percussion carry it. Creole is primarily brass, that sharp, signature…"

Lily let her search for the word before she gave it to her. "Coronet?"

"Yes! That's it, although Louis Armstrong was the standout on that. But they both have that low country sway, you know?"

"I know." Lily nodded, tracing the edge of the board with her finger. "Like evening settling over the streets in Havana. There's always the sound of falling water like drums in the background, and music spilling out of the cafés on San Rafael Boulevard on the way to go—"

"Dancing barefoot in Neptuno Parque?" Alex leaned back slightly, her eyes intense. "How do you know about that?"

Lily bit her lip and ran a hand through her hair, trying to wrap words around an accidental experience that had shaped the edges of her writing since. "It's a long story, but I went to Havana for a weekend and ended up staying for a month. I fell in love with…I don't know, it's hard to describe. The heartbeat of it, I guess." She looked up as the warmth of Alex's hand settled on her thigh. "I still feel like a part of me is there. I was never the same after."

It was a long moment before Alex spoke. "What did you go there looking for?"

"It was work. I was thinking of setting a b—" Lily stopped, her heart pounding at almost giving away her real life, the one that now suddenly seemed like a memory. "It was just supposed to be a work thing."

Alex held her eyes as Lily slipped her thigh between Alex's knees.

"That's a bold move." Alex's voice was intimate and teasing at the same time. "Especially since you haven't told me your name yet."

Lily smiled, taking a long second to look her up and down. "And what have you done to deserve that?"

"You might have to trust me on this." Alex smiled, gently biting her bottom lip. "But I've got skills worth your name."

"Fine. You can have my name and the answer to one more question." Lily's heart raced as Alex slid a hand up the outside of her thigh. "But this is rare, so choose carefully."

Alex's gaze didn't waver as she spoke. "When was the last time you kissed someone you wanted to melt into?"

"Wow. Well played." Lily took a deep breath when she realized the answer and instantly regretted her offer. "It's been...five years. Since I left McCall last time, actually." She paused, speaking more to herself. "I meet a lot of people with work, too many, and I guess it's just overwhelming sometimes."

"Can I wrap this up for you?"

Lily jumped at the sound of the bartender's voice. She shook the fog from her head as she attempted to pay the bill, but Alex waved it away and gave him her card. After she signed, Alex took her hand and led her through the crowd, and as they walked out into the cool night air, bright stars filtered through the fir trees, the tops brushing slow texture into the lush velvet sky.

Lily pulled her keys out of her pocket and stopped at the Jeep. "This is me."

"It looks like you."

"The Jeep is just a rental." Lily peered over Alex's shoulder at the car next to hers, a restored antique Ford Thunderbird convertible, painted in the classic slick turquoise color with chrome accents and white leather interior. "What I'd really like is a car like that."

Alex turned and leaned into the Thunderbird, pulling the keys from the ashtray and starting it with a flick of her wrist. The engine purred to life and settled into a low, contented rumble as she leaned back against the door.

"You're kidding. This is yours?"

Alex nodded, smoothing her palm lovingly over the shiny chrome strip along the top of the door. "Don't be too impressed. She was a mess when I found her."

"It reminded you of home, didn't it?"

"Exactly. Cuba banned American imports after the fifties, so if you didn't learn to fix up the antiques, you didn't get to drive at all." She switched the car off, then turned back to Lily, lifting her hand and bringing it to her mouth to kiss. "Miss Lily, it was a pleasure. Maybe we'll see each other again one day."

Lily nodded, not trusting herself to speak, then turned toward the Jeep door. She hesitated. She wanted to say something, do anything but leave, but as usual, she had no words. She'd just started to open the door when she felt it shut again. Alex spun her around smoothly and pressed her back against the Jeep, holding her face gently in both hands for just a moment before she brushed Lily's lips with hers. Lily melted against her, and Alex kissed her like heat, like lust, like hot Cuban nights, pulling every inch of her body against the hard lines of her own, hands moving like slow fire from her waist to her neck.

She slowed, finally, then gently bit Lily's bottom lip as she pulled away, holding her eyes before she turned and walked back toward the bar. It was a long few seconds before Lily remembered to draw a breath.

CHAPTER THREE

B y the time Lily pulled into the Lake Haven retreat, the designated parking area was full, so she drove down to the main lodge and parked next to a massive fir tree that silently filtered the moonlight as she zipped up her vest and locked the Jeep. The lodge was a sprawling, two-story log cabin with a wraparound porch, glossy red Adirondack rockers scattered across the split pine porch, and milky-white jars of yellow roses perched on small tables between them. The grounds glowed with warm lights that illuminated the path to the main buildings, then down the slight slope to the lakeshore. The woods to the right of the lodge held a handful of tiny cabins with screened-in porches, each with a green Coleman lantern on an iron hook next to the door.

Lily wasn't sure what she'd been expecting. Maybe nothing; she hadn't even thought about it until she'd boarded the plane out of LA, but this place was unexpectedly gorgeous with its rustic lakefront style. Beyond the lodge, a shimmering path of moonlight sparkled on the water, and Lily fought off an insane urge to run down to the shore, strip off all her clothes, and swim to the barely visible island she knew was on the other side of the water. The air was sharply cold and clean, and she slipped her hands in her pockets as she drew in a breath and held it, unwilling to let it go. She'd been breathing LA smog for the last five years, and she felt the metallic scent of it start to fade as she exhaled.

"Lily?" A husky voice behind her caught her off guard. She spun around to see Sam leaning out of her truck and squinting in her direction. "Is that you?"

Lily nodded, and Sam parked and ran to her, scooping her up in her arms. "What the hell are you doing here? Sara didn't tell me you were coming!"

Lily looked into Sam's dark eyes and hesitated, unsure of how to explain why she was there at all. She realized too late she wasn't prepared to see Sam, and feelings she'd buried years ago rushed toward her like water. She'd never been in love with her, but she'd forgotten how handsome Sam Draper was in person. Even the scent of her, like fresh air, brought back memories of the last time they were together like a silent movie reel jerking to a shaky start in the background. "That's because I didn't tell anyone." She paused, searching for words. Any words. "I mean, I don't even know what I'm doing here. I haven't been in McCall since your wedding. I've kept in touch with Sara, but—"

"She tells me all about your books," Sam cut in. "I'm so glad you two have stayed close."

"Honestly, she's kept me sane for the last few years when I was struggling…" She paused. "With all the parts of being an author that have nothing to do with writing."

Lily felt the tension in her shoulders return with the memory and rubbed her eyes with the pads of her fingers, trying to stave off a sudden headache. Sam pulled her into a hug again, her words gentle against Lily's cheek. "She told me about the panic attacks. That's got to be rough."

Lily nodded, reluctantly thankful for Sam's strong arms around her.

"I know you're a hermit at heart. Fame was never what you wanted." Sam let her go slowly and glanced in the direction of the lodge. "Tomorrow is the first day of our couples retreat. Did you bring someone with you?"

"Oh no." Lily shook her head. The thought that the retreat might be for couples only hadn't even crossed her mind. "I didn't know it was just couples. You're probably totally booked, and I should have called, but I just, I don't know, I…"

Sam smiled. "Lily, you're always welcome here. And Sara is going to be thrilled." She paused, her voice thoughtful. "Actually, this might be perfect timing for her." Lily smiled as Sam pulled the flashlight off her belt and shone it into the woods. "The bears have been relentless this year, though. They must have known you were coming."

Lily smiled, falling into step behind Sam as she led them down to the lodge. The overhead lights lit up the evergreens with a Gothic mix of light and shadow, and a choir of owls cooed in the distance. Before she even knew one was close, it swooped down out of nowhere, almost close enough to touch, its feathers a thousand muted shades of ash and charcoal. She hovered above them for a long second, then glided to rest on the top of the flagpole, turning her head slowly to follow Lily with deep gold eyes.

Sam dropped her voice to a low whisper. "Still charming the locals, I see."

Lily tilted her head to the right, and the owl followed suit, then pierced the air with a deep, resonant hoot as she extended her wings and took off toward the water. The air shifted, and Lily watched her disappear into the darkness before she finally looked toward the lodge door. "So who's in there?"

Sam leaned in to peek through the window. "I have no idea. I've been down at the station all day, so it's a crapshoot, really. Registration is over, but the retreat starts tomorrow, and we have a full house." She turned on the light over the door as she spoke. "It's late, though, way past dinner, so we might get lucky and miss most of them." Sam winked as she opened the door. "But if not, you'll be the only one in there with a personal bodyguard."

Lily laughed and walked through the door Sam held open. The lodge's central area was flooded with golden light and decorated in the same masculine style Lily remembered from the evenings she'd spent in front of the fire at Sam's lake house. Supple leather couches and a sparkling antler chandelier gave the space a ski chalet vibe, along with the custom bookshelves that lined the walls and wide-plank floors creaking underfoot.

"You built all this on the property your dad left you?"

Sam nodded, stopping at an expansive walnut desk in the far corner, illuminated by an oiled bronze mica lamp standing behind it. "Yep, I realized I was never going to sell it, and it seemed a shame not to put it to good use somehow." She searched the key cabinet behind the desk, then slipped two bronze keys onto a brass loop and dropped them into her pocket. She paused, peering out into the darkness through the window next to the desk. The lake shimmered just beyond the shore, and Sam's voice dropped as if she didn't realize she was speaking. "Something's still missing, though. I love the idea of the retreat, but I want it to be more…meaningful, somehow. I just can't figure out what that means to me."

Lily looked around at the expansive main room. She'd gone to the Sundance Film Festival last year in Park City, Utah, and this lodge rivaled the understated luxury of the lodges and ski chalets she'd seen there. "How did you find the time to do all this? Sara told me you got promoted to chief, but I can tell from looking at this place that your style is all over it, so don't even try to tell me you hired someone to do it for you."

"Hey, I never said doing the interior design myself was a smart decision." Sam winked and nodded toward the tall door to the right. "But enough about that, let's figure out whether the chef ordered any decent beer this season."

She closed the cabinet, and they walked through the swinging doors to the dining hall, where one long main table, lit up with mason jars of fresh herbs and fragrant mint, was surrounded by several mismatched smaller tables that reminded Lily of Sara's diner. One end held a retro turquoise party bucket piled high with ice and bottles of beer, and Sam popped the top off an IPA with her hand and handed it to Lily. "Charlotte Tuttle is our activities director. You'll meet her eventually. She must have left these here for any stragglers."

"I can't believe we're the only ones here," Lily said, looking around. "Where's Sara?"

"She made a last-minute run with Mary down to Boise for some supplies, which usually means Mary was dying to go to Olive Garden." Sam looked at her watch as she flicked the cap off her bottle of Sam Adams. "But she should be back soon."

There was a small picnic basket with a red gingham cloth next to the beer. Lily realized too late she was staring at it, but by then, Sam had smiled and nodded in the direction of the basket.

"Go ahead and look. With any luck, she left some snacks. I'm starving too." Sam took a long swig of beer and pulled out one of the chairs for Lily and one for herself. "We had a little situation at Moxie Java today that I wasn't expecting, so I haven't had time to eat since breakfast."

Lily unwrapped the cloth to reveal a basket of snacks: sandwiches wrapped in kraft paper and tied with white twine, each with a sprig of fresh rosemary tucked into the bow; brownies and lemon bars in clear cellophane tucked along the side; even a cloth bag of homemade potato chips. Or at least, that was what the hand-lettered denim label on the outside said they were.

"Oh my God. You weren't kidding about having a chef. Look at this stuff. I feel like someone from the Food Network is about to pop out of the kitchen and hand me a cocktail."

Sam laughed, running her hand through her hair as she leaned back in her chair, then unwrapping a fancy BLT the size of a deck of cards.

Lily and Sam had met five summers ago when Lily was assigned a temporary job placement as the receptionist at the Lake Patrol Headquarters. Lily was twenty-three that year, which made Sam exactly twenty years older than her *and* her boss, so they did their best to keep their attraction under wraps. It had worked for the most part because despite their fiery chemistry, it was never a love thing. They never talked about it; it was just an understanding.

Sam started on the second half of her sandwich and pulled the bag of chips out of Lily's reach with a teasing look. Despite the silver hair at her temples that made her look, well, handsome, Sam looked exactly the same as the day they'd said good-bye.

She'd come over to Lily's rental house in McCall to help her pack up her car, and when it couldn't hold anything else without warping a door, Sam had shouldered it closed and leaned slowly into the driver's window. Lily could still smell the faint scent of sunscreen and lake water that lingered on her skin, and she'd closed her eyes, holding her breath and letting it burn into her memory.

"I know you just signed that contract, and you're freaked out about this writing thing." Sam's voice had been deep, achingly familiar and tender at the edges as she'd leaned closer and kissed Lily's cheek. "But if you need me, I'll be there. I promise."

She still remembered Sam in her rearview mirror as she'd pulled out onto the road, the dust rising around her in a translucent swirl as she'd forced herself to look toward her future.

Sam crumpled up the paper wrapper and smiled from across the table as she pulled the two brass keys out of her pocket and handed them over. "I figured, even if I invited you to stay at our house with us, you wouldn't, so with that in mind, we have one option left."

"The ropes course platform I saw on my way in?"

"Very funny." Sam grinned as she packed up the rest of the food and handed it to Lily. "Here, take this to your cabin. I think we were the last stragglers tonight anyway, so you might as well have something to feed the raccoons."

"What?" Lily attempted to shift her face into her best innocent look and held the door open as Sam hit the lights on their way out. "I have no idea what you're talking about."

"Lily." Sam smiled and glanced over as they stepped out onto the porch. "I used to come over to your house late at night, remember? And they'd literally be standing on your windowsill tapping the glass to get you to feed them more of that trail mix you made. It was in a jar in your kitchen labeled with their names."

"Yeah. I miss that." She looked up at the stars as they headed toward her Jeep parked at the edge of the woods. "There isn't a lot of wildlife where I live in LA, just a few coyotes that visit every once in a while."

"And by 'visit,' you mean they pretty much sleep on your porch?"

"Yeah. Kinda." She laughed, taking the arm Sam offered as they stepped away from the reach of the floodlights and closer to the edge of the forest. "The harder it is for me to be around people, the more animals come out of the woodwork to circle around me. I've never figured it out."

"That doesn't surprise me in the least, Snow White." Sam bumped her shoulder as they walked. "You're an amazing soul. They're just protecting you." Sam grabbed her bags out of the Jeep and nodded for her to follow as she walked in the opposite direction of the other cabins and led her down a path toward the water. "Although, there's a slight possibility that you may miss sleeping with the coyotes after a few nights with—"

"Honestly," Lily interrupted, exhaustion draping itself around her shoulders like a weighted blanket. "I couldn't care less who I have to share a cabin with. I'm just grateful you have a spot for me."

Sam squeezed her shoulder and guided her down a darker path, only steps away from the gentle lap of the lake water. She pulled the flashlight off her belt and clicked it on, and Lily caught sight of a small wooden sign marked with an arrow: *Staff Only*.

"All of our staff double up in the cabins, but we have one empty spot this season. One of our waterfront staff decided to stay in her parents' lake house this summer on the East Shore, so it worked out perfectly."

Lily stopped in her tracks, anxiety creeping into her mind from the back and rolling to the front like dark water. "But the other person here…they don't know I'm coming?"

"They will in about one minute." Sam paused as if she'd just remembered something. "By the way, I handed you two keys before: one unlocks your cabin, the other unlocks the kitchen door. I figured you might not want to eat with everyone until you actually meet some people and get settled."

"Well, as long my new roommate is okay with it, that works great." She matched Sam's stride and looked up at her as they stopped outside a small log cabin with a screened-in porch. Gold light warmed the windows and spilled out onto the path, glossing the tops of her Docs. Lily could almost make out a faint melody of Ella Fitzgerald, which seemed to soften and meld into the background music of the lake water.

"Sam…" Lily trailed off. Sam pulled her into a tight hug, kissing her cheek as she let go. "Just…thank you for this. You really saved me today."

"Are you kidding? I love that you're here, and I can't wait to tell Sara. She'll be thrilled. She's been having a tough time lately, and I think you're just what the doctor ordered."

"The fertility thing?"

A bat swooped between them with a *whoosh*, then circled back again, hovering in midair for just a moment an inch from Lily's nose before flitting off into the darkness.

"I'll leave you to settle in." Sam opened the cabin door and quickly looked around before she rolled Lily's suitcase inside. "Which is code for 'I don't want to get divebombed by the welcome wagon.'"

Lily smiled, catching sight of the same bat hovering a foot behind Sam's head.

"Breakfast is in the lodge at around seven, and both Sara and I will be around for the full two weeks, so we'll have lots of time to catch up. Sara put her kitchen manager in charge at the restaurant, so she got a break to do something fun for a change, and I took some vacation days." Sam paused and rolled her eyes. "Apparently, I had no choice. They keep threatening to lock me out if I don't take some time off."

Lily nodded, remembering the handful of guest cabins she'd seen just down from the lodge. "How many couples are here?"

"Ten couples total, plus the staff that run the waterfront, programming, and activities. We'll get you up to speed on everything in the morning so you can sign up for some classes if you want to get out there." Sam flashed her a wide smile as she turned toward the path to the lodge. "I've got something I've got to get to, but you've got my number, so call me if you need anything, okay?"

Lily nodded as Sam hugged her, then disappeared down the trail. Lily was so tired, the door felt too heavy to pull shut behind her as she stepped into the cabin. The scratchy Ella Fitzgerald lyrics reminded her of an old record player, and sure enough, a vinyl record was spinning lazily on a vintage wooden box player, lit from above with a single pendant Edison bulb.

The cabin was one room but open and spacious, with pine-and-iron bunk beds along one side and a small sitting area with overstuffed bookshelves covering the wall behind it. Lily wandered over to the shelves and picked up one of the books. It was an antique, an old guide to camping in Yellowstone, the pages yellow and brittle under her fingers. The scent of aged paper drifted to her nose and melted the tension from her shoulders. She'd always loved the enveloping silence of books, with their whispered promises to fade the world around her with every word, until the only sound that existed was the smooth, dry brush of the page under her fingertips.

A bathroom with fluffy white towels and a surprisingly large tiled shower took up the back portion of the cabin, and Lily wandered back into the main room, noting that the bottom bunk was taken. The beds looked handmade, wider than typical bunks, with a wooden ladder that connected the two levels. A small brass lamp was attached to the wall beside each, and both were outfitted with fluffy green duvets and plaid sheets. Lily shrugged off her vest and rubbed the ache from her forehead with the tips of her fingers.

"Well, I'm certainly not in LA anymore."

"No, ma'am."

Lily looked up to see Alex striding through the door in board shorts and a Speedo swim top, shaking the lake water from her dark hair and sweeping Lily from top to bottom with the same intense gaze. "Welcome to Havana."

CHAPTER FOUR

M urphy?" Sam strummed the steering wheel of her Land Rover with her thumb as she swept past the speed limit sign just outside the resort. "Can you stall the judge for five more minutes? I got caught up at the camp. I'm on my way in now, though."

Sam didn't wait for an answer, just clicked her phone off and tossed it on the seat beside her. She had a headache the size of a Kansas tornado threatening to explode and not a single Advil in sight. Or at least, none she could spot in the glove compartment while she took the last curve into McCall on what felt like two wheels. Her truck finally skidded to a stop at the station as Sam leaned over to take a last look for the bottle that should be there, but no luck. She'd pilfered her stash too many times in the previous few weeks. She couldn't remember the last time she didn't have a headache. Between being promoted to chief and supervising the development of the retreat center, Sam felt like she hadn't downshifted once in the last three years.

The station's main doors were still unlocked, and Sam jogged to her office, tucking a manilla file she'd prepared earlier into her bag, then sprinted up the hill from the station to the small courthouse at the end of the main street. A hurried glance at the dark windows as she passed Gus's Place told her that Sara was likely on her way home.

They'd had a brief conversation earlier. Sam had called her with the story about what had happened in Moxie Java just as Sara closed up the restaurant. She'd given as many details as possible, then had tossed out the thought she hadn't been able to shake all afternoon. Even with a mountain of positive thinking, her idea was rough at best or, more realistically, fraught with potential disaster, but it was't going anywhere, so the only thing to do was put it out there.

Sam had waited as Sara's initial shock had settled into a long pause on the other end of the line. She'd resisted the urge to throw words into the silence to shape and sand the edges of it to make the idea seem plausible. She'd only rubbed her temples and waited, listening to the familiar sounds of the restaurant staff in the background closing up the kitchen for the night.

Sam had spun a pen in her fingers, still waiting for Sara to answer. Her plan was rash, random at best, and she was asking her wife to agree to it with virtually no background information and an almost nonexistent chance of success. Sam had put the pen back on her desk closed her eyes, trying to gather her thoughts. It was starting to seem like she had no choice but to go in a new direction.

"Of course, baby." Sam had felt Sara smile on the other end of the phone and had realized she'd been holding her breath. "Of course we can do that. I would have come up with the same idea."

Sam had breathed a sigh of relief, and they'd made a few quick plans before Sara had to finish closing up. As she'd hung up the phone, Sam had remembered again how lucky she was to have married a woman who could roll with an unexpected punch like that, how lucky she'd been to have married Sara.

She rounded the last corner in front of the courthouse and spotted her brother-in-law's truck in the parking lot. "Jesus, what have you been doing?" Murphy grinned and jumped up to hold the double glass doors open. "Get your ass in here!"

Sam rolled her eyes playfully and passed him at double speed, turning around and running backward as she asked in a low voice if everyone was still in the courtroom.

"Nope, they're in chambers now, but I stalled them for you. I got Sara to bring Judge Hanson one of those steak sandwiches he loves. He's still chowing down, I think."

"You're a genius, man. I owe you one." Sam slowed as she approached the judge's chambers, knocking lightly and opening the door only when she heard a muffled invitation to enter.

Judge Hanson was just finishing one of Sara's flame-grilled steak sandwiches, washing it down with what looked like Sara's famous

Savannah sweet tea. He wiped his hands on his napkin, motioned Sam in, and nodded toward one of the tweed chairs across from his desk.

Sam sat quickly with a nod in Moxie's direction, who was sitting stiffly in the other chair, holding a white paper bag from Gus's Place on her lap with both hands. She was pale and nervously tucked her chin-length dark hair behind her several times, her eyes focused only on her hands.

The judge finished clearing the last of his dinner off his desk, and Sam smiled at Moxie, whispering behind her hand. "Relax. It's going to be okay."

Moxie nodded, her grip on the white paper bag in her lap tightening by the second. "Is he really a judge?"

"I really am a judge." Moxie jumped as the judge cut in with a warm smile "Although, I understand the confusion there. This is an unusual meeting, to be sure. Chief Draper asked me to stay late today and hear your case." He leaned back in his leather desk chair, thumbing through the folder Sam had placed on his desk as she came in.

Moxie looked like she might be sick, and Sam noticed a sheen of sweat had broken out on her upper lip. She looked up, and Sam held her eyes with a quiet steadiness, which, surprisingly, seemed to help. Moxie drew a breath and loosened her grip on the bag as the judge started to speak.

"So I understand from the chief we had an incident at the coffee shop this morning?"

Moxie nodded, lifting her chin slightly and meeting his gaze.

"And you relieved the deputy transporting you of his gun?"

Her reply was so soft it sank in the air, but she didn't lower her eyes. "Yes, sir."

The judge was silent again, stacking the papers and sliding them back into the folder as he turned to look at Sam. "Chief, you gave me some information this afternoon that led to a few phone calls regarding Deputy Wilson and his service record. I'll make sure there's an investigation regarding his performance today, specifically the racial slurs he aimed at you, Maria. There is no excuse for that." Judge Hanson paused, leaning forward on his elbows and lowering his voice. "And just for the record, I see here that your first name is Maria, but the chief called you Moxie. If you prefer that, I'll note that on your file."

Moxie looked at Sam, but Sam just nodded in the judge's direction. "Yes, sir." Moxie said, refocusing her attention on the judge. "I mean, Your Honor."

"Just out of curiosity, how did you get that gun? They're almost impossible to pull from the holsters if you're not wearing them." Judge Hanson sat back and waited, watching as Moxie gathered her thoughts before she answered.

"It wasn't in the holster. The deputy took it out and laid it on the table between us when I turned down an offer he thought I'd jump at." She paused, wiping her damp palms on the leg of her jeans. "He chose the wrong girl, I guess."

Sam looked at the judge, who shook his head and glanced at the clock on the wall. "Can you tell me what that was?" He asked the question like he already knew the answer.

Moxie looked down and picked at a thread on the sleeve of her jacket. She waited a few seconds, then just shook her head.

The judge paused, then looked at Sam. "Do you think you might be able to tell Chief Draper at a later date when you're more comfortable?"

Moxie looked over at Sam, her face pale and tense. She didn't shake her head this time, but she didn't nod, either.

"Just think about it. If there's something we need to know, I trust that you'll make us aware of it." He paused to finish the tea in his to-go cup, then dropped it in the trash beside his desk. "I know you've had a long day, Moxie, and frankly, I'm looking forward to going home to my second dinner, so I'm not going to waste time here telling you what you did was dangerous." He paused, tapping his pen on the desk. "We both know it was a poor decision. But based on what the chief said, I don't think for a minute that you intended to hurt anyone, and because of the deputy's actions before the event, it's entirely plausible you believed your safety was in question."

Moxie nodded, some of the color returning to her face as she waited for him to go on.

"I'll get to the point." The judge shuffled the papers on his desk until he found the one he needed. "Because you're in the system already and underage, the obvious choice would be to find you another foster placement, but the chief here says she thinks that's not the best choice for you."

Moxie looked up at Sam in surprise, then nodded, swiping at a tear on her cheek with the heel of her hand.

"And frankly, I'm inclined to agree." The judge glanced at Sam and went on. "I was a personal friend of her father's, who was the chief of police here in McCall for over twenty years, and he and I cared a great deal about changing the way the foster system works." His voice dropped to a softer tone. "It's not working at all in your case, and I think it might be time to do something different, don't you agree?"

"What do you mean?" Moxie looked at Sam, then back at the judge. "I'm not going to jail?"

"Well, I'd give Moxie Java a swerve for a while if I were you, but I'm not sending you anywhere, actually." He picked up a small white bag and slid a chocolate chip cookie onto his desk. "I'm not overlooking what you did today, but I don't see you as a true danger to the community." He paused until Moxie raised her gaze to his. "And I also don't think justice will be served by transferring you into our overloaded juvenile detention system just because that's the obvious option. I'm sending you to a counselor here in McCall, and you'll also need to do fifty hours of community service before this time next year."

Judge Hanson cleared his throat and signed the document in front of him, passing it across the table to Sam. "So with that in place, I'm granting Chief Draper's request to be your temporary foster placement. I'll make sure she has all the details concerning counseling and the community service as well. We'll revisit this in six months and see where we are then."

A tear dropped to Moxie's cheek, and she looked from Sam to the judge more than once before she spoke again. "Are you kidding me with this?" Her voice caught, and she swiped at her cheek with her sleeve. "I thought my life was over after today."

"Miss Moxie, your life is just beginning." Judge Hanson leaned forward and caught her eye with an unexpected smile. "And I can't wait to see what you do with it."

❖

Lily had just stepped aside to let Alex into the cabin when there was a sharp knock on the other side of the door. Alex returned to the door and peeked out the window before opening it again. A blonde leaned against the door frame, her bright golden ponytail swishing over her shoulder. She glanced past Alex to Lily, then promptly dropped her gaze to Alex's mouth, whispering a few words that Lily tried not to hear as she busied herself unzipping her suitcase.

The day washed over her again, and she couldn't even remember if she'd packed a toothbrush. Or if she had, where that might be. She sighed, running her hand along the side pockets of her suitcase more than once as she heard the door shut again. The sound of peeper frogs rose and fell outside the windows as she struggled with the main zipper, and the familiar sweep of mountain air, never still after nightfall, brushed itself against the black glass of the windows.

Alex grabbed some clothes from the chest of drawers next to the bed and smiled, walking backward toward the bathroom. "Sorry about that. That was Charlotte, the program director. I should have introduced you, but I'm sure you'll meet her at breakfast. She said you're here as a guest of Sam and Sara?"

"That's okay. I don't have the energy tonight anyway." Lily paused, too tired to choose her words carefully. "Is she your…"

"Girlfriend?"

Lily nodded, unzipping the bag just far enough to reach the interior pocket but not so far that the entire contents would tumble out.

"No, not my girlfriend." Alex stopped at the bathroom door, leaning against the door frame, a sheen of lake water still glossing the sharp cuts of muscle in her arms. "She was here to give me the heads-up on your arrival, but she was late on the draw. I saw Sam dropping you off when I came out of the water."

"Yeah, Sam and I have been friends for years. Coming here was a spur-of-the-moment thing." Lily gave up the toothpaste hunt for a moment and blew a lock of hair out of her eyes as she looked up. "In fact, I didn't exactly tell them I was coming, so it was a bit of a scramble to find me a spot." She paused, unsure of how to address the elephant in the room. "Look, I would never have kissed you if I knew you had a thing with someone." Her voice dropped off into the memory of Alex pressing her back against the Jeep, the warmth of her breath melting into her neck.

"You didn't kiss me." The record player jerked to a pause between songs as if holding its breath, then came to life again with a scratchy whisper. Alex's dark eyes sparked as she raked her hand through her damp hair. "I kissed you."

Lily pulled her toothbrush and paste from the pocket and zipped it back up, but by the time she'd looked up, Alex was in the bathroom and reaching into the shower to start the hot water. She looked down at the toothbrush in her hand, unsure of whether to go in or not until she remembered the clear glass shower door. She watched as Alex turned and stripped off her Speedo top, revealing a beautiful phoenix tattoo covering her from hip to shoulder, deafening and silent in sheer shades of fire, fading into tendrils of shaded smoke at her shoulder.

Lily hesitated as she turned back to the bunk. There was definitely a vibe between Alex and Charlotte, and the last thing she needed was to get involved in drama while she was here. She heard the bathroom door close gently and turned back around, realizing too late she was biting her nails, a childhood habit that had made a fierce comeback recently.

Why would Alex kiss me like that if she was involved with someone? She closed her eyes, trying to push back the memory. *And why did it have to be so undeniably hot?*

Her mind was still spinning as she pulled a water bottle out of her bag, brushed her teeth outside, then glanced around the cabin for a book to lull her to sleep. Now that she was really looking, she realized books were everywhere, stacked neatly in the bookcase and in random piles around the cabin. Even the record player on the corner table was perched on a somewhat precarious stack of antique novels. Lily glanced into the bathroom to make sure Alex was still in the shower and scanned the titles stacked on the windowsill beside the door. Lesbian pulp fiction by Ann Bannon, with characters like Beebo Brinker and titles like *Women in the Shadows* and *Odd Girl Out*, as well as books by Cuban and French philosophers, in addition to several library books she could only assume were permanently overdue.

The sound of the shower stopped abruptly. Lily walked back to the bunks, grabbed the first book she found on the small nightstand, then tossed it onto her bed without looking at it. She folded her jeans and placed them on her still-packed suitcase with a sigh, clicking on the small paper lamp on the chest of drawers on the way up to her bunk. The weirdness of fleeing LA with no plan and ending up in a tiny cabin in McCall with someone she'd randomly kissed was beginning to swirl around her like she was watching a movie of someone else's life in fast-forward. She felt slightly dizzy as she climbed the ladder to the top bunk, thankful the door to the bathroom was still shut so she at least didn't have to talk about it.

Lily felt her bones slowly unfold onto the bed as she lay back and stared at the gabled plank ceiling, too exhausted to read anything at all. The window beside her was open, and the muslin curtain stirred, brushing her cheek as the breeze came in off the lake. She closed her eyes, breathing in the scent of silver birch bark, cooling and shifting in the night air.

She was sinking into velvet layers of sleep by the time she realized the book she'd tossed on the bed was jutting into her back, so she reached for it as she climbed under the warmth of the duvet, turning it over in her hand in the amber lamplight.

Embers Into Fire by Lily Larimar.

CHAPTER FIVE

Mary slipped a pan of warm brownies under the counter in the drugstore, then plucked a cup off the mug tree in the window and poured a steaming cup of coffee from the pot next to the cash register. She'd owned the drugstore in McCall for over thirty years, and there had only been a handful of days that she'd missed *Days of Our Lives*. She had a routine. She locked up the shop every day at 2:00 p.m., opened the cabinet that hid her television, and switched on her soaps. Over the years, the snacks had gotten a bit more indulgent, but other than that, the routine was the same, and that was the way she liked it.

Mary had just switched on her show and was headed toward the front of the store with her keys when a slight, tomboyish girl slipped through the door. She walked with her head down and navigated quickly toward the back of the store. Her hands were shoved into the pockets of her threadbare hoodie, and the muted footfalls of her black Converse were the only sound in the shop.

Mary watched her for a moment before locking the front door and taking a seat behind the counter. She sighed as she dumped sugar in her coffee and waited for the little delinquent to get the hell out. If she didn't hurry, she'd miss the recap from yesterday's episode, not that she hadn't already watched it. The girl reappeared after about a minute, eyes still on the floor, and lingered for a second by the Snickers bars before she headed to the door, pulling on it several times without success.

She finally turned to Mary only when it was clear there was no other option. "Um…the door is locked."

Mary poured hazelnut creamer into her coffee and stirred, tasting it twice before adding more. The girl shifted her weight from one foot to the other, her eyes darting around for another exit. Any other exit.

"You have to let me out."

"I think you'll find, young lady," Mary blew on the surface of her coffee and sat back on her stool, "That I don't have to do shit."

The girl hesitated as she laced her fingers behind her head, looking as if she might cry.

"But you might get farther with that door if you pull whatever you just shoved in your grubby little pocket and set it here on the counter."

The girl's head dropped, and Mary half heard her mutter a curse word before she shuffled back to the counter. She looked up for only a second before her gaze turned longingly to the carefree tourists passing the shop windows, and the thought crossed Mary's mind that she just might make a run for it and try to body slam the glass.

She knew most of the teenage troublemakers in town and watched each one like a hawk when they ambled through the door in loud groups after school. They lingered around the candy, pocketing what they could get away with, but word had gotten around, and they'd developed a healthy respect for Mary over the years. Probably had something to do with the paintball rifle she kept behind the counter.

This girl didn't have that kind of swagger, though, or whatever the kids called it these days. She'd come in like she was on a mission and had pocketed something before Mary had even made it back behind the counter, which was a bold move, considering she was the only one in the shop.

"So let's have it." Mary took a sip of coffee and glanced longingly at the pan of cooling brownies under the counter. "I don't have time for this bullshit. I've got my stories to watch."

The girl looked up from under her hood and stepped back a couple of steps. "I can't, I…"

"You're going to want to reconsider." Mary sat back on her stool, coffee in hand. "What exactly do you think your options are here?"

She glanced again at the door, then pulled a small blue box out of her hoodie pocket and placed it carefully on the counter. "I'm sorry. I guess I just needed them."

Mary looked at the small box for a few seconds before she came back around the counter. The girl flinched as she stepped out of the way, then watched as Mary grabbed a handful of Snickers bars and dropped them into a small paper sack along with the box of tampons. She handed the bag to the girl and reclaimed her stool.

"I can't take this," the girl said, her voice soft. She looked steadily into the sack for a long few seconds, which Mary knew right away was an obvious attempt to hide the tears in her eyes. "I don't have any money."

Mary glanced up at the clock and pulled the tray of brownies out from under the counter, still warm and gooey, with a thick caramel swirl on the top. "I'll tell you what. We'll call it even if you help me eat these brownies while I watch my show. God help me if I'm left alone with that pan." Mary hit the button on the remote, and the theme song to *Days of Our Lives* played in the background. She put two brownies on a napkin and pushed them over the counter. "What's your name? And you can't be from around here. I know a Southern accent when I hear one."

"It's Moxie, and I grew up in Arkansas. My mom dragged me to Boise because she followed some guy out here a few years ago." Moxie finished half a brownie in one bite and swallowed hard, meeting Mary's eyes for the first time. "Why are you being so nice to me? I just tried to steal from you."

"I'm Mary, by the way. And, honey," Mary said, pushing up her sleeves as she cut an oversized hunk of brownie and plunked it down on a napkin for herself. "I raised four daughters. I know you wouldn't have taken those if you had any other choice." She paused. "And that's just different."

An hour later, the pan of brownies was almost empty, and Mary had even seen Moxie smile once or twice. She was too thin, and the freckles across her nose made her look like she was barely in her early teens. Moxie had a sadness about her that reminded Mary of Sam Draper as a child, although that had worn off a few years after Gus, the police chief, had officially adopted her. The poor thing had been left at the county fair to fend for herself overnight, and when the authorities had finally caught up with the mother, she couldn't sign away her rights to her daughter fast enough. Gus and Mary had been friends since high school, so she'd seen Sam grow up and loved her as fiercely as she loved her own daughters.

Moxie picked up her bag and reluctantly stood as the show ended and the credits rolled. "Um, Mary?" She looked up, the top of the bag crinkling in her hand. "Would it be okay if this just stayed between us? It's a long story, but the last thing I need is to get in trouble right now."

Mary smiled as she picked up the keys and came around the counter to unlock the door. "If you ask me, people talk too damn much anyway. This ain't nobody's business but ours, Moxie."

Moxie nodded, slipping through the door that Mary held open and out onto the sunny sidewalk. The wind ruffled her hair, and she tucked it behind her ear, looking as if she wanted to say something. Finally, she bent to tie her grubby shoelace, then stood, tucking the bag under her arm. "You watch that show every day?"

"Every weekday at two o'clock." Mary smiled, brushing a brownie crumb from the shoulder of Moxie's hoodie. "But get here on time. I don't want to have to be explaining what you've missed the whole time."

Moxie flashed a sudden smile and turned to go. Mary watched her walk down the sidewalk for a good while before she propped the door open to let in the summer breeze and went back in to finish the last brownie.

"Hey, Sam?" Charlotte, Lake Haven's program director, leaned against the door frame of Sam's office in the main lodge. "I just got a call from the lake that you might want to know about."

Sam turned in her chair, rubbing her eyes. This was only the second season for the retreat, and the permit and insurance paperwork alone had her pulling her hair out. She'd taken two weeks of accumulated vacation time for the retreat this year, but the officers still called her for literally everything, so between that and catching up on all the logistics at Lake Haven, the last couple of days had felt like the furthest thing from a vacation.

"No problem, I was about to call it a night anyway." Sam motioned her in. "Everything okay?"

"At the moment, yes, but I just got a call from a couple registered at the retreat, and they seem to be lost in a canoe with zero idea how to get back to the docks. I think they lost their bearings as the sun went down."

"Ah, man, you're kidding. Did you call Lake Patrol?"

Charlotte swung her blond ponytail over her shoulder, and Sam noticed Charlotte's gaze had dropped to her mouth. "Not yet. I thought I'd ask you first."

Sam stood and grabbed her jacket. "Do me a favor? Call my wife and let her know I'll be a little later getting home. I'll go get them myself. They can't be too far out." She slid her arms into the jacket and turned off the lights, shutting the door behind her. "Did they give you any idea of where they are?"

"Yeah, they can see that huge blue slide on the dock at the kids' camp, and I told them just to stay there. I figured that might make them easier to find."

"Thanks, Charlotte." Sam found her boat key and glanced at her watch. "Keep your phone on you. I'll take it from here. How did dinner go tonight?"

"Great, some of the couples had questions, but I answered them. It sounds like everyone loves the activity options this year. They can do yoga or watersports or just be together, although I always recommend taking advantage of everything. Speaking of which…" She paused, her voice soft as she continued. "Is there anything else you need from me?"

Sam said no politely and excused herself. Charlotte had been an instant success as program director this season. She'd taken a huge load off Sam's shoulders for the same reason she also irritated the hell out of her: everything Charlotte said was dripping with a Georgia accent and the invitation to flirt. She was gorgeous, with tight curves, a cheerleader personality, and a deep love for attention, but she routinely failed to remember Sam was married. Well, it didn't seem to matter to her that anyone was married, to be fair.

The darkening lake water lapped at the side of the dock as Sam untied her speedboat, clicking on the running lights before she stopped to send a quick text to Sara. The sky was a deep lavender, the first stars just starting to twinkle behind the treetops as Sam pulled the boat smoothly out onto the water. The wind blew her jacket around her as she stood behind the wheel, accelerating onto the lake's mirrored surface, carving a path from her dock to the camp she'd attended as a kid.

She'd taken over the position as Chief of Police when the previous chief had retired; it was supposed to be temporary, but before she knew it, her name was on the door, and that had been that. But the truth was that she missed being out on the open water. Being stuck behind a desk had never been her thing, and no two days at Lake Patrol were ever the same, which was exactly how she liked it. But as police chief, her hours were longer than ever, the responsibilities were endless, and she and Sara had started to feel like ships passing in the night.

Sam cut a deep curve around the point of North Beach as the lavender tint of sunset darkened to an expanse of black velvet sky, and the chill reminded her to zip up her jacket. Even in June, the temperature dropped quickly on the water, turning crisp and sharp as the sun sank behind the mountain. Once the darkness settled, all the shorelines started to mirror each other, and it was easy to get turned around, so she wasn't surprised when she caught sight of the lost canoers waving their paddles like they'd been stranded on a desert island.

After returning them safely to the resort, Sam came through the door at home just in time to watch her wife take a bubbling casserole dish out of the oven. Sara's wild blond waves were longer now, like constant sunlight hovering around her face, but the pale gold freckles and deep lake-water eyes were the same. Sam dropped her keys soundlessly onto the entry table and leaned back against the door, watching as Sara pulled a spoon out of the drawer and leaned into the dish, breathing in the scent for a moment before she pried a bite off the crispy edge.

It was Sam's favorite—white truffle lasagna—but what she really liked best about it was watching Sara taste it right out of the oven. Somehow, despite being thirty-seven years old and a professional chef, she seemed genuinely shocked every damn time that it was too hot to eat.

Right on cue, Sara dropped the spoon in the sink and frantically fanned her mouth with her hand. Sam walked up behind her and wrapped her arms around Sara's waist, and Sara smiled up at her, leaning back into the warmth of her chest.

"Thank God you're here." Sara turned and wrapped her arms around Sam with an angelic look. "Did you see that lasagna reach out and attack me?"

"I did, baby," Sam whispered against the soft ivory slope of her neck. "And it was brutal. In fact, there might be an arrest later. I'll keep you posted." Sam pressed Sara up against the refrigerator, tracing the delicate line of Sara's bare shoulder with her mouth as she unbuttoned her shirt. The black linen slid down her body as Sam dipped her mouth to one pale pink nipple, circling with her tongue before pulling it lightly into her mouth and working it achingly slowly with the slow, wet heat of her mouth.

"Seriously, no bra?" she whispered. "Are you just trying to drive me crazy while there are people in the house, and I can't do anything about it?"

"Well, Moxie is upstairs on the computer, and Jenn and Murphy aren't supposed to be here for another few minutes, so…" Sara trailed off as Sam moved back up to her neck, her breath warming the soft skin just below her ear.

"You don't have to ask me twice." Sam laughed as she scooped Sara up in her arms and started carrying her toward their bedroom. "I mean, let's be honest, you don't even have to ask me once—"

Her next words were lost as the doorbell and the oven timer blared simultaneously. Sam laughed as she set Sara gently back down, buttoning her shirt with quick fingers as she watched her brother-in-law lean over and peer into the entry window.

"I'm guessing that timer went off for your garlic bread, and if that doesn't make an appearance, Murphy may never recover, so I'll just follow up on this tonight." Sam buttoned the last button, tipped Sara's face up, and kissed her gently. "To be continued, my love."

❖

After dinner, Murphy finally laid his cutlery on his plate and sighed, rolling up his sleeves as he leaned back in his chair. "Seriously, Sara, what's *in* this? I'm not sure I've had anything that good in my life."

Sara laughed as she pushed the last of the garlic bread closer to Murphy's plate. Even after all these years, he always made her feel like a celebrity chef. "It's nothing that complicated, really. Just bechamel sauce with some chanterelle mushrooms I sautéed in butter, chardonnay, and thyme. It's the crispy sage on top that makes it special, I think."

"Well, it's delicious." Jennifer smiled and smoothed a hand over her belly. "I highly recommend that every pregnant woman get themselves a chef for a sister."

Sara laughed as she started to gather the plates, but Sam gestured for her to sit as she and Murphy stood to clear the table. "I already had it in the oven when you called, and I made way too much anyway.

We're cooking for more people now with Moxie, but she wasn't hungry tonight."

"Is she okay?" Sam put the plates in the sink and hit the button on the coffee maker. "I haven't seen her since I dropped her off at the pickup basketball game this afternoon in town. I offered to drive in to get her in a couple of hours, but she wanted to walk back." Sam pulled four mugs out of the cupboard and handed them to Murphy. "I should probably be checking in on her more, but I got snowed under some paperwork at Lake Haven."

"She's fine, I think. She just probably wanted some time to explore." Sara dropped her voice, glancing up the log stairs to the office door that was still closed. "I was telling Mary about her this afternoon, and she said Moxie has already been into the store, so that's a good thing. Everyone needs a little Mary in her life."

"Gospel truth right there." Jennifer nodded as she took the cream and sugar set Sam handed her and placed them in the middle of the table. "Moxie is your foster placement, right? I can't believe we haven't talked about this yet. Tell me everything."

Sara nodded. "Last night was her first night with us, and I almost screwed it up. She had a panicky moment when she walked into her room, and her stuff wasn't on her bed."

"I'll have to tell you the story another time," Sam said, lowering her voice to a whisper and glancing up the stairs. "But everything she owned was shoved into this beat-up plastic trash bag. I promised her it would be in her room when she got to our house—"

"But I wanted it to feel like home," Sara cut in with a sigh. "So I unpacked all her clothes and washed them, then put them away in the dresser." She leaned back in her chair and glanced at the coffee maker as Sam poured the steaming pot into a carafe. "When she realized that no one had taken her stuff, that it was just clean and put away, she just stood there for a moment. Then she sighed and put her hand over her chest like she'd been holding that same breath all day." Sara paused, her voice more thought than words. "When I took her a sandwich a few minutes later, she'd fallen asleep on the bed, still wearing the same thing." Sara paused. "She looked exhausted and pale, like she hadn't slept in days."

"I can't wait to meet her." Jennifer stirred a spoonful of brown sugar into her coffee. "To be honest, I can't believe you guys haven't gone this direction before now."

"I guess I just never thought about it." Sam winked at Sara and took an almond-dotted amaretto cookie from the plate in the center of the table. "That's what happens when I'm too busy trying to knock up your sister."

Everyone laughed at that, and it was a moment before any of them realized Moxie was coming down the staircase. She stopped short when she looked up and seemed to realize that Sam and Sara had guests over. When she finally spoke, her voice was low and tentative. "Um…Sam?"

"Hey, Moxie." Sam pushed her chair back from the table. "Feel like eating yet?"

She shook her head, her slender shoulders almost lost in the black Adidas hoodie that would have been too big for Sam at nearly six feet. "I'm sorry, I didn't realize you had people over. I can ask later." Her voice faded as she turned, her footsteps as silent as her thoughts.

"Wait, do you need to talk alone? We can do that." Sam stood and nodded toward the chairs around the fireplace, her voice gentle. "But while you're here, this is Sara's sister, Jennifer, and her husband, Murphy. Murphy works with me down at the station."

Moxie stopped on the stairs, motionless, then turned slowly around. "So you're both cops?"

The air shifted, and all eyes were on Moxie as Sam pulled out a chair at the table for her. She sat, tucking a glossy lock of hair behind her ear and looking steadily at Jennifer and Murphy. Sam didn't even try to hide her smile; it was exactly how she'd stared Sam down over the barrel of the gun in Moxie Java.

Moxie took a few seconds, as if to choose her words, before she started talking, tugging at the hair elastic around her wrist. When she finally looked up, she spoke directly to Sam, her voice hesitant but determined in the same breath. "I have a friend from my neighborhood in Boise, another foster kid. Her name is Kylie. She told me a few months ago that she was getting transferred to my caseworker, and since then, she's been in two different placements." She looked at her wrist again, and this time, Sara watched as Sam noticed the fine white scars across them. "And in both, she's had the same trouble with, like… her bedroom door at night."

Murphy shook his head, and Jennifer held her gaze with kind eyes. Even though Sam was the only one with the backstory, Moxie's meaning was clear.

"I just got an email from her, and now she's headed somewhere else." Moxie faltered, glancing at Sam. "It's the same place that deputy thought he was leaving me before I met Sam in Moxie Java." Moxie traced the grain of the table with her thumbnail.

Sam nodded, glancing across the table at Sara before she spoke. "Actually, it may help us going forward if everyone knows what happened. Is it okay to tell them?"

Moxie nodded, then locked eyes with Jennifer and Murphy, leaning forward on the table as she spoke. "Or how about I just save us some time and give you a highlight reel."

"God, I love this kid already." Murphy laughed, settling back in his chair. "Go on, Moxie. Hit me with the highlights."

"Okay." She pushed up the sleeves of her hoodie and leaned back in her chair. "The Boise deputy who was supposed to take me to my new foster placement in McCall tried to leave me at this massive house on the lake that didn't feel right. I made him leave and take me to town, and when I told him I wasn't going back to that place, he took out his gun and put it on the table like a threat or something. By the time Sam walked in, I was up front with the gun, and everyone in there was scared to death, me most of all." Moxie took a breath, her voice softer, unsure. "I didn't know what I was doing. I know it looked like I was robbing the place, but I didn't want money or anything. I just knew that if he left me there, something bad would happen again, and I figured nothing was worse than that. Even jail."

"So..." Sam pulled a notebook out of her pocket but dropped it back in as soon as she caught the look on Sara's face. "The place he took you is here in McCall?"

Moxie nodded. "Remember when I told you he was so angry because he thought I would jump at an offer, and I didn't?" She shook her head as if to clear the memory from her mind. "I just refused to let him leave me at that house. He didn't know what to do, and both of them were pissed off."

"Wait, who is them? There was more than just that deputy?" Sara got a small plate from the cupboard, dished up some lasagna and salad, and pushed it down the table.

Moxie pulled it toward her and picked up her fork. "You really want me to eat this, don't you?"

"I mean, no pressure." Sara smiled, her palms in the air. "But I might not be able to sleep tonight if you don't."

Moxie picked up her fork, her eyes thoughtful. "You should really have kids. You're, like, already a mom."

Sam put her hand over Sara's and squeezed it, and Jennifer smiled at them from across the table.

"Oh God." Moxie put down her fork and bit her lip. "I probably just said the total wrong thing. I just meant you've been so nice to me and—"

"It wasn't wrong, not by a long shot." Sara looked up at Moxie and smiled. "That was actually the perfect thing to say."

Moxie smiled and ate most of her lasagna in just a few bites. She even picked at her salad before leaning back in her chair and pulling her sleeves down over her hands. Sam picked up her plate and returned with a cold bottle of Coke, which she opened with a flick of her thumb before setting it down.

"So," Sara said gently. "I think the story you're telling might be really important. I'd love to hear more whenever you're ready."

Moxie nodded, tracing the white outline of the Coca-Cola logo with the tip of her finger. "I guess I started putting it together in my head when the deputy took me to that place on the other side of the lake." She paused as if choosing her next words one by one. "But it wasn't a normal house, you know? Something just felt off. Like, it was right out of Hollywood or something."

Sara nodded. "Was that supposed to be your new foster placement?"

"I mean, I guess. But that place was huge, with, like, people who worked there and stuff. Not even close to a normal house."

"Had your social worker told you anything about the placement?" Murphy's voice was gentle. "Like who your foster parents would be?"

Moxie shook her head. "This was the fourth placement she'd put me in. She never told me anything about the ones before, so that wasn't a surprise, but each was worse than the last. It was like she was looking for ways to make me miserable or something." She took a sip of Coke and set it back down, her eyes on the table. "I mean, I never did anything to her. I don't know why she sent me to such bad places."

Sam nodded, tapping her thumb silently on the table as she spoke. "How long have you been in the system?"

"Since my mom went to prison two years ago, and she'll be there for the next forty years before she's even eligible for parole, so she lost custody, and the judge says I belong to the state now. She was my only family, so I got sent to a group home first, then my social worker got assigned to me and kept moving me around."

"I get it." Murphy's words were soft, as if he wanted Moxie to know they wouldn't hurt her in a world where everything else had sharp edges. "So life went to shit, and you've pretty much been alone since, huh?"

"Yeah." Moxie looked up and let out a wavering breath, as if she'd been holding it the whole time. "That's exactly it."

"You mentioned that you 'started putting it together' when you got sent to the fancy house in McCall." Sam leaned forward, catching Murphy's eye. "What did you mean by that? What started to come together?"

"I don't know how to describe it." Moxie pulled her glasses out of the front pocket of her hoodie and put them on, the overhead light glinting off a vertical crack spanning the entire left lens. "Maybe it's just a coincidence, and I'm not trying to get anyone in trouble, except..."

Sam cut in when she faltered. "Except you're starting to realize it isn't a coincidence?"

"It's not." Moxie's jaw flexed, and her gaze was steady as she looked back at Sam. "I know it's not."

Murphy cracked his knuckles loud enough to make her laugh and smiled warmly at her. "I'd bet a stack of money Moxie's smarter than me, so I'm going to need someone to explain what you guys are talking about. Take me back to the beginning."

"That's the thing. I don't know." Moxie took another sip of Coke, then pushed it slowly away with the tip of her finger. "I think my social worker knew my placements weren't safe, but I got sent there anyway. She always told me I just needed to blend in and not cause trouble, to just 'do whatever they say, and you'll be fine.'"

"I can't imagine she had much luck with that." Sam tried to suppress a laugh and almost choked on her cookie. "She's *met* you, right?"

"Exactly." Moxie's smile was like a sudden flash of sunlight. "So it all started to come together when I walked into that big fancy house and talked to the rich guy who lived there. The woman who answered the door just looked me up and down for a long time, then took us upstairs to his office, and right away, I knew something wasn't right."

Murphy leaned forward on his elbow. "What tipped you off?"

"Well, I could tell the rich guy and the deputy knew each other already because the deputy called him Travis, and they were both just staring at me and not saying much." She paused, shoving her hands back into the front pocket of her hoodie, her jaw tense. "So I asked to go to the bathroom, just to get a minute to think. On the way there, I passed this huge window that overlooked the pool, and there were a bunch of girls just lying out by the pool, some in bikinis, some topless." She paused. "No boys. Just girls."

Sara's phone rang, and everyone jumped. Sara excused herself to take it as Moxie went on.

"So anyway, the whole situation was just so weird that I never did go to the bathroom. I just went back to the office and stopped at the door. I hadn't closed it all the way, so I just stood there and listened to them talking."

Murphy and Sam leaned forward. "Could you hear what they were saying?"

"Yeah, unfortunately." Moxie paused, then lifted her chin before she went on. "Something about me looking like a boy. And the guy said my skin was too dark for something."

"Well." Murphy shook his head and reached across the table for another amaretto cookie. "I have loads of shit to say about Dumb and Dumber, but I'm a professional, so I'm just going to just shelve that for a different time."

Sam dropped her face into her hands and shook her head before she finally looked back at Murphy with a smile.

"Oh, right." He sighed, rolling his eyes, which made even Moxie laugh. "And I'll just be over here, not swearing." He winked in her direction. "Carry on, tiny badass."

Moxie laughed, but her smile faded quickly as she sank back into the memory. "Anyway, I realized what was happening then, so I just told them I wasn't staying and that he had to take me back to Boise. That's why the deputy was so pissed off at Moxie Java."

Sam nodded. "Correct me if I'm wrong here, but I'm guessing you're worried Kylie will end up at the same place, right?"

"Right. Except there's no way they'll let *her* leave, even if she wants to. I don't think that guy cared if I stayed or not, but Kylie's way younger than me, skinny and blond. She looks like a model, and I don't know how to describe it." Moxie paused. "But she's way less likely to throw a fit than I am."

"Oh damn," Murphy said, running a hand through his hair as he leaned back from the table. "That's not a good combination."

Sam nodded, pulling another Coke out of the fridge and handing it to Moxie. "Would you know how to find this place again?"

"I've thought about that, but honestly, I wasn't paying attention on the drive there. But I would definitely recognize that stupid pool out back. It's shaped like some cheesy heart."

"Jesus." Murphy shook his head. "Lifestyles of the Rich and Tasteless."

"I remember that place." Sam paused. "Remember? Harvey Johnston, that used to own the hardware store in McCall, sold it a few years ago, and the new owner applied for a permit right away to build a heart-shaped pool."

"Do you remember if the pool is on the lakefront side?" Murphy's question was directed at Moxie. "Like close to the water, maybe?"

Moxie nodded. "Yeah, totally. The back of the house and the pool back up to the shoreline. You wouldn't be able to miss it from the water."

"Well." Sam leaned over to kiss Sara as she walked back in, then retrieved a decanter of scotch and four glasses, reaching for Moxie's bottle and pouring Coke into her glass first.

"I believe we have a little adventure to go on tomorrow." Sam raised her glass toward the center of the table. "Anyone care to join me?"

CHAPTER SIX

L ily rubbed her eyes with the heels of her hands as she walked through the door of the main lodge, still groggy from her nap. It was clearly too quiet to have made it in time for dinner. She'd gone to two activities she'd signed up for that day but had missed her last one due to an unplanned three-hour nap she didn't remember agreeing to. A fire was still crackling in the central fireplace, but the flames were sinking into embers, and the lodge was still and silent. The last waft of what must have been dinner lingered in the air, and she glanced through the small window in the dining room door.

The sensible thing to do was settle in on one of the leather couches to read, but the audible growl from her belly sparked the thought that the program director, Charlotte, might have left snacks out for the latecomers like she had the first night. She checked the time as she pushed through the door, then stopped in her tracks when she heard the sharp *thwack* from the other side.

"Oh no!" She peeked around to see Alex holding a hand to her head. "I'm so sorry. I should have looked to see if anyone was coming from the other direction."

"That sounded way worse than it was," Alex said, flashing Lily a smile as she lowered her hand. "Besides, you were gone by the time I got up this morning. I was wondering if you'd hopped a plane back to California."

Lily stepped up to Alex and examined the angry red welt rising on her forehead. "Jesus. I really got you." She looked past Alex to the kitchen. "Listen, we need to get some ice on that, or I really will be on my way back to Cali. Sam's going to bounce me from the retreat for beating up on you."

Alex laughed, picking up the scattered remnants of the sandwich she'd been eating and tossing them into the trash by the door. "Don't be silly, I'm fine." She paused, glancing down at the stainless-steel diver's watch on her wrist. "What are you doing here so late, though?"

Lily started to answer, only to be interrupted by another insistent growl from her stomach. "Well, that about sums it up. I somehow slept through most of the afternoon, including dinner, and I may die if I don't eat something." She paused, making her voice sound as serious as possible. "Like, for real."

"Come on. I'll show you around the kitchen. I need to make another sandwich anyway...this one had a scuffle with the door and lost."

Lily smiled and followed Alex back to the kitchen, breathing in her scent. Clean notes of leather, dark evergreens, and whatever it was Alex slicked into her hair instantly brought back the raw memory of the night they'd met. She'd gone to sleep since thinking about being pressed against the cold metal door of the Jeep, Alex's hands wrapped around her waist, and the sharp contrast of gentleness and power in her touch that had reminded her of Sam.

Clearly. Her gaze settled on Alex's defined back and broad shoulders as she headed toward the walk-in refrigerator. *I have a type.*

Alex grabbed an armful of sandwich stuff, fruit, and a handful of cookies from the walk-in and laid them out on the kitchen island. "Oh God." Lily reached for a cookie. "These look delicious. It's always a good sign when there's more chocolate than cookie dough. It's all about the golden ratio."

"Sara made those," Alex said, taking one bite before they went on. "I think she's missing being in the kitchen, but the chef this season is great so it frees her up to do activities and mingle with the guests."

Lily laid out her bread and chose one of the chunky slices of ham to go on it. "I have a date for breakfast at Gus's Place with her tomorrow morning. I can't wait to catch up in person. I got to hug her this morning at breakfast and chat for a few minutes but nothing in-depth."

"Sam told me you guys were close." Alex slid the mustard and mayo down to Lily and handed her a knife. "How did you meet?"

"Well, Sam is my ex. Although, I'm not sure if I'd say we were dating at the time." She paused, reaching for the pickles and arranging four dill slices on the ham as she tried to think of words to wrap around their relationship that summer. "It was more like…"

"More like fucking than dating?"

Lily laughed, plopping a tomato slice on her masterpiece and cutting it in half. "Well, damn, you don't mince words, do you?"

"Not usually." Alex grinned, dropping a handful of cookies into a paper bag and folding it over. "Especially about relationships."

"It was tense for a minute, but the three of us came through it fine, and we've all stayed close. Sam was the one who encouraged me to get off my ass and sign my first book contract."

Alex raised an eyebrow and took a bite of her sandwich.

"Yeah, I saw my latest book on your nightstand. You're busted." Lily looked up as she dropped her sandwich into a sack. "Especially since my picture takes up the entire back cover."

Alex just smiled, then hopped up to sit on the kitchen island. "Listen, you look like you look." Alex paused to let her gaze drop to Lily's shoulders briefly, then folded over the top of Lily's sack. "I know you have to have women hitting on your constantly, so I let you have your space."

Lily smiled, bumping Alex's knee with her hip as she bit into a cookie. "Not that I wanted much space in the end, as it turns out."

Alex got a bigger canvas bag from underneath the island and loaded in the cookies and fruit. "Speaking of which, are you ready to go?"

"Go where?" Lily looked at the clock and back to Alex. "Am I late for something? I swear, my sense of time has been warped since I've been here. I don't know what it feels like not to be constantly working."

Alex hopped down and put the cheese and meat away as she shot a wink over her shoulder. "You're not late for anything unless you want to be down at the campfire bowl with Charlotte and all the couples."

Lily rolled her eyes. "So far, they've been great, but it's a hard pass on all the loved-up couples tonight."

"Hard pass every night for me." Alex hit the lights and guided Lily out, one hand warm on the small of her back.

Darkness had fallen in the blink of an eye, and the shimmering Edison bulbs that crisscrossed the center of the property seemed like endless strands of golden stars strung end to end. The air had cooled enough to bring out the fresh scent of the lake water, and peeper frogs chirped and warbled from the dark edges of the forest. Alex led them down the hill to the dock and, ten minutes later, had nearly convinced Lily to step into one of the canoes.

"So," Alex said, zipping her jacket and running a hand through her hair. "Just so I'm clear, what's the holdup here, exactly? Canoe phobia?"

Lily gazed with distrust at the dark, glittering water. "Just that literally *anything* could be out there. What if McCall has their own version of a Loch Ness Monster or something?"

Alex dutifully scanned the water with a serious look she just managed to pull off without laughing. "Well, I've got a flare, a lantern from the boathouse, and my cell phone. And if we're going to the island, Sam is literally a hundred yards away. Like, less than a minute by speedboat."

Lily paused, carefully weighing her options, then gingerly stepped into the boat with a single foot only to pull it back out again. "And if I agree to this ludicrous night trek to a dark, mysterious island where I'm virtually certain to become *Dateline*'s newest episode…" She paused for dramatic effect. "Then I get sole custody of the bag of cookies?"

"Agreed." She held out a paddle for Lily and motioned her into the boat.

"You think I'm rowing?" Lily smiled, taking the paddle with her thumb and forefinger and laying it back into the bottom of the canoe. "That's adorable."

Alex laughed, pushing the extra paddle to the side. "Well, technically, it's 'paddling,' but I stand corrected."

"That's what I thought." Lily stepped carefully into the canoe and sat gingerly on the back seat, looking warily into the inky water. "Pass those cookies back here just in case I don't make it to the island. I'm not taking any chances."

Alex shook her head and laughed, pulling smoothly out into the water. As they got farther and farther from the docks, the stars above their heads became a glittering expanse of diamonds scattered across a bolt of black velvet. A duo of spotted brown owls followed them, swooping in a crisscross pattern over their heads, undoubtedly amused by Alex's nervous dramatics when they came too close.

"I feel like I'm being divebombed by rogue bird assassins." Alex ducked as one of the assassins dove close enough to ruffle her hair with the breeze from her wings. "I mean, damn, did you just see that? And that was a flashing neon sign that they speak English too. Fantastic."

"Gonna have to toughen up if you're going to hang out with me. I'm a wildlife magnet for some reason."

"Well, I'm not about to have a calm conversation with a grizzly bear, if that's what you mean." Alex turned back around to wink in her direction. "I heard a story about you taming the wild beast that decided to hang out on Sam's porch a few years back."

"What?" Lily leaned back and picked the chocolate out of her cookie to eat first. "That's almost certainly a lie." She was thankful she was sitting behind Alex as she tried to feign indignation. "Who was telling the story?"

"That's would be Sam. She and Sara took my Latin dance class today just for fun." Alex's oar cut smoothly into the black water, the motion soundless and rhythmic at the same time. The pattern was slick, almost hypnotic.

Lily trailed her fingers over the side of the boat into the silky ripples of water, watching as her touch carved its own path through the cool darkness.

"Although, clearly, she added some details for dramatic effect. Like, that you did it topless. Not that I minded."

"I did do it topless." Lily smiled when Alex's head whipped around to look back in her direction. "I'd just eaten dinner at Sam's house, and my shirt smelled like barbeque sauce and the burgers we'd grilled earlier on the upper deck. Not a great combo to be wearing when approaching a bear, if one has a choice." Lily paused to dig into the cookies and held her prize up to the moonlight before she continued. "Besides, something had to be done. The bear had us cornered on the deck and was blocking the only exit."

"Well, then, she's one hundred percent correct in her assessment. You are a badass." Alex shook her head. "My choice would have been to run like hell back into the house and lock it up like Fort Knox, but you decided to whip your shirt off and have a calm conversation with a three-hundred-pound wild animal. Why not?" Alex pulled the canoe smoothly onto the wet sandbank of the island, then extended a hand and helped Lily jump onto the beach beyond. "You might want to leave your shoes in the boat. The sand is amazing this time of night. It's absorbed all the sun from the afternoon heat, then when the air cools down in the evening, it releases it."

Alex pulled a rolled-up blanket from the front corner of the canoe, along with a steel flask she tucked under her arm.

"What's in that?" Lily said, taking the blanket and laying it out on the warm sand next to the water. "And how did that just magically appear?"

"In the flask? I come out here all the time, so I keep a few things in the boathouse out of self-preservation." Alex shrugged off her jacket, put it around Lily's shoulders, then pulled the cookie bag over between them.

Lily reluctantly put her half-eaten cookie down and started on her ham sandwich.

"So," Alex said, brushing a bug off her leg with a sweep of a hand. "Now that you realize I know who you are..." She paused as if choosing each of her words carefully. "I remember at the bar, you said you weren't working at all right now. Why is that?"

Lily swept her bare foot over the sand as if all the answers she needed were there, and she just had to uncover them. "I don't know how to put it into words. It's like I pushed myself to write more and go harder for so long that I felt overwhelmed, like I was drowning under the weight of it all. I went on medication for anxiety attacks, and they just kept getting worse." She wrapped up the remnants of her sandwich and put them beside her on the blanket. "I just finally had to get out of LA and back into the air I could actually breathe, I guess."

"What made you choose McCall?"

"It was the last place I remembered being truly happy." Lily pulled her hair to the nape of her neck and wound it around an elastic. "And I was running out of experiences to write about. I think I need to just be present in my own life for a while."

Alex nodded, passing the flask to Lily, who peered into it like it might contain a grenade. She took a sip and almost held back a cough before she handed it back.

Alex leaned back on her elbows and looked at the sky. "It seems that you'd have to drain your soul a bit for every scene to write like you do. You can only do that for so long before there's nothing left to give. No soul and no passion means no real magic on the page." She paused, her eyes as dark as the sky. "It's the same on the dance floor."

"That's it, I think. I've always said that writing is alchemy. It's a little of my soul and memories, plus a little of the reader's soul and imagination which ignites into...magic." Lily took a long swig from the flask and handed it back. "So I guess the short story is, I lost what makes the magic."

"Well, that answers the question about your books, but the real question is"—Alex took off her shoes and tossed them into the canoe with a clatter—"why is your love life so dismal?"

"Damn, Alex." Lily lay back on the blanket and laughed. "I mean, don't mince any words on my account."

Alex leaned up on one elbow and pointed past Lily into the darkness. Lily turned to find two little gold eyes and a black nose edging past a wide tree trunk to look at them. She unwrapped her sandwich soundlessly and whispered, "You're not afraid of a little raccoon, right?"

"You do you. I'm just a spectator here."

Lily broke off a piece of the bread and tossed it into the space between her and the raccoon, who carefully padded forward, toes disappearing entirely into the sand as she walked.

"And remember," Alex whispered, her breath warm against Lily's neck. "If you feel like you need to whip your shirt off for this, I totally understand."

Lily rolled her eyes and lay quietly on the blanket, facing the raccoon, making herself as small as possible. The little bandit inched forward until she pounced on the bread Lily had tossed, turning it every few bites in her nimble black paws until every crumb was gone. Lily made a high-pitched whirr and held out the remainder of the sandwich. The raccoon slunk closer, took the rest of the sandwich in both front paws, and sat on her hind legs to eat like a tiny human at an invisible picnic table.

"What did you say to her?" Alex whispered. "This is the cutest thing I've ever seen."

Lily didn't answer; she just reached behind her for a cookie and pried all the chocolate chips out of it before handing it over. "None of your business. But I'd think twice before you get into the ocean with me."

"Are you trying to tell me you're a shark magnet? Because I happen to have a thing for shark magnets." Alex took a swig from the flask and shot Lily a serious look. "In fact, that's the number one thing I look for in a girl."

"Ah. That explains why you're out here by yourself all the time."

Lily smiled as the raccoon snatched the last cookie from her extended hand and waddled back into the woods. She settled back on the blanket, feeling calmer than she had in days. Animals always seemed to appear out of the woodwork when she needed them.

"Now why would you assume I'm by myself?"

"That's an excellent point." Lily laced her hands behind her head and stared at the sky, hazy with silver stardust and hovering low over the endless, glittering expanse of dark water. The breeze drifting in from the surface of the water smelled clean and faintly sweet, like the green honeysuckle that draped itself over the curved stone doorways in Cuba. The scent unfolded in the rain and hung in the air only for a few moments at a time until the cobblestones dried in the sun. "Let me guess. Charlotte's favorite rum is Havana 7 Reserve?"

Alex raised herself up on an elbow and waited to speak until Lily met her eyes. "I wouldn't know. She came to my cabin a few nights before you got here and said all the right things, but I turned her down."

Lily nodded and bit her lip. It was clearly none of her business why Alex would turn down a blond bombshell who was practically throwing herself in her direction, and asking about it would clearly be inappropriate. "Why did you give Charlotte a pass? Tell me everything."

Alex laughed, the sound skipping like stones across the water. "I knew you weren't going to let that one slip past you." She picked up Lily's hand and turned it over, then held her palm just above it. "Do you feel that?"

Lily closed her eyes, reminding herself to breathe as she felt the warmth of Alex's hand just above her own. "It's heat. Like a late summer afternoon, when the heat is so intense you can see it moving like water in the distance."

"Exactly."

Lily opened her eyes at the sound of Alex's voice, deep and soft beside her, more touch than sound.

"Chemistry." She trailed a finger across Lily's palm. "It's a prerequisite."

❖

Sara looked up as Moxie came back from the bathroom. She shut the dishwasher door with one hand and picked up a pink tea rose saucer of chocolate chip cookies with the other, holding it out for her.

Moxie took it, then looked around and hesitated. "Where do you want me to put these?"

Sara just smiled, nodding at the door. "They're for you, silly. Sam left to pick something up at the retreat, and I'm headed to bed. I thought you might want to take these up to your room. They're from the cookie jar on the counter. Sam is in it constantly, but I try to keep it filled so it's there whenever anyone needs a snack."

Moxie's gaze dropped again to the saucer as she said good night and started up the stairs. Sara turned off the living room lamps and was headed upstairs too when she remembered the appointment she'd made for the following morning.

"Hey, Moxie?"

Moxie turned, already halfway through one of the cookies. "Yeah?"

"What are you doing tomorrow?" Sara picked up her glass of scotch from the table. "Do you have time to go into town with me?"

Moxie nodded and pushed her glasses up on her nose, finishing the last of her cookie.

"I called and got an appointment for you with my eye doctor. He's going to update your prescription, and you can pick out some new glasses."

Moxie shook her head, a slightly panicked look on her face. "Glasses are expensive. And mine are fine. They've been cracked for two years. I'm used to it."

Sara poured a quick mug of milk and handed it to her on the stairs. "I know everything is different, and that has to be scary. But just because you've had broken glasses for two years doesn't mean you didn't deserve better than that." Sara paused, her voice softening. "And just for the record, it's okay to eat. All you want, in fact. It's okay to take up space. And it's more than okay to need to see where you're going."

Moxie nodded, the way one nodded when listening to a foreign language.

They climbed the stairs together. Moxie put the milk and cookies on her nightstand, then sank down on the edge of her bed and looked up at Sara. "Thank you." She looked exhausted as she rubbed her eyes with her fingertips. "For the glasses and the clean clothes and stuff." Moxie looked at the ceiling and steadied her voice. "My mom was pretty wasted most of my life. I mean, she tried hard..." She trailed off, and Sara watched her fingers tighten around her glass. "But I think I was always taking care of her, you know?"

Sara reminded herself to breathe. The first spark of trust was shimmering in the space between them, and she didn't want to do anything to break the spell.

Moxie sighed, the lines of her shoulders thin and sharp under her hoodie. "Anyway, I just wanted to say thank you." It was all Sara could do not to hug her. She looked so small on the edge of the bed, folding her glasses carefully on the nightstand and pulling her hair out of the worn ponytail holder she slipped onto her wrist.

Murphy was right. Moxie was a little badass, but that was because she'd had to be. Everything inside Sara longed to make things easier for her, to hold the world off long enough to give her some space to be a kid.

Sara said good night and closed the door quietly behind her. She stood at the top of the staircase and listened as Sam's keys turned in the lock downstairs, then went to meet her in the kitchen.

"Hey, beautiful," Sam said, picking up the scotch Sara had set on the counter. "I thought you'd be in bed by now."

"I realized something tonight." Sara trailed her fingers down the back of Sam's neck. She felt her world shift with every word, like a boat turning into the path of the bright gold sun setting over the water. "And I wanted to see how you felt about it."

"Hit me." Sam wrapped her hands around Sara's hips and pulled her close.

"Baby, you know I've never wanted anything more than to have a family with you, but..." Her voice cracked, and Sam pulled her into a hug, only letting go when she found her words again. "But I'm done with the fertility drugs and in vitro treatments. I'm just...done."

Sam seemed to hesitate as she ran her fingers through Sara's hair, then led her to the table to sit down. Sara searched her eyes, her hand warm on Sam's thigh. "How do you feel about that?"

"Honestly?" Sam paused, lifting Sara's hand to kiss her palm, then settling it over her heart. "I'm relieved. I've wanted a family with you since the day we got married, but seeing you go through everything that requires is tearing my heart up." She fell silent, as if choosing her words one by one. "But you've wanted this for so long. Are you really sure you want to give that up?"

"Love makes a family." Sara paused, glancing up the staircase behind her before turning back to Sam. "We don't need a baby to make that happen."

It was a long moment before Sam spoke.

"Sara Draper." Emotion welled in Sam's eyes, and she pulled Sara close, tracing the soft slope of her bottom lip with her thumb as she spoke. "That's the most beautiful thing I've ever heard you say."

Sam held her close for a moment, then slid a hand around to the small of her back. Sara shivered as Sam whispered into the nape of her neck, the heat of her breath warming her skin. "We should keep trying, though, right?"

Sara laughed as Sam scooped her up in her arms and carried her down the hall to their bedroom where she kicked the door shut and laid Sara on the bed, fingers already working the tiny shell buttons on her black linen shirt.

Sara's breath caught as the warmth of Sam's tongue swirled around her nipple, pulling it gently into her mouth. She let Sam slip the shirt off her shoulders, then laughed as she watched her reach to the head of the bed and drape the shirt carefully over the bedpost, arranging the folds until it hung just so.

"What?" Sam said. "I know how you feel about linen."

"First of all, it's true." Sara watched the taut muscles in Sam's shoulders ripple as she pulled her own shirt off and dropped it into a puddle at the foot of the bed. "Wrinkles in linen are permanent." She pulled Sam back down and wrapped her legs tight around Sam's hips. "But I love that I said that once, the summer we met, and you never forgot it."

"Baby." Sam's breath was warm as she traced the lines of Sara's hip with her mouth, pulling off her shorts and a delicate scrap of blue lace underwear with one swift motion. "Everything you say is important to me. Also, I've also lived with you long enough to know that linen anxiety is real."

Sara laughed again as Sam playfully bit her inner thigh. She wove her fingers into Sam's hair, closing her eyes as her words turned to the familiar slick of Sam's tongue over her skin. She lifted Sara's thigh onto her shoulder and traced every inch with her mouth, slowing as she reached Sara's center, touching her clit with only the heat of her breath before doing the same to the other side.

"Sam," Sara said, reaching up to settle her hands on the headboard, her words so soft they melted in the air between them. "I need you inside me."

"Anything you want, baby." Sam moved up to kiss her, then whispered into her neck as she got off the bed. "But I got us something yesterday. Want to see what it is?"

"Maybe." Sara pretended to consider her options. "Only if it involves you getting back into bed."

Sara pulled back the covers and slipped under the fluffy duvet, settling back against the pillows. Sam smiled as she struck a match to light the ivory candles beside their bed, then switched off the lamps. The wind outside brushed invisible rain against the windows, and distant thunder rumbled, stirring the lake enough to hear it lap against the shoreline below their bedroom window.

Sam turned back to Sara. "Look under my pillow."

Sara pulled their new toy out from under the pillow and slowly turned it over in her hands. It was surprisingly heavy and double-ended, but in the shape of an L, with a smooth, velvety finish. Sara secretly loved how Sam surprised her with gifts that showed their sex life was a priority; she'd heard her friends describe exactly the opposite in their own relationships over the years, so the fact that Sam actively nurtured this aspect of their marriage made her feel loved in a way she'd never experienced before.

"I love the look of this, but I've never seen anything like it." Sara wrapped her fingers around the longer end, tracing the lines of it with her fingertip. "What is it?"

Sara looked up to see Sam watching her, hands laced behind her head on the pillow. Her gaze was intense as Sara brought it to her mouth, her swirling her tongue over the end of it until Sam groaned and bit her lip. "Baby, you're killing me."

"Oh, really?" Sara smiled and laid the toy on Sam's abs, her voice dripping with the honeyed Memphis accent that five years in the North hadn't seemed to touch. "Well, I'm just getting started, so unless you want to watch me try it out while I have you handcuffed to the bed, I'd start setting up that little show-and-tell I asked for."

"Oh, that's adorable." Sam laughed as she flipped Sara onto her back with one swift motion and slipped her hands under Sara's hips. "I love it when you think you're in charge."

Sam winked as she settled between Sara's naked thighs. Sara arched her back as she felt the slow melt of Sam's tongue across her clit, then held her breath as Sam started to work her in slick, warm circles. Sam spread her hands over Sara's inner thighs, lifting and holding them above her head as she stroked every inch of her with the flat of her tongue before returning to her clit.

❖

After five years loving Sara's body, Sam knew the meaning of every breath, the way her thighs tensed over Sam's shoulders when she was close, even how she reached behind her at the last second to grab the headboard before she came. Sara still turned her on more than any woman ever had, and more than once, Sam had come without even being touched as she went down on her, tongue stroking Sara's clit as the breathy urgency of her voice pushed Sam over the edge. Sam paused as she realized how close she was now and held her mouth just above Sara's clit until she begged.

"Baby." Sara's voice was sultry, her fingers white and tense against the headboard. "Please."

Sam groaned and sank back into the warmth of her, her shoulders edging Sara's thighs farther apart, moving her tongue slick and strong over Sara's clit. Sam breathed her in, bracing against the orgasm building as she buried her tongue deep inside.

"Let it go, baby." Sara's voice was breathless, her fingers soft and light on Sam's shoulders. "Come for me."

That was all Sam needed. She let herself sink into it, felt her body surrender as it crashed over her in a silent wave, knocking the breath from her lungs and leaving her gasping and shaken between Sara's thighs. When her breath finally slowed, she moved back up Sara's body, kissing her and whispering all their sacred words, love shimmering like heat between them. She wrapped her hands around Sara's waist and lifted her as she turned over, settling Sara to sit across her hips like she'd done a thousand times before.

"God." Wild waves of sunlit blond fell around Sara's shoulders in the darkness as she circled her hips against Sam's, her wetness slick between them. "It's so sexy how you just pick me up and put me where you want me." She smiled and bit her lip as she remembered. "The first time you did that, I was instantly wet. I think it was that night we spent in the treehouse, and it still works every time."

Sam smiled, her hands sliding up Sara's thighs. "Well, take a breath because we're just getting started, baby."

Sara reached for the forgotten toy, turning it over in her hand. "I'd love to be cool and worldly here, but I seriously have no idea how we're supposed to use this." She paused, then dragged her tongue from one end to the other, her eyes locked on Sam's. "What does a girl have to do to get a show-and-tell?"

Sam's voice was a low scrape as she took it from Sara, sliding her back from her hips to sit between her thighs. "Let's just say we don't need the harness tonight." Sam slid the short end of the L-shaped toy inside her, and Sara wrapped her hand around the other end as she knelt above Sam's hips and kissed her, easing back on it slowly.

"Take your time." Sam paused, waiting for any hint that it might be too much. "It's more than what you're used to." Sara closed her eyes, taking a deep breath as she leaned back to take the last few inches. She bit her lip, and Sam squeezed her thighs gently. "Baby, if it's too much, just—"

"Sam," Sara interrupted as she started to rock her hips gently. "I love it. It feels amazing to have nothing between us like this." She leaned back, her eyes sparkling. "But will you do that other thing I love?"

Sam slipped her hand between their bodies and found Sara's clit as she rocked her hips. She arched, moving deeper into Sara as she watched her lean back, her hands behind her on Sam's thighs. Sam watched every move, memorized every curve from her hips to her breasts, her body flushed and damp, her pale pink nipples tense and straining.

Sam wrapped her hands around Sara's hips, pulling her down with every stroke to grind against her.

"Baby…" Sara's voice was breathless. Her eyes fluttered shut as her hair dropped behind her, her hips moving in perfect circles between Sam's hands. "Do you want to watch me come for you?"

Sam's eyes were locked on Sara. "Fuck yes, baby."

Sam sank into the rhythm of her hips, drinking in the sensual curves of Sara's naked body. She tried to speak, but the words faded into the orgasm that swept between them, shaking Sam to her core and making her wonder if she could draw another breath. Sara's rhythm faltered as the intensity crested, and Sam took over, guiding her hips into the deep strokes she knew Sara loved, grinding against her clit as Sara arched back and shuddered to her second climax, her hips rocking in a slick rhythm against Sam's.

As the intensity faded, Sara melted into her arms, and Sam turned her over and pulled her close, wrapping her body around Sara's from behind and pulling the duvet over them.

"Sam?"

Sara's voice was already fading into sleep, and Sam smiled as she waited for her to continue.

"I still love you more every day."

Sam kissed her neck and whispered, "Me too, baby." She listened to the rhythm of Sara's breath and settled her hand over Sara's heart. "Every damn day."

CHAPTER SEVEN

Well, would you look at that? You survived the late-night canoe ride." Alex winked at Lily as she unlocked their cabin door, then held it open for her to go in. "We didn't even have to call Sam." She dropped the keys beside the record player and turned on the lamps. "Not that I wasn't looking forward to calling your ex to rescue us in the middle of a date, but whatever." Alex looked up at Lily and grinned. "I can wait till next time, I guess."

Lily shrugged off her jacket and tossed it up onto her bunk, mentally sifting through her cache of clever retorts. "So that was a date?"

"Well, yeah." Alex thumbed through a pine box of records under the player. "I mean, I didn't have a lot of time to plan, so it's not one of my best, but we did have rum. So technically, it was a date."

"Actually, I loved that rum. It almost tasted like…" Lily trailed off as she tried to wrap words around the scent but came up with nothing.

"Smoke?" Alex set up a record and it dropped under the needle, the familiar scratch giving way to a sultry jazz quartet that made Lily feel like she was wandering the dark alleys of New Orleans.

"Yeah, smoke." She paused. "But rum isn't smoked, is it?"

"Other than being aged in charred oak barrels, the smoke element is usually added after the fact." Alex slipped her shoes off and set them just inside the door of the cabin. "There's a cocktail in Havana that uses scorched rosemary and sage garnish to give it that flavor, plus a smoky simple syrup. It's my favorite thing in the world."

Lily pulled her sky-blue silk pajamas from underneath her pillow and placed them on the bathroom sink, then started the shower and waited until the water turned to swirling pewter steam before she came back into the main room.

"You miss Havana, don't you?"

Alex was still at the record player and didn't turn, just traced the edge of the record sleeve with her finger, her words soft as ash when she finally chose them. "Every day."

Lily walked back into the bathroom and started to close the door, then stopped and propped it open as she turned toward the shower and unbuttoned her shirt. She felt the weight of Alex's gaze warm her skin as she unzipped her jeans, stepping out of them and slipping off her underwear. She heard Alex cross the room, then felt hands circling her waist and warm breath close at her neck.

"Lily." Her voice was soft as she said something in Spanish.

Lily realized she was holding her breath and made herself exhale before she spoke. "What does that mean?"

"It means you're so beautiful that I don't have the words. In either language." Alex kissed the other side of her neck, brushing her lips against her skin so softly, Lily thought she might have imagined it. "And that thought has been on repeat in my mind since I met you."

Alex kissed her, tracing the edge of her ear with the tip of her tongue, her hand warm and light against the base of Lily's neck. And then she was gone, the space behind her empty, echoing like the sound of the door closing softly behind her.

Lily stepped into the shower and let the water run over her face, her thoughts racing. It felt so natural, being with Alex. Women hit on her constantly in LA, but there was something calm about Alex, something quietly respectful. She listened when Lily talked, her dark eyes searching for every nuance of meaning. Even her touch was familiar, as if they'd been lovers for a thousand years.

Lily's fingertips brushed the nape of her neck where Alex's breath had been as she stepped out of the shower and wiped the steam from the mirror. As she stared into her reflection, she realized what was different, why she finally felt safe to exhale.

Alex held space for her. She created the space for her to unfold, to relax and soften. For the last few years, she'd felt herself shrinking, disappearing, somehow reduced to her own words on paper. The paper had been passed through a thousand foreign hands, crumpled into a ball, and compressed into something unrecognizable. Alex held the space she needed to smooth out the paper and remember the shape and space she'd once inhabited.

She was playing a live recording of low country jazz when Lily finally walked out of the bathroom, the steam that followed her instantly rising into the cool breeze that shifted the curtains over her bed.

Lily drew in a slow breath, her eyes closed. "I love the scent of sand when the sun sets." The sound of her own voice jolted her back into the present, and she looked up at Alex, who'd turned toward her to listen, her gaze soft and constant. Lily paused, wishing she could gather the words she'd just scattered into the air, but there was nothing to do now but go on. "It's just…during the day, the sun heats the lake water, and the scent of it travels everywhere, but as evening cools, the wet stone scent of the sand has space to rise."

She dropped her clothes into her laundry bag and turned back toward the bunk, wishing she'd remembered that her words often didn't make sense to anyone else. When she was a child, she'd overheard her mother on the telephone with her second-grade teacher one evening after dinner. The memory was almost twenty years old now, but that moment still played like a grainy retro movie in her mind.

She'd been coming down the staircase when she heard her mother's voice, the polished railing cool and smooth under her palm. She'd stopped still, listening as it shifted from friendly to coolly polite as the conversation progressed. Lily sank down onto the stairs and leaned her forehead against the railing, listening; there was a long stretch of quiet, and Lily had heard her mother's nails strumming the counter when she'd finally replied to whatever her teacher had taken so long to explain.

"Lily doesn't have her head in the clouds, Miss Morrison. You're just wrong here."

Lily had leaned against the railing and listened hard, the hardwood stair cold and unyielding under her corduroy cutoffs. Dust motes had hovered in the late evening light streaming through the glass panels in the front door. She'd waited, afraid to breathe in case she missed something.

"With all due respect, she learns by memorizing her entire world, not just two-dimensional words on a page like everyone else." There was a long sigh, a pause, then just two more words. "She's different."

Somewhere along the way, Lily had realized her mother had been right. Her brain worked differently than most, and over the years, she'd learned it was easier to be silent than judged. Everything about her was different. How she experienced the world, how she responded to it, even how she described it in her writing.

The sound of cracking ice snapped her back to reality, and she turned to watch Alex as she chipped jagged shards off a square block, then wrapped it back in a cloth and returned it to the freezer tucked inside what Lily previously thought was a dresser.

"So that's an icebox?" Lily walked over to look, her damp feet leaving footprints on the raw plank floors. "I swear that was a dresser yesterday."

"That's what I thought for the first week. The dresser face is actually just a door that swings open." She pointed to the brass hinges on the side, and Lily leaned down to look, holding the front of her silk pajamas to her chest. "There's one in every cabin. Sam had someone build them to hide a mini fridge so the staff had somewhere to keep drinks that wouldn't ruin the mid-fifties aesthetic of the cabin 'interior,' or whatever the hell she said." Alex laughed, dropping ice shards into two glasses and the remainder into a dented copper cocktail shaker. "I mean, I've got to give it to her. You wouldn't know it to look at her, but Sam could give any self-respecting gay man a run for his money in the design department."

Alex poured rum into the shaker, then added something from a separate flask she tucked back in the fridge. Lily watched as frost gathered on the outside of the shaker, mesmerized as Alex flicked it with her wrist, spun it on the flat of her hand, then uncapped it and strained it into the glasses. Alex nodded toward the opposite window.

"Will you pinch a couple of sprigs of mint from that plant in the windowsill?"

"You grow cocktail herbs in your cabin?" Lily smiled as she handed them over and watched as Alex placed them carefully in each glass. "If you're trying to seduce me with your weirdness, it's working."

Alex winked and handed her one of the glasses, then motioned for Lily to follow her outside to the two slatted wood folding chairs set up by the door. The lake sparkled in the moonlight, framed by the massive, ghostly reflection of the dark grove of firs on the north shore. A slate-blue heron swooped low over the water, scanning the surface for fish, then dropped into a pure vertical dive and emerged from the dramatic splash with a reflective prize in its grasp.

Alex looked over at her and pushed the glasses up on her nose. "I could say the same thing, you know."

Lily had noticed the contact lens case on the bathroom shelf, but it hadn't occurred to her that Alex would wear glasses occasionally. They were perfectly round tortoiseshell spectacles with a Harry Potter vibe—if Harry had been a tall, intensely sexy Cuban dance instructor.

As if on cue, Alex handed over her glass for Lily to hold while she zipped up her black hoodie. The first ghostly vapors of steam started to rise and hover above the lake as the air sank into a cooler temperature than the water. She was wearing men's jeans, faded to the lightest sky blue, and stretched out her legs in front of her as she glanced back to Lily, who had just remembered what Alex had said to her.

"What do you mean, you could say the same thing?" Lily sipped from Alex's glass instead of her own before handing it back to her. "About what?"

"You asked if I was trying to seduce you with my weirdness. You've been doing that to me since the second I saw you."

Lily's heart sank, and she looked out over the water as the only cloud in the sky moved hesitantly across the hazy surface of the pewter moon. She didn't have to ask; she knew what Alex meant. She'd known since that night on the stairs, although as an adult, she'd tried not to notice when others perceived her as different. But now, all she wanted was for Alex not to answer. She just wanted another moment to let herself think that everyone around her didn't see it.

Alex touched her knee to Lily's. "Do you remember the first night we met? At the bar?"

"Of course." Lily forced herself to smile, and her stomach tensed as she took a sip of her drink. Then another.

Alex turned to face Lily and laid a warm hand on her thigh. Lily swallowed hard and looked up. "I sat down beside you as the bartender was pouring your whiskey. You were so intent that I don't think you noticed me. You just closed your eyes and brought it to your nose, breathing it in. I just sat there and watched you experience it with your whole body."

Lily looked up and met Alex's eyes. They were sparked with gold and glittering with the reflection of the lake water.

"It was the sexiest thing I've ever seen."

Lily smiled and slipped her hand under Alex's, still warm on her thigh. Relief settled in her chest as the music stopped, and Alex squeezed her hand.

"Your turn, Ms. Larimar." She nodded in the direction of the record player just inside the cabin. "I'll just sit right here and see what you come up with."

"Oh, great." Lily rolled her eyes. "At least there's no pressure." She shot Alex a wink as she went inside, where she found the rustic pine box full of Alex's albums and started thumbing through them. She was looking for something specific, something she knew would be there, and it was. Lily dropped the vinyl out of a cardboard sleeve with worn, sun-faded edges and centered it on the player, dropping the needle onto the record carefully. Music filled the cabin, instantly warming the air with a sultry Cuban vibe.

"I knew it." The door opened, and Alex smiled as she came back into the cabin with both drinks in one hand. "Buena Vista Social Club. I knew that's what you'd look for."

"I just love it. It feels like you could just wander down a street in Cuba and find them playing in some club with the doors thrown open and the audience sitting in random chairs on the sidewalk."

Alex put their drinks on the stack of books in the windowsill, then offered Lily her hand.

"What?" Lily tilted her head for a split second before it dawned on her. "Oh no. I can't dance. I mean, I've literally never done real dancing."

Alex just smiled, her hand still extended between them.

"Like...ever."

Alex slid one hand warm around the small of her back, pulling Lily lightly against her. "You don't have to know how to dance." She paused, then bit Lily's lower lip, soft as air, brushing it gently with the warmth of her tongue as she stepped back. "You just have to trust me enough to follow."

Lily took Alex's hand again as she taught her a basic salsa step, which turned out to be a repetitive step forward with one foot, then back with the other. The acoustic Cuban rhythm melted into the air around them, pushing their bodies closer, until Alex took her hand in hers and raised them to shoulder level.

"Hold your frame." Alex looked at Lily's arm and pushed against her hand until Lily pushed back slightly. "There you go. Keep me in my place."

Lily arched an eyebrow as Alex started the step for them again, holding her eyes. Their bare feet were silent against the wood floor, and Alex's rhythm was sure and constant. The heat between them shimmered, as real and tangible as the music.

"I'm going to spin you into a half turn. Just keep that basic step going."

"Wait, what?"

Alex spun her so that Lily's back was against her body. They both were still doing the same basic salsa step, only now Lily felt every inch of Alex behind her as she moved. Alex's breath brushed the delicate skin of her neck, and she closed her eyes as she listened. "Now we're going to spin back." Lily nodded, focusing on the heat of Alex's body behind her. "Just let me move you."

Alex spun her back, but this time there was no space between them, and the rhythm of the music hung in the air as if they were dancing under last shards of a sunlit Havana evening. The energy between them was intense as Alex slipped one thigh between hers while the music dripped heat in the background. Time was slow and silent as Alex pushed her hand slightly forward, and Lily leaned back from the waist until her hair touched Alex's hand at her hip.

"Goddamn." Alex's voice was raw, as intense as the music behind them. She brought her slowly back up, unfolding Lily's body onto hers, until only breath hovered warm between their lips. "That was unbelievably beautiful."

Lily closed her eyes. Alex traced her cheek with her thumb as the music stopped, and the needle fell silent against the record as dawn started to shimmer against the windows.

❖

Lily pushed open the door to Gus's Place later that morning and spotted Sara in the corner, settled onto one of the cozy couches by the windows with a white ceramic diner mug of coffee in hand. She hurried over and sank down on the couch beside her, leaning in for a hug. It was so good to see Sara, although Lily had almost slept through her alarm.

After the dance, she'd slept for a couple of hours in Alex's bed, her still damp hair warm against her chest, and the last thing she remembered was Alex's fingertips trailing over her back as she fell asleep.

"I'm so sorry I'm late." Lily settled back into the plush cushions and sighed as a server handed her a latte in an identical mug. "Last night was a late one, and it was hard to get out of bed this morning."

"So tell me everything." Sara laughed and pulled her feet up underneath her on the couch. She took a sip of coffee and leaned in. "What's happening with Alex?"

"What?" Lily just managed not to spray latte foam across the coffee table in front of them. "How could you *possibly* know about Alex?"

Sara laughed, leaning back and cradling her mug in her hands. "Well, when Sam came home that first night and told me you were here, I couldn't understand why she hadn't invited you to stay at the house, but she said she put you in with Alex." Sara winked at Lily over the rim of her cup. "She didn't seem to get it, but I saw this coming from that moment on."

"Well, not that I hate being in a cabin with the hotness that is Alex." Lily reached up to take the menu that the waitress handed her and shook her head. "But there's no way I would have wanted to intrude on your house. It's bad enough I showed up out of nowhere and expected you two to have a place for me at the retreat."

Sara laughed, sweeping her blond hair up into a makeshift bun that she quickly speared with a pen from her pocket. "Are you kidding? That was the best news I'd had in ages." She stopped short and nodded at the server, who was power walking back to their table. "Do you know what you want to eat?" She laid her menu on the table and dropped her voice. "My new server Allison has the tableside manner of an Olympic sprinter. She's a godsend when we're busy, though, so I'm not complaining."

Sure enough, Allison reached them just a few seconds later and waited silently with her pen hovering above her order pad.

"Oh God. I have no idea." Lily scanned the menu. "I haven't eaten here since just before your wedding."

"The menu is actually pretty much the same. You always ordered the biscuits and gravy, right?"

Lily handed her the menu and nodded. "God lives in that gravy recipe, so that'll do it."

Allison scurried away, and Lily turned back to Sara. "What do you put in it, anyway? *Food and Wine* magazine included it a couple of years back in their Heaven on Earth issue, right? One of my chef buddies in LA was raving about it."

Sara refilled her coffee from the carafe on the table and smiled. "I hinted at it, but the recipe is so simple, I didn't dare tell them the actual secret."

"Going out on a limb here," Lily said, reaching for a sugar packet. "But bacon grease and bourbon?"

Sara threw her head back and laughed, which made all the senior citizens at the Formica bar look up over their newspapers to check out where the noise was coming from. They smiled warmly when they realized it was Sara, and she lowered her voice to whisper, "How did you know that?"

"Sara, we've been close for a few years now. I think that would be the answer to most questions one might ask about you."

"Well, you're not wrong." Sara smiled at Lily over the rim of her cup. "Which segues perfectly back to hot Latin dance instructors. Tell me *everything*."

"That doesn't segue in the slightest." Lily laughed as she shrugged off her jean jacket and folded it beside her. "I don't know what's happening, to be honest. I know I've only been here a few days, but she's sexy as hell and makes me feel…"

"Safe?"

"Yeah, that's exactly it. How did you know?"

"Because that would have to be true for you to be thinking about getting into something. I know you spend too much of your time feeling the opposite." Sara dumped two packets of sugar into her coffee, barely pausing before reaching for a third. "Besides, I don't know what it is, but she definitely has this old-world gangster vibe to her. I have a feeling she could handle just about anything she encountered in a dark alley."

"But…" Lily hesitated, picking up an empty sugar packet and folding it into a square as she spoke. "Last night we had this amazing date, danced together, stayed up all night…"

"But didn't sleep together?"

"Exactly." Lily tossed the packet and laughed. "And how the hell did you guess that out of the blue?"

"Let's just say I wouldn't be surprised if Sam and Alex have a few things in common." Sara shook her head, dropping her voice to a whisper. "The first time Sam and I were together, she actually stopped us right before it happened. I was literally naked in the back of my boat when she sat up and said that she just couldn't do it."

Lily's mouth dropped open. "Jesus Christ. Did she say why?"

"Not till a few days later." Sara shook her head, tucking a stray blond wave behind her ear. "And I can tell you, it took me that long to find the shattered pieces of my ego on the floor of the boat."

"Damn." Lily paused. "Sam is usually so smooth. I have a hard time picturing her telling a gorgeous—"

"And naked," Sara cut in.

"Excellent point." Lily nodded. "I have a hard time seeing her saying no to a gorgeous naked woman she was already in love with."

"Well, that's the interesting part of the story. She took me on a little food tour of Idaho after an impromptu tasting for this place crashed and burned. We were drinking whiskey the first night when I told her that it was okay if she wasn't attracted to me, that she could just say it. I think I even said that I wasn't going to jump off a bridge or anything."

"Oh God." Lily leaned forward, completely immersed in the story despite knowing how it eventually panned out. "What did she say?"

"She told me that she realized at that moment in the boat that she couldn't risk losing me—"

"Which is the most romantic thing ever."

"Right? So the reality was that she waited until she was sure." Sara turned the diamond band on her finger. "And the rest is history."

"Speaking of that, what's happening with this last IVF attempt?" Lily took a sip of her latte and put it back down on the table. "The last time we talked, your appointment was the next day."

Allison appeared out of nowhere just as Sara opened her mouth to speak, and soon the table in front of them was loaded with biscuits and gravy, bacon, and two dishes of fresh watermelon mint salad, as well as an alarmingly tall pile of chilaquiles for Sara.

Lily picked up a thick slice of crisp bacon and sat back, allowing Sara to answer when she was ready. She just watched as Sara took a moment to arrange the plates on the table, then sank back into the pillows beside her.

"I got my period a few days ago."

Lily squeezed Sara's arm but stayed silent.

"I told Sam last night that I don't want to try again. I think I knew it was the last time for me, you know?" She took a bite of the chilaquiles and the tension showed on her forehead, as if she was searching for an explanation that didn't exist. "I don't know why I knew. I just did."

"You don't have to know why." Lily paused, her voice gentle. "And you don't have to explain it to anyone."

Sara looked up at her, the tension in her jaw visibly softening. "I don't, do I?"

"Nope." Lily shook her head, a slow smile spreading across her face. "You don't have to say one single word. This is your experience, and no one else has a right to details unless you want to give them."

"Thanks. I just needed to hear that, I guess." Sara let out a long breath. "Exactly that."

The two of them suddenly remembered their food, and it was a few moments before Sara turned back to Lily to ask how the promotion was going for *Embers into Fire*. "I love that book, by the way." Sara smiled, reaching for another napkin. "I read it twice in one week when you sent it to me."

"It just landed in bookstores last week, actually. I sent you my copy, the one they call the author's copy, so you got to read it before everyone else."

"Oh, man." Sara bumped her shoulder to Lily's as they finished up the last of their breakfast. "I wish you would have told me that then. I lost like two months of quality bragging time about how I know the author."

"Oh, good Lord." Lily rolled her eyes and laid her silverware on her plate. "You'd better be joking."

"I am, of course." Sara smiled up at Allison as she came to take their plates, leaving them with just their coffee cups and cozy couch. The sun warmed the plate glass window behind them, and the sidewalk sounds of McCall were just audible over the clink of cutlery and scrape of chairs over the diner floor. "How's everything going with that, by the way? Did you just leave the press junket for the book and hop a plane to McCall? Clyde has to be losing his ever-loving mind."

"You're telling me." Lily rolled her eyes and looked at the ceiling. "I mean, Jesus. I know it's not easy being my agent, but he's really got to chill out before he has a heart attack."

"Yeah, well, it's good for him. Character building." Sara refilled their cups from the carafe and sat back into the pillows. "How are you really doing? You had to be at the end of your rope if you just ditched LA and Clyde with no warning."

"I was." Lily shook her head to clear it. "I mean, I still am, really. I've got to find a way through this, but he wants to know when I'll be back, and I don't know how to tell him that I don't know yet."

"And how have you been since you've been here?" Sara looked over at Lily. "I know it's only been a few days, but are the panic attacks getting better at all?"

"You know, I actually haven't felt like that since I left LA, but I can't really explain why. I'm still stressed about all the same things, but there's just something about McCall that...helps, I guess."

"Someone really wise told me once that I don't owe anyone an explanation." Sara elbowed lily softly. "And I didn't have to understand what was going on all the damn time."

Lily looked up with a wink. "Well, she sounds fantastic."

"She is, as a matter of fact."

Sara's phone buzzed, and she had a short conversation while Lily finished her coffee, then dropped her phone back into her bag and leaned in, one eye on the front door of the diner. "So, I didn't realize it was getting so late, but I need to tell you about Moxie. She's coming in to meet me in just a few minutes."

Lily glanced out the window and down the street to the coffee shop. "Java?"

"Nope. We have a foster kid who's living with us, and that's her name."

"Whoa." Lily shook her head to clear it. "I swear, your life has more twists and turns than my storylines. You have a foster kid? When did this happen?"

Sara's face softened as she pulled a twenty-dollar bill from her wallet and laid it on the table. "She's only been with us a few days, but she's the sweetest, toughest girl on the planet. She reminds me a little bit of you, actually."

Lily nodded, noting the slight, hesitant teenager walking through the double glass doors at the front of the diner as if on cue. She was wearing faded jeans with a rip in one knee, a threadbare tee that said *Jasper Crystal Festival 2018*, and a pair of black Chuck Taylors. When she caught sight of Sara in the back, her face brightened, and she walked toward them.

"Hey, Moxie." Sara smiled, zipping her bag closed and glancing at Lily. "This is Lily, a good friend of mine who's here from LA for a while."

Lily smiled and said hi, but Moxie looked instantly nervous and stumbled over her words. When she finally answered, her voice sounded as if she'd sprinted from the resort to the diner. "You're Lily Larimar. I have your picture." She shook her head and tried again. "I mean your book. The one that you wrote."

"I'm so flattered." Lily reached out from the couch to shake her hand. "It's great to meet you, Moxie."

Moxie shook Lily's hand and paused, seeming to consider her words more than once before she said them. "I saw your book in the window at Barnes and Noble right before my mom went back to jail." She paused, pulling her sleeves down over her hands. "I bought it the next day and it…kinda saved me."

"Books have saved me since I was a kid." Lily's face softened as if she were looking at a forgotten picture of herself at that age. "That totally makes sense."

"You know, I have a copy of Lily's latest, *Embers Into Fire*," Sara said with a glance at Lily. "If you want to read it, I'll leave it on your bed."

"Really? There's more than one?"

"Actually, I flew here straight from a signing in LA, so I have an extra copy with me. I'll sign it for you personally and drop it by the house if you're interested." Lily smiled warmly up at Moxie, who suddenly looked like she didn't know what to do with her hands. *I can relate*, Lily thought as she felt herself warming to the quiet girl with the crack in her glasses. "That way, it's all yours."

"That's amazing." Moxie shoved her hands into the pocket of her jeans. "And thanks. I'll find some way to repay you."

"Nope." Lily shook her head. "I wouldn't even be able to do this if there weren't readers like you who really love the stories, so you can just consider us even."

Moxie smiled, which somehow caused the cracked left lens of her glasses to drop to the floor and break into three jagged triangles.

"Perfect timing." Sara laughed, picking them up and dropping them on the table.

"Let's go get you some new glasses so you can read that book."

CHAPTER EIGHT

Sam reached for the last bolt with her wrench just as her cell phone buzzed in her pocket. She tightened it quickly and retrieved her phone, holding it between her face and her shoulder as she climbed back down the ladder.

"Hey, Alex." Sam dropped the wrench into the back pocket of her jeans and wiped a smear of grease off the back of her hand with her T-shirt. "How can I help you?" Sam hit the speakerphone button and leaned against the ladder, enjoying the late afternoon breeze sweeping in off the lake. Once she was away from both the station and the retreat, there seemed to be more fresh air and space to breathe it.

"Hey." Alex's deep voice echoed in the wide-open space. "Do you happen to have time for a chat? I'm done with the last class of the afternoon, and there's something I want to run by you."

"Yeah, of course."

"Great, are you at home? I can walk over, if that works."

"Yeah, of course." Sam looked at her watch. "Just come to the front of the house and follow the stone trail that leads to your right down to the water. You can't see me from the driveway, but I'm right beside the barn."

Just as Sam was hanging up, she saw a text from Sara: *Moxie and I are picking up dinner before we head home. Still meeting Murphy in town tonight?*

Sam replied and ran both hands through her hair as she looked out over the lake to the island, shimmering with iridescent greens and blues under the low-hanging afternoon sun. Lately, she'd been leaving her clothes on the dock every evening and swimming to the island. Years ago, the water had saved her in the first few months after her father died. She'd swum from her house to the island over and over, letting it smooth and cool the rough edges of grief that had threatened to consume her like fire. Now she felt drawn to it again, but this time, there was no obvious reason, which somehow bothered her even more. When her dad had died, she'd known on some level that swimming to the island was helping her work through her grief. This time, she just had a vague feeling that something was missing, and she didn't have a clue what that was.

After a few minutes, she saw Alex striding down the stone pathway in loose khakis rolled up at the ankle and an unbuttoned tropical shirt over a white tank.

"Damn, Alex," Sam called. "You couldn't look more Cuban if you tried."

Alex laughed, stopping to tie her shoe as she answered. "Yeah, well. Occupational hazard." As she stood, she looked around before meeting Sam at the bottom of the path. "I knew you had a barn, but I swear, when you showed me around at the start of the summer, there wasn't a lighted half-court basketball setup down here."

"Good eye." Sam smiled and stepped off the concrete. "I actually had someone from town frame it out and pour it a couple of days ago, and I just set up the goal before you got here."

"Nice." Alex scanned the empty square. "But did you remember the basketballs?"

Sam nodded to two new balls at the north end of the court. Alex picked one up and stepped onto the court in a slow dribble, alternating hands several times before she tossed it in Sam's direction.

Sam caught it and shot a perfect basket, retrieving it quickly and tossing it back. "You said you had something you wanted to run by me?"

Alex nodded and went for a layup, which bounced twice around the rim just to fall away. She tossed it over, rolling up her shirtsleeves as Sam tucked it under her arm. "Yeah." Alex paused. "It's about Lily."

"Lily?" It took Sam a few seconds to remember she'd given Lily the only available spot open at the retreat in Alex's staff cabin. "Sure, what's up?"

"Well, she speaks highly of you, and I know you two had a..." Alex paused as if searching for the word.

"Thing?"

"Exactly." Alex laughed, holding her hands out for the ball and sinking it through the net with a satisfying swoop. She bounced it back, then shaded her eyes as she spoke. "I'm starting to realize I'm really into her. I just wanted to give you the heads-up. I know you two are still close, so I imagine you still care about her."

Sam dribbled to center court and managed to keep the ball out of Alex's reach just long enough to shoot and swish. She turned to Alex and smiled, tugging off her T-shirt and tossing it to the side of the court, leaving her in just a black Nike sports bra.

"I know she's searching for something right now, for balance, maybe, so she's vulnerable." Sam held Alex's gaze as the wind ran its fingers through the treetops behind them. "Can I trust you to guard her heart? Even if it doesn't work out?"

"Of course." Alex's gaze was steady. "You have my word."

Sam nodded. "That's good enough for me. And I appreciate you letting me know. She'll always be special to me, and she's actually one of my wife's closest friends." She glanced up to the house, making sure Sara and Moxie hadn't returned. "And on a different note, I have a question for you."

The wide gold beams of afternoon sunlight fell over Alex like stage lights as she waited for Sam to continue.

"I know this is going to seem out of left field," Sam said, swiping the sweat from her forehead with the back of her hand, "But do you ever get misgendered in everyday life?"

"Like, do people ever think I'm a man?"

"Yeah, I mean, if you don't mind me asking." Sam tilted her head to the side, looking Alex up and down. "You've got some serious shoulders and a good inch on me, and I'm almost six feet."

"Oh yeah. Every damn day." Alex laughed, placing the ball carefully back where she'd gotten it on the side of the court and tossing Sam her T-shirt. "Mary from the drugstore in town does it on purpose, I swear."

Sam didn't reply for a long moment, just looked Alex up and down. "So do you have plans tonight?"

"Why?" Alex laughed, looking behind her for effect. "Are you asking me out on a date?"

"Yes, sir." Sam laughed and pulled her shirt over her head, nodding for Alex to follow as she walked back up the path toward the house. "That's exactly what I'm doing."

❖

Sam laughed and shook her head as she walked up the pine needle strewn path to the Other Place, McCall's only real bar. She knew exactly what she'd find when she got there, and sure enough, Murphy was already at one of the patio tables with the cast-iron tabletop cauldrons, gleefully piling a handful of marshmallows onto a tiny roasting stick.

"Dude." Sam rolled her eyes as she shrugged off her jean jacket and dropped it over the back of her chair. "I was hoping last time was just a one-off. Don't tell me you brought your own…" Her voice trailed off as she took in the tiny mason jar of strawberry jam and silver spoon on the table. "What the hell is all this stuff?"

Murphy shot her a withering look as he pulled a handful of individually wrapped Reese's peanut butter cups out of his jacket pocket and lined them up in a perfect row next to a stack of graham crackers. "I would tell you, but I know from experience, you don't appreciate the finer things in life."

Sam leaned back and laughed as she watched Murphy painstakingly drop a dollop of strawberry jam onto a cracker with a tiny silver spoon, top it with a Reese's cup and a smoking hot marshmallow, then bookend his masterpiece with another graham cracker. He held it up and eyed it from every angle like a jeweler inspecting a diamond, then leaned back and dropped the entire square into his mouth with a look of pure bliss.

The server stopped by to get Sam's order and shook her head as she watched; this was clearly not her first experience with Murphy the S'more Connoisseur.

Sam winked and whispered in her direction, "I'll just have a Guinness. Also, I'll be tipping big for both of us."

She laughed, leaving them to it as Murphy's little moans of

pleasure slowly faded, and he brushed the crumbs from the front of his shirt.

Sam directed his attention to a tourist at a nearby table filming the entire episode. "Dude. You're my brother-in-law, and I love you, but hanging out with you is putting a major dent in my street cred." Sam grinned and put the cap back on the dainty jam jar. "I'm just sayin'."

"Well." Murphy smiled and winked at the tourist. "When I start to give a single shit about street cred, I'll let you know."

The server returned with Sam's Guinness and the drink Murphy ordered: a frosty, pale pink cosmo in a martini glass. Sam shook her head and tried to stifle a laugh. "I swear to God, if you drink that thing with your pinkie in the air, I'm leaving."

"Do what you gotta do, Chief. I'm secure in my masculinity." Murphy sipped his cosmo with his little finger lofted as high as possible, leaning back in his chair with a satisfied sigh. "Why did you want to meet tonight? Not that I'm complaining about getting out. Jennifer is in major nesting mode and is currently repainting the nursery for the third time. Apparently, the yellow she picked out last week is too 'buttery.'"

"Yeah, good luck with that one, man. How's Jen doing, by the way?"

"She's great, other than the doctor telling her she needs to slow the hell down. But we only have a few weeks to go, thank God, so I think we might be in the clear at this point." He leaned forward and dropped his voice. "Does this have anything to do with what we talked about at dinner…with Moxie?"

Sam nodded, popping one of the peanut butter cups into her mouth.

"Good. I'm glad you called." Murphy's face dropped. "I haven't been able to sleep since she told us about that whole thing."

"I know, right?" Sam lowered her voice and glanced around before she continued. "I mean, I realize this stuff happens in big cities like New York and Miami, but it never even crossed my mind that we'd have to deal with possible sex trafficking in McCall."

"That's the thing though, right?" Murphy swiped the sugar from the rim of his glass with one finger. "If you think about it, it's genius. No one would think it could happen here, and those lake houses are all gated and so far apart that they're the perfect hiding place." He seemed lost in thought as he stoked his tiny cauldron fire with a few more cedar sticks, blowing on it gently to fan the flames. "I got your text this morning that you and Moxie went to see if you could find that house at the crack of dawn. How did that go? Did she verify that it's the one at the old Johnston place?"

"Yeah. I didn't want to take the chance of someone seeing her on the boat, so we had to go before it was really daylight." Sam reached for her Guinness and took a deep swig. "We found it right away, and she's right, that heart-shaped pool is unmissable, just as tacky as it sounded when he applied for the building permit. That's it, though. I don't want her anywhere near this in the future. In fact, I worry about her even being in town and that dude running into her."

"I wouldn't worry about that." He loaded another marshmallow onto his stick. "People like that don't do their own shopping. I'm sure he has people to do everything for him, and they wouldn't recognize her."

Sam nodded, begrudgingly taking a perfectly roasted marshmallow off the stick Murphy offered and popping it into her mouth.

"So," he continued. "What's your plan here? I mean—"

Murphy stopped short when Alex approached and looked at Sam as Alex sat down at the table. Sam didn't say anything, mostly because she knew Murphy would, and that was part of her plan.

"So," Murphy said, right on cue. "Are you going to introduce me to this dude, or should I give him my burger order? Help me out here."

Sam leaned back and laughed, high-fiving Alex. "Murphy, this is Alex Suarez, and *she* works at the retreat as our Latin dance instructor." Sam nodded in Murphy's direction. "And this is my brother-in-law, Murphy, who also works with me down at the station. He's married to Sara's sister, Jennifer."

Alex stuck out her hand, and Murphy shook it. "Alex, that's my bad. I should have clocked that you weren't a guy. You look just like the chief here."

"Actually, we set you up," Sam continued, subtly gesturing for the server. "I wanted to see if an average Joe would mistake Alex for a guy, which is what we're going for, actually."

Murphy looked at Sam with an irritated expression, falling silent and sulkily poking at his fire with the roasting stick.

"What?" Sam said, confused. "What did I say?"

"I mean…" Murphy shook his head in disbelief. "I can't believe you just called me an 'average Joe,' but whatever."

All three laughed and the server took Alex's drink order before disappearing back into the bar. The patio was nearly empty as night fell, and the sounds of tree frogs ramped up as fireflies hovered above their table, listening in. The breeze was cool and still carried the fresh marine scent of the lake, and they were close enough to the community docks that the sounds of distant speedboats and wakes breaking on the shore whirred in the background.

"So," Sam said, looking around to be sure the last table had left the patio. "I've briefed Alex on the situation in general terms, and I'm considering including her as part of an undercover operation."

"You're kidding me, right?"

"Nope." Sam leaned back in her chair so the server could drop off Alex's pint. "I'm dead serious. I talked to Boise headquarters about it, and they're on board as long as we are just gathering evidence. Idaho is a one-party consent state, so a civilian can legally video conversion with someone if they are a contributor to it."

"Which means that she would have to get into that mansion somehow with no invitation and get them to reveal something to her through direct conversation." Murphy popped the cherry at the bottom of his martini glass into his mouth with a deadpan expression. "Well, that's easy. Can't see any potential pitfalls there."

"Yeah, yeah. I know it's going to be tricky, but we'll have backup on land, and we're going to be on the lake doing surveillance, so if she does get into a problem, we can signal backup to move in and get in there quickly." Sam finished the last of her pint and unbuttoned the top two buttons on her shirt. "Alex doesn't come to town often, so the chances of her having met this guy are minimal. I don't think it will occur to him that she's actually a woman, and that Cuban accent will be easy to spin into a cover story."

Murphy looked up at Alex. "And how do you feel about all this?"

"I mean undercover stings aren't a hidden passion or anything, but once I heard what may be going on up there, I was immediately down to nail his ass."

"Damn straight." Murphy laughed and clinked his glass to Alex's. "I like this guy already."

Sam nodded. "It's important to realize that with this kind of operation, they're guaranteed to have guns and be inclined to use them. Keeping this secret before and after is a given, and your acting skills have to be on point because they'll be looking for a reason to doubt you."

"Look, if I didn't think I could do this, I wouldn't get involved." Alex shook her head slowly. "I grew up with *primas*, and this kind of thing happens in Cuba all the time. They promise the girls 'work' in America, and by the time the girls figure out what they're expected to do, the bastards have taken everything: their phones, their passports, and even the confidence they'd need to actually find help." Alex picked up her phone and pulled up a picture of three teen girls on a beach, dark hair flying across their laughing faces, the sun radiant in the background. "This was years ago. My sisters are older now, of course, but it's getting to be an epidemic in my home country. I want to do something to stop it, even in a small way."

"And I'm about to have a kid myself," Murphy said, his voice uncharacteristically subdued. "What if something like this happened to them? I'd have to kill somebody."

Sam nodded, kneading the back of her neck with one hand. "You know how I feel about it. Moxie hasn't been with us long, but she's been through a lot already for fifteen. I can't believe they're targeting vulnerable foster kids for this kind of thing. For me, that's the most disgusting thing about this particular operation."

"Yeah, as if those kids don't have enough to worry about." Murphy dropped his jar of strawberry jam carefully into the jacket of his pocket. "The foster care system is already challenged, to put it lightly."

"Um…Murphy?" Alex didn't suppress a laugh as she seemed to realize finally that the s'more accouterments were part of a carefully curated kit that Murphy brought to the bar himself. "I let the cosmo and pink swizzle stick slide, but tell me that isn't your tiny silver spoon and jam jar."

Sam coughed into her hand and suddenly became very interested in the cuff of her jacket.

"Listen." Murphy sniffed. "Clearly, you two need some in-depth lessons of how to be comfortable in your masculinity, but fortunately for you, I have the patience to give you some pointers on your journey." He stood and patted the pockets of his loaded jacket and dropped a stack of bills on the table. "Now, if you'll excuse me, I have a nursery to decorate with tiny, fluffy bunnies."

❖

It was late when Sam finally came through the door at home. The scent of Sara's dark chocolate walnut cookies enveloped her as she hung up her jacket and wandered into the kitchen, where Sara was attempting to teach Moxie how to dip half the cookie in chocolate ganache.

"I'm just not sure about this," Moxie said, looking doubtfully at a pile of broken cookies on the waxed paper beside her. "I've never made cookies before that didn't come from a mix, and something tells me I don't have what it takes. This dipping thing is, like, a whole different level."

"It's okay." Sara turned and leaned back to greet Sam with a kiss. "Fortunately for us, I'm married to a cookie-eating machine, so there will be zero evidence of any failed attempts in about five seconds."

Sam swooped in and scooped up the entire pile, opening the fridge door and grabbing the milk while she started on the practice cookies. By the time the milk was poured, Moxie was pulling her first whole cookie out of the molten chocolate dip and laying it carefully on the tray to cool.

"Yes!" Sara hugged her. Moxie looked thrilled, staring at her creation like she'd just found the cure for global warming. "I knew you could do it. It's way trickier than it looks to keep it in one piece after the dip, and you nailed it."

"Is this a good time to steal Moxie for a chat?" Sam looked at her watch and flipped a switch on the wall. "I want to show her something."

"Absolutely." Sara took the chocolate off the heat and grabbed the tongs. "I'll dip the rest of these while you're gone, and they'll be ready to eat by the time you get back in."

Moxie followed her through the front door, but Sam realized she'd stopped when she got to the last step and looked back.

"Are you okay?" Sam felt the silence settle heavy and dense between them. "You look pale."

Moxie dug the toe of her shoe into a groove in the brick entryway and nodded. "I just need to know if I need to get my stuff." She paused, shoving her hands into her pockets, which Sam knew by now she did whenever she was uncomfortable. "You know, like, my stuff that's upstairs."

Sam realized what she meant and held out a hand that Moxie took, confusion clouding her face. "I have to show you something for you to understand, but just trust me, it's not what you're thinking." Moxie's hand was ice-cold as Sam led her to the rock path and then dropped behind, letting her walk ahead at her own pace. As they rounded the corner, the spotlights outside the barn bathed the new basketball court in golden light, and she watched from behind as Moxie slowed to a stop on the path.

It was a long moment before Moxie continued to the court and bent down, running her fingertips over the surface of the freshly poured concrete. Her hair covered her face, and she tucked it behind one ear as she stood and looked back at Sam.

"This is new." It wasn't a question.

"You're right." Sam walked the rest of the way down the path and joined her at the edge of the court. "I had them pour it a few days ago."

"But why?" Sam's eyes followed as Moxie caught sight of the brand-new backboard and net on the other side of the court. "Why would you do that?"

"Do you remember when we were sitting on the floor of Moxie Java, and you tossed that paper cup into the trash that was all the way across the room?"

Moxie nodded, biting her lower lip and turning back to the court.

"I could tell you loved playing basketball." She paused. "And that it broke your heart when you had to leave your team."

Moxie turned back to Sam, tears gathering in her eyes as she waited for her to go on.

"I wanted you to have something here that was yours. Something solid to remind you, when you get scared, that we want you here."

When Moxie finally spoke, it was just a whisper. "How do you know I'm scared?"

"Because I know how it feels." Sam paused, carefully choosing the right words to wrap around the memory she kept at the farthest edges of her mind. "My mom left me at the county fair when I was six years old, and I went to a foster family here in McCall. I don't remember a lot of it, but I know I didn't make it easy on them. They couldn't get me to stop dragging all my blankets out into the hall to sleep at night."

"Why did you do that?"

Sam laced her fingers behind her head and looked at the stars for a moment before she answered. "Because I knew they couldn't leave if I slept in front of their door. That, at least, if that happened, I'd know they were leaving me." Sam felt her voice crack, and she stopped for a moment before she went on. "I just didn't want to wake up alone again."

Moxie cropped her face into her hands. Sam held the silent space between them until she was ready, and when she finally looked up and nodded, Sam folded Moxie into her arms and held her while she cried, the night air still and protective around them both.

CHAPTER NINE

A lex shut the door to her car as quietly as possible, but with a restorec Thunderbird from the fifties, it still reverberated across camp like a Top Gun flyby every time she did it. Two owls sharing a bare cedar branch took off toward the water as Alex clicked the flashlight app on her phone to illuminate the trail to the staff cabins. A twig cracked underfoot, and she kicked it away, breathing in the sharp ash scent of woodsmoke that drifted in from the campfire bowl.

The conversation she'd had with Sam and Murphy felt like a physical weight on her shoulders. They'd been worried about her safety, but that was the last thing on her mind. She knew enough about sex trafficking operations to know that they were alarmingly sophisticated, and there was a lot riding on getting this undercover role right. The one thing she had on her side was the secret: the one thing that no one yet knew about her that might make all the difference when the rubber actually met the road.

Alex smiled as she rounded the corner and saw Lily through the window, perched on the top bunk with her laptop in front of her. She watched from outside of the cabin as Lily stared at the screen, her face illuminated by the blue light. She started to type several times, then stopped and looked to the ceiling, rubbing her temples with her fingertips.

Alex opened the door quietly and stepped in, tossing her jacket onto the turntable.

"Am I going to be disturbing your writing if I come in and take a shower?"

Lily smiled, shaking out her hands and closing her computer. "There's no writing to disturb. I've been sitting here for two hours, and I officially have less now than I started with." She sighed, the tension visible in her neck and shoulders. "It's like my mind is hiding the words from me."

Alex opened the door again, framing the endless expanse of dark lake water glittering with reflected starlight. The moon hung heavy and low over the island in the distance, the tree line at the edge shadowed like a distant mountain range.

"Well, I find most of my answers at the island." Alex unbuttoned her overshirt and hung it on the top post of the bunk bed. "Have you looked there?"

Alex watched as Lily's eyes follow the lean lines of her body down to the khaki shorts slung low at her hips. Alex gathered her white ribbed tank in her hand and pulled it over her head, leaving her in just a spare white sports bra.

"Ready?"

Lily slid off the bunk and followed Alex outside, where she took off her T-shirt and dropped it on the chairs beside the door. "The question is, are you ready?"

"Oh, come *on*." Alex laughed, trying not to all-out stare at Lily's bra, if you could even call it that. "That's not even in the same league."

It was the exact color of her skin, with narrow ribbon straps and a sheer mesh fabric just a touch more transparent than glass. Alex took a second to drink in the graceful angles of her collarbone and perfect rosy nipples before she reluctantly dragged herself back to reality.

"You're expecting me to remember how to swim when you look like that?"

Lily tossed a wink over her shoulder and dove into the dark water, emerging a second later with a perfect freestyle stroke. Alex waded in and swam after her, thankful for the silent reprieve of the water around her. It gave her a few more minutes to stop thinking about what she'd just gotten herself into and shift her mind back into the present.

She reached the island well before Lily and settled herself on the sand, digging her toes into a drift that still held the heat of the sun. The full moon bathed the water in a silver glaze, brushing a floating gray heron's wings with dusky light before it disappeared into the tree line to watch from afar. A warm breeze ruffled through her hair like a lover before it floated back out to the water, and the scent of cooling earth drifted by in layers from the grove of trees and wildflowers behind her.

Lily finally reached the island and walked up onto the sand, water glossing every dip and curve of her body. Her nipples were tense and dark, and it was all Alex could do not to peel that sheer bra from her body and toss it back into the lake. Lily sat down beside her on the sandbar and lay back, unfolding onto the soft surface as water streamed down her body and disappeared into the warm sand. Alex followed suit, bracing herself on her elbow, close enough to feel the heat coming off Lily's body like steam.

"So," Alex said, silently memorizing every curve of Lily's breasts as she spoke. "Why were the words not coming today?"

"I don't know." Lily gazed up at the inky sky for a moment before she shook her head. "Actually, I take that back. I do know. It's just too soon. There isn't space in my head yet for stories to take shape." She sighed. "It's like trying to carve a path through a room crammed with people."

Alex nodded, running a hand through her wet hair. "What does that feel like, when the words do come?"

"It feels like walking through a movie I'm creating minute by minute." Lily closed her eyes. "It's…magic. And that's what I'm missing." She paused, drawing in a long, slow breath. "There has to be space for the magic."

Alex sank down on her back beside Lily so they were both looking at the same stars.

Lily turned to her, her pale blue eyes a metallic pewter in the moonlight. "Did you always want to be a dance instructor?"

Alex laughed at that, and from the scuffle coming from the darkness, it startled whatever was lurking just beyond the tree line.

"No, I guess you could say I sort of fell into it by accident. It keeps me connected to Cuba, and I guess I've needed that. My normal life is usually pretty intense."

"I believe that. You have an intensity I felt before we'd finished our first whiskey. It must come from somewhere." Lily leaned up on her arm and trailed a wet fingertip from the base of Alex's neck to her abs.

Alex closed her eyes, soaking in the delicate sensuality of her touch as Lily leaned in and followed the same path with the warmth of her tongue. Alex's fingers tangled hard into Lily's damp hair as she traced the outline of Alex's nipple through the sheer fabric of her sports bra, then finally shifted it to the side, holding the warmth of her breath over Alex's skin for a few long seconds before she pulled her tense nipple into her mouth, stroking it with in an insistent rhythm.

"Jesus." Alex hesitated as Lily scraped her nipple lightly with her teeth. "Christ."

Alex bit her lip as Lily moved over her, shifting her body so her thighs were on either side of Alex's hips. When she leaned in to take Alex's nipple into her mouth again, the deep curve from her shoulders to her waist was insanely hot, and Alex struggled not flip her over in the sand and take her right there.

Lily's breasts brushed hers as she reached for the hand that Alex had slung across her forehead. Alex closed her eyes, sinking into every slick inch of Lily's mouth as it closed over her middle finger. Lily circled it with her tongue, taking it all in her mouth, stroking it lightly up one side and down the other, then scraping the sensitive tip through her teeth before she let it go.

That was all she could take. Alex groaned as she stood, picking Lily up with her and wrapping her legs around her waist.

"We've either got to swim back now, or we're staying on this island all damn night." Alex waded into the water up to her waist and kissed Lily's neck before she went on. "I want to taste every single inch of you, and once I start, I'm not going to stop."

The swim back to the cabin was much quicker than going out to the island, but as they walked out of the water, something felt different, and Alex had a sinking feeling she knew what that was. "Did we put a record on the player before we left?"

Lily looked tilted her head to peer through the window. "No, but I think I can see who decided to put some music on, and I'm guessing it isn't for me."

Alex took a moment to breathe through her annoyance and reached for the door, holding it open for Lily to go in first. Lily headed straight for the bathroom, pulling the door shut behind her.

"Charlotte."

Charlotte looked up from her perch on the arm of the chair, Alex's whiskey and an ice cube clinking around the glass in her hand. She tilted it to her lips and held Alex's eyes. "Yes?"

"Why the hell are you in my cabin?"

Charlotte held up her phone, then tucked it slowly into her bra, loosening another button on the white men's shirt she was wearing over a pale yellow bikini top. "I saw that you'd called me today, but you didn't leave a message, so I just thought I'd drop by."

Alex took a measured breath and stepped back, pulling on the shirt she'd tossed on the bunk earlier. "You can't just walk into my cabin uninvited. Sam has something she needs me to do next week, and I just needed to let you know so you can rearrange the schedule."

Charlotte finished the whiskey in her glass and set it among the books in the bookcase. "Are you sure that's all you want?"

Alex held her gaze. "I think I've made that very clear."

"Fine." Charlotte glanced at the bathroom as she walked toward the door. "When you finally get bored of what's-her-name, you know where to find me."

Alex bit back her response and locked the door behind her, then dug Louis Armstrong out of the record bin, clicking on the lamp as she headed for the bathroom. Lily was turning on the shower, and Alex stepped up behind her, pulling her body back against her own. "Lily, I'm sorry about that. I've made it clear to her, but she just—"

Lily turned in her arms and put a finger on Alex's lips. "I was listening at the door, and I could tell you've had that conversation. You're not responsible for what she does after she has that information."

Alex slid a hand around the back of her neck and kissed her, pulling Lily's body tighter against hers and unhooking her bra with a quick flick of her fingers.

"Christ." Lily let the bra fall off her breasts and tossed it onto the sink. "That was hella smooth. If I wasn't already planning on getting naked with you, that would've sealed the deal."

"You'll be shocked to know…" Alex slipped her clothes off and reached over to test the water before she turned back to Lily. "That it's not my first bra clasp, Miss Larimar."

Lily smiled, dropping the rest of her clothes and turning back to Alex. "Oh yeah, I'm fainting with shock over here."

She stepped into the shower, and Alex watched the water run over her naked body, her nipples tightening as Alex stepped in with her and closed the door. Lily melted into her as soon as Alex's mouth met her neck.

"You're so fucking beautiful, Lily," Alex whispered, her words rising with the steam and hovering between them.

Lily's moan when she ran her hands along the deep curve of her waist and down to her ass made Alex's clit ache, and the light scrape of Lily's nails up her back was intense, enough that she knew that if Lily touched her, it would take her over the edge. Alex stepped back just far enough to let the steam rise between them, holding her eyes as she traced Lily's mouth with her finger, then slipped it inside. Lily closed her eyes, pulling it deeper into her mouth, holding Alex's wrist and licking the tip of it as she slowly let it go. She smiled when Alex raked a hand through her hair and picked her up, wrapping Lily's legs tight around her waist and backing her up against the white-tiled shower wall.

"Goddamn, girl." Alex held Lily against her body with one arm and slid her first two fingers back into the warmth of Lily's mouth, closing her eyes as Lily slicked her tongue between them. "I want to take this slow, but I don't think I can."

"Slow burns..." Lily let her fingers go and leaned in, biting the soft skin of Alex's shoulder. "Are overrated."

Alex leaned slightly back and looked deep into Lily's eyes. "I'm dying to take you, but I need you to tell me you want this."

Lily nodded, her eyes half-closed with the heaviness of desire.

"Tell me," Alex whispered, the hot water streaming over her shoulders. "Let me hear you say the words."

Lily licked Alex's lower lip, lingering until Alex touched the tip of her tongue to hers. "Alex," Lily whispered. "I need you to fuck me."

The last word was lost in a sudden breath as Alex slid her fingers deep inside, her mouth warm and wet against the nape of Lily's neck. She paused, holding her against the wall until she whispered that she wanted more. Lily's thighs tightened around Alex's hips, and she moaned as Alex started fucking her, leaning her head back against the cool tile. Alex's touch was intense, gentle, and unrelenting in the same breath. She snaked her tongue into Lily's mouth with the same rhythm, then slid her mouth down her neck, listening to Lily breathe and memorizing the pace she needed, then taking her just beyond it.

"Don't stop." Lily's head sank to Alex's shoulder, and Alex felt a shudder move through her. "Just don't stop—"

"Shh." Alex's voice was slick and molten between them. She moved to Lily's ear, her words as ethereal as the haze of steam between them. "I've got you."

Lily leaned back, her hands tangled into Alex's hair, her lips open and flushed, hips circling against Alex's hand. Alex curved the fingers inside her slightly and slicked her thumb over Lily's clit, swollen and responsive under her touch.

"Tell me what you want."

"Alex." Lily's words and breath melded and scraped like liquid metal as she found each one slowly and strung them together. "Make me come for you."

That was it. That was all Alex needed to press her back against the tile, pinning her there with the heat of her mouth, hips setting the pace for the fingers that were still deep inside. She angled her hand to stroke Lily's clit with every thrust, and Lily whimpered for more as her orgasm crested inside her. Her cheeks were flushed a deep pink, eyes closed, and the curves of her breasts glistening with steam as she grabbed at the wall behind to anchor herself in a spinning world of intensity.

"Come for me, baby," Alex said, watching as Lily tensed and bit her lip. "Just let go."

She watched as the orgasm surged through Lily and felt her body tremble deep inside as it shook her, wringing out the last of her breath. Lily leaned forward on Alex's shoulder and wrapped her legs around her waist again, still shuddering with the last delicious waves as Alex opened the shower door and carried her out of the bathroom to the bed.

"Morning, handsome."

Sam opened one eye and then slung her forearm back over her eyes. Sara set the tray of croissants and jam on the nightstand and poured Sam a cup of coffee from the carafe, smiling as she watched Sam's eyes flutter open. Sam sat up slowly and leaned back against the headboard, rubbing her forehead with the heel of her hand.

"God." Sam took the steaming cup of black coffee from Sara and squinted through the wide beam of sunlight that seemed unnecessarily robust for early morning. "Waking up to you looking like that never gets old." She pulled Sara closer by the front of her robe that was still damp from her shower. "Come here."

Sara leaned in for the kiss and then another before she stood to get her own cup of coffee. "Right back at ya, Draper." Sara eyed her rumpled dark hair, tight white tank top, and black boy shorts, then pulled up her shirt to get a better view before Sam playfully swatted her hand and reached for a croissant.

Sam had been part of every aspect of building the retreat over the last two years, and the definition in her abs and shoulders reflected it. The salt and pepper starting to show at her temples in the last few years had seemed to double recently, which Sara loved, but lately, she'd started to worry that Sam was struggling with something. She'd watched her walk down to the dock, drop her clothes, and swim to the island a few times after dinner in the last week, which was always a clue she had something heavy on her mind.

"I can't believe I slept so late." Sam picked up her phone from the bedside table and looked at the time. "What are your plans for the day?"

"I'm driving Moxie into town to help Mary out with some things at the drugstore, but nothing other than that."

"Oh, I see how it is." Sam smiled and shook her head, settling back against the headboard. "Mary has her hooked on *Days of Our Lives* now too?"

"Well, she won't admit it, but yes." Sara pulled apart her croissant and topped it with a smear of fresh butter, the steam melting it instantly and glossing the tips of her fingers. "Actually, Moxie asked if it was okay to start working there for a few hours a week."

Sam accepted the bite that Sara put in her mouth, catching her thumb to lick the butter off before she kissed her palm. "What did you say?"

"I told her that that was fine, but when I called Mary for the scoop, she did that sniffing thing she does and said it was nobody's business but theirs." Sara smiled, glancing back at their bedroom door and lowering her voice. "Secretly, I love that they've bonded. Mary could run a damn country, and she raised four girls, which is similar, to be fair."

"Mary is one of the most solid people I know, so I love that idea. Besides, it'll give her a little spending money since she won't take any from us."

"I know, right?" Sara twisted her hair into a low bun, settled cross-legged on the bed, and took a leisurely sip of her coffee. "I tried again to leave some on her nightstand, and she just gave it back to me."

"Did she say anything?" Sam reached for a strawberry from the bowl on the breakfast tray and popped it into her mouth. "And just as an aside, that kid couldn't be more like me if I'd birthed her myself."

Sara laughed. "She even looks a little like you. She just said that she appreciated it but that she'd find a way to earn her own."

"I get that," Sam said, licking strawberry jam from the silver knife, a classic move to drive Sara crazy. "But you were right when you said that when she starts high school in the fall, she's going to need some clothes. I want to take her to Boise for a weekend, if that's okay with you. Let her shop at all the tomboy stores you and Jennifer know nothing about."

"Fine, but we're coming too. If I leave you two to your own devices, she'll come back with nothing but jeans and hoodies."

Sam smiled and set her croissant on the tray. "Oh my sweet, sweet, femme…why would anyone need something besides jeans and hoodies?" Sam playfully pulled Sara down onto the bed and into the fluffy duvet, kissing down the slope of her neck to her shoulder. "Baby, of course you'll be there. In fact, I'm telling her it was your idea in the first place. The thought of shopping for clothes outside of Patagonia sounds like the ninth circle of hell to me."

Sara snuggled in closer and laid her head on Sam's chest. The sound of her heart beating was as familiar as her own. She waited for a moment, then looked up at Sam, tucking a wild lock of hair behind her ear. "So when are you going to tell me what's got you so worried?"

"Damn." Sam took a long breath, running her fingers through Sara's hair. "How did you know?"

"Because I know you," Sara said. "You're my whole heart. I know when you're not okay."

"I don't know what to say, or I would've told you sooner, love." Sam rubbed the deep crease between her brows with her fingertips. "It's been driving me crazy that I don't know how to describe it, and the last thing I want is to get it wrong and have you think it's about us. It's not…I just can't figure out what it is."

Sara looked up through her eyelashes and laid her hand, warm and soft, over Sam's heart. "We made the promise on our wedding day that if something was ever wrong between us, we'd stop everything right then and untangle it. I trust you. If it was something to do with me, you would have told me a long time ago." Sara slid her hand up into Sam's hair and traced the silver at the edge of her ear. "You don't have to know how to talk about it. Or even what it is. Just tell me three words that get the closest to describing how you feel."

Sam was silent for a long moment, trailing her fingers up and down Sara's back. "Disappointment, maybe?"

"Okay. That's the first one."

"But…" The edge of frustration was raw in Sam's voice. "I don't know why, I—"

"Shh…" Sara said, reaching up to put a finger on her lips. "Don't worry about that. You don't have to know yet. What's the second word?"

"Emptiness, maybe?" Sam said hesitantly. "And the third is probably frustration."

Sara just listened, knowing that if she didn't try to throw her own words into the space between them, Sam would unravel the feelings herself.

"I mean…" Sam raked a hand through her hair and rubbed at the tired lines at the corners of her eyes. "I guess it has to do with Lake Haven. I knew I wanted to do something for our community, build a place where people felt safe to come and be themselves."

"And do you feel like you've done that?"

"That's just the thing. I do." The frustration was now nakedly apparent in Sam's voice. "But I think I need Lake Haven to have a more meaningful purpose, you know? It's turned out better than I ever could have imagined, but something's missing."

Sara nodded and waited for her to go on.

"Yeah, it's perfect." Sam paused, thoughts drifting across her face like blown storm clouds. "And people love it. It has the potential with more advertising and staff to be one of the most successful retreats in the country. I mean, we already have a waiting list for next summer, and with Charlotte running the show, it's been solidly successful."

"Okay," Sara said, leaning up on one elbow. "Let's go back to that second word you said."

"Emptiness?"

"That's it. Tell me more about that."

"I guess sometimes. Because when I think about doing this for another twenty years, it just feels…"

"Empty?"

"Yeah." Sam brought Sara back down and wrapped her in her arms. "That's exactly it." Sam's phone pinged on the bedside table, and she reached over to pick it up. She scanned the text and put it back down. "Do we have plans for dinner tonight?"

"None that I know of. Did I forget something?"

"No, but I think we do now. That was Alex, and she says she has something to show us."

"Is it about the undercover thing you guys were talking about with Murphy?"

"She didn't say, but I can't think of anything else unless she's coming over to break in Moxie's basketball court."

Suddenly, Sara caught the beside clock out of the corner of her eye and bounced out of bed. "I'm supposed to be taking Moxie to town in five minutes, and my hair is still wet. If I don't at least blow-dry, I won't be able to fit it in the car with us."

Sam sat back and smiled, reaching for the last of her croissant as Sara scrambled into jeans and a summer-weight cashmere T-shirt, then slid on a pair of white Tretorns at the last second as she attempted to smooth back the wisps of hair that had escaped from her bun.

Sam tilted her head and looked her up and down. "You look beautiful."

"You know what makes me love you even more?" Sara stopped in front of the mirror, turning to look at Sam over her shoulder. "I can tell you mean that, even when I look like one of those weather people caught in a hurricane."

Sam tossed Sara her cell phone and winked. "I happen to like having my own little blond hurricane blowing around the house." She got out of bed and pulled on a pair of jeans from their walk-in closet. "Don't worry about dinner. I'll pick up some steaks to grill this afternoon."

"Don't you dare," Sara said, opening the door and leaning on the frame. They both heard Moxie coming down the stairs at the same moment and smiled. "The kitchen manager at work keeps telling me I'm on vacation and won't let me get back there to cook anything. Dinner is all mine tonight. I adore Cuban food."

Sara blew Sam a kiss and ducked out the door, only to stick her head back in a second later. "Sam?"

"Yes?" Sam walked out of their bathroom with a toothbrush dangling from her mouth. "Did you forget something?"

"How did you feel when you finished Moxie's basketball court yesterday?"

Sam paused, and her shoulders relaxed. "So happy." She lowered the toothbrush slowly, a slow smile spreading like sunlight over her face. "Happier than I've been since we opened Lake Haven."

Sara smiled, quietly pulling the door shut behind her.

CHAPTER TEN

The heat settled quickly that evening, and the cool breeze coming in from the water brushed the treetops with the first light of golden hour as Sara put the finishing touches on dinner. She dabbed at the front of her sleeveless white linen dress with a clean towel and club soda with one hand and stirred the Arroz Amarillo on the stovetop with the other.

"Sam?" Sara spun around to find Sam at the table opening a bottle of Chilean Chardonnay. "Would you take over rice duty here while I sort out this spoonful of black beans I just dropped down the front of me?"

"Of course, hang on." Sam crossed the kitchen in two strides and took the wooden spoon. "How did you manage to do that?"

"You just mind your own business, Draper," Sara teased, pouring a bit more soda on the front of her dress. "Although, I may have to change. This dress is getting more transparent by the second."

Sam did the sexy growl Sara loved, and she laughed, rubbing the wet spot with a fluffy kitchen towel. "There. I think I've basically gotten it out, and I don't seem to look too naked."

Both looked up when they heard the front door open, and a few seconds later, Moxie walked in with an easy smile and pushed her cute new glasses up on her nose. "Hey."

"Hey, Maximillion." Sam turned, still stirring the rice in front of her. "I feel like I haven't seen you all day."

"Yeah, I kinda stayed with Mary most of the day. She closed the drugstore because she wants us to paint it. Or…" Moxie grinned, pulling at her paint-stained T-shirt. "She wants me to paint it, anyway."

"Let me guess," Sara said, taking over at the stove. "While she eats cinnamon rolls behind the counter and gives you directions?"

"Well, it was pecan brownies again today, but yeah, that's right." Moxie reached for a cookie out of the cookie jar on the counter and put the lid back carefully, leaning over to check out what Sara was cooking. "It's okay, though. She's paying me, and I like her a lot."

Sara took the frosty glass of pale gold wine Sam offered her and glanced over her shoulder at Moxie. "Mary was my first friend when I landed in McCall, and I actually bought my first house from her."

"She's still your best friend, isn't she?"

Sara smiled, dipping a small silver spoon into a bubbling shrimp dish on the back burner and blowing on it before she tasted it. "She absolutely is, but how did you know?"

"Because she says that she loves you like she loves her daughters." Moxie smiled, finishing the last of her cookie and wiping a smear of chocolate on the back of her jeans. "She told me the whole story of how you came here one summer from…Georgia, right?"

"Yep, Savannah."

"Well, she said you came in and opened up the diner, stole Sam's heart and—" Moxie paused, eyes flicking skyward as if trying to remember Mary's exact words. "Oh yeah, I remember. She said that you 'brought the color back to McCall.'"

Sara turned to Sam, and they both smiled as their eyes teared up. Sam folded her into her arms and hugged her tight. As Sara pulled away, she nodded toward Moxie eyeing the cookie jar, and Sam smiled.

"All right, Moxie," Sam said, motioning her toward the counter. "I mean, I hate to call you out here, but you're going at this cookie thing all wrong."

A flash of worry crossed Moxie's face for just a second until Sam winked in her direction. "Okay," she said, her face relaxing into a smile. "I'm listening."

"It's a common mistake, but what you're experiencing here is a simple volume problem."

Moxie tilted her head and looked back to the jar. "A what?"

"Well," Sam said, sliding the drawer under the cookie jar open and directing Moxie's attention to a small stack of paper bags. "You're taking them one at a time. What you want to do here is maximize your volume by dropping a few of those bad boys in a sack"—Sam dropped three cookies into a bag and folded it over—"and *boom.* Now you've just minimized your return trips to the jar. You can even tear the bag open for an instant disposable plate later."

"That's genius."

Moxie grinned, then shoved the bag into the pocket of her jacket and started to go upstairs but paused at the bottom and looked back at Sara. "You know, my mom had a cookie jar in the kitchen when I was growing up." Moxie ran her fingers over the worn cuff of her jacket, then finally shoved her hands into the pockets. "When I was little, I'd climb up on a chair every day to check if there were cookies yet, and there never were. I thought cookie jars were just magic. I didn't realize someone had to bake them and put them in there." She pulled the little brown bag of cookies out of her pocket and turned it over in her hand. "I know this must sound stupid, but I can't believe that there are always cookies in your jar. Like, every time I look." She paused, meeting Sara's eyes. "It's kind of a big deal."

"Moxie there will always be cookies in our kitchen for you." Sara leaned back into Sam's chest. "Always."

Moxie smiled and went upstairs to her room, closing the door softly behind her.

"Well, Mrs. Draper," Sam said, leaning against the counter and uncapping a beer she'd just pulled from the fridge with a flick of her thumb. "Let me ask you something."

"And what is that?" Sara said, glancing back up the stairs and smiling.

"How do you feel about what Moxie just said?"

Sara smiled, the meaning starting to sink in. She picked her wineglass up and clinked it to the rim of Sam's bottle.

"Happy." Sara said, leaning into the warmth of Sam's chest and wrapping her arms around her waist. "Happier than I've been since the day we decided we wanted to make a family."

❖

A couple of hours later, the doorbell rang, and Sam went to answer it, realizing too late she had a knife in her hand. Sara's favorite music, the Gypsy Kings, played in the background, and the air was warmed by a deeply savory spice that Sam was fairly sure had something to do with the pots covering every burner in the kitchen.

"Whoa, man." Alex took a step back as Sam opened the door. "You said Sara was cooking, so I brought her some flowers, but you can have them if you put that knife down."

"Smartass." Sam laughed and waved Alex through the door, leading her to the kitchen and dropping the knife back into the Wüsthof block in the kitchen. Alex gave Sara a quick hug and handed her the bouquet of wildflowers, which Alex mentioned she'd rowed to Rock Island to pick.

"Damn, dude, you're making me look bad here," Sam said, holding up a handful of tiny key limes in a green mesh bag like they'd just committed a crime. "But I'll forgive you if you can tell me what the hell a Caipirinha is and how to make the damn thing."

"Are you joking?" Alex did a dramatic swoon with her hand over her heart. "We're making my favorite drink from Cuba? It's Brazilian, actually, but we claim it." She did a quick inspection of the liquor bottle on the counter and punched the air in excitement. "And you got actual Cachaça?"

"And…" Sara looked up from filling a vase for the flowers. "Amber agave to sweeten it."

Alex reached for a chair to steady herself in dramatic flair. "I've literally never been so happy in this country. Step aside, Chief Draper, the Cuban has landed."

"Gladly." Sam laughed, wiping her hands on the kitchen towel and heading for the table. "I've got real limes, too, if you need them. Those seem kinda tiny."

Alex and Sara both turned slowly around to face her, rolling their eyes in unison.

"Nope?" Sam tried again. "And what about some actual sugar? I mean, what could possibly be wrong with that?"

"Have a seat, Draper." Alex grinned as she halved one of the key limes and sliced it into paper-thin rounds on the woodblock cutting board, then rolled the rest of the tiny bright green citrus carefully under the heel of her hand. "I've got this."

"Take your time," Sara said, sprinkling spicy flaked salt over the steaming pan of rice. "Dinner won't be ready for another fifteen minutes at least."

Alex hummed along with the acoustic Spanish guitar as she muddled some of the citrus with agave and a touch of caster sugar that Sara had in the cupboard, then added some freshly cracked ice, the agave, and several squeezes of the key lime juice. A generous shot of Cachaça completed the masterpieces, and Alex handed Sam and Sara their glasses and proposed a toast.

"What should we toast to?" Sara said, popping the lid back on the shrimp dish as richly scented steam swirled around her.

"Here's to..." Sam raised her glass. "Nailing those bastards."

"Couldn't have said it better myself." Alex grinned, sipping her cocktail and pulling out a chair at the table. She'd dropped a leather bag over the back of it as she'd come in and now reached in and pulled out her laptop. "Is Moxie joining us tonight?"

"No, she's playing basketball with a friend, so I made them some sandwiches and drinks to take down there. My kitchen manager has a daughter going into her junior year of high school too, so I introduced them the other day at the restaurant, and they were like, instant friends."

Alex looked at her watch and sat back in her chair. "The reason I wanted to talk to you both is that I may have something that will help us infiltrate that mansion."

"Well, I'm all ears." A vein in Sam's forehead throbbed, and she tightened her jaw. "Because short of sending Moxie back in, which I would never do, I haven't been able to come up with a plausible scenario."

"Well, you told me the other day that this is basically a fact-finding mission, right? We're in there to gather evidence, not bust the place up?"

"Right. Just info." Sam held up her glass to admire Alex's handiwork. "And damn, this thing goes down smooth. I love it. Tastes like key lime pie."

"They're small but mighty." Sara took one of the pans off the heat and set it on a trivet to cool as she fluffed the yellow rice with a fork. "Those things knocked me on my ass the first time I had them."

"Same here," Alex said, taking a deep sip. "And you don't feel it till you stand up, so you've been warned, Draper."

"Note taken." Sam grinned and tapped the tabletop with her thumb. "Okay, I'm dying to know what you've got for me because I was starting to think there was no way in there."

"First off, can you get this guy's number from his address or property records?"

"Already done. I even found a picture and asked Moxie if that was the guy she spoke to, and she recognized him right away, so I'm fairly certain we have the right info."

Alex took a deep breath, glancing again at her watch.

"Okay, when my family immigrated to the States when I was in my early teens, it was mostly so my mom could join her sister Margherita in Florida. They grew up together and then raised their kids together, so I was super close to my cousins, one in particular." Alex picked up her phone and clicked on a text, then continued. "Alejandro and I are only one month apart, and we were inseparable growing up. They even called us 'the twins.'"

"That's adorable," Sara said, bringing a covered dish of bread to the table and swatting Sam's hand when she reached for it. "You two were that close?"

"Well." Alex looked at her watch and opened her laptop, clicked a few keys, and looked up as Sara and Sam both leaned closer to screen. "There was that and something else."

Alex clicked an icon at the top of the computer screen, and a live video unfolded onto the screen. Someone who looked like an exact replica of Alex flashed a bright smile and launched into an excited streak of Spanish, which Alex returned, then turned and nodded to Sam and Sara and began speaking in English.

"This is Sam Draper, the chief of police here in McCall, and Sara Draper, her wife and restaurateur." Alex stopped to take a sip of her drink and nodded in the direction of the screen. "And guys, this is my cousin Alejandro. He's calling from Hawaii but lives in Miami."

"I can't *believe* this," Sara said, leaning closer to the screen. "You two literally look like the same person. Even your haircut is exactly the same."

"Well, actually, I am an inch taller than you." Alex flashed an innocent smile at her cousin. "Just in the interest of accuracy."

"I'm telling you for the last time, man, I was having a bad hair day the day we measured. I just didn't have my volume game on point." Alejandro's accent was slightly thicker than Alex's but otherwise identical. "But more importantly, is that a Caipirinha in your hand?"

"Yes, sir, and a perfectly made one, thanks to Sara."

"Well," Alejandro said, smiling at Sam and Sara. "I like you guys already." Alejandro paused, then sat back in his desk chair, the smile fading from his face. "So Alex says you may have a sex trafficking ring up there?"

Sam nodded. "Almost sure of it." Sara excused herself to put the finishing touches on dinner, and Sam sank into the chair next to Alex. "I assume Alex has given you the scoop on the few details we know already?"

"Yeah, she has. I want to help however I can." He glanced to Alex and continued. "And we may have come up with an idea."

Sam raked a hand through her hair. "Thank God, because I've been staying up nights worrying about this, and I don't have shit to show for it, to put it politely."

"So," Alex started with a glance at her cousin. "Alejandro has been a club promoter for almost twenty years in the Miami area, and along the way acquired several multi-million-dollar clubs right on Miami's main strip, in addition to a few smaller niche clubs and restaurants directly on the beach."

"Damn." Sam shook her head. "That's seriously impressive."

Alejandro arched an eyebrow and looked pointedly at Alex. "Well, it didn't do me a damn bit of good. I still don't stack up next to the golden child over here. I dropped out of college to become a promoter, and my mom didn't speak to me for an entire year. She still tells people I plan parties for a living."

"Whatever," Alex said with a wink. "You now make more money than God, and that beach house you bought them last summer got you back in her good graces, to say the least."

"Oh, we both know I won't be getting there until I marry a nice Catholic girl and give her some grandchildren. But let's get back to the point." Alejandro rolled his eyes good-naturedly and focused his attention back on Sam. "We were thinking that it's logical that someone like me might be interested in a little company for myself and also my constantly rotating VIP guests."

Sam nodded slowly. "And you obviously don't want to use someone local who will recognize you, so you're outsourcing to a smaller, safer operation that a contact tipped you off to?"

"Exactly." Alejandro tapped a pen on the desk in front of him. "That way, if he googles me, my name and long history will pop up, and most importantly, every picture he sees will look exactly like Alex."

Alex grinned. "Only shorter, of course."

Sam laughed as Alejandro threatened to come through the computer and teach Alex how to use a tape measure. He also mentioned his unfortunate hair situation yet again, this time with entirely unconvincing details about the effects of humidity.

"All right, all right," Sam said as the two volleyed playful insults back and forth. "That actually is a solid start. Is there any way we can borrow the chip from your phone while we're pursuing this so that info matches as well? In that culture, it follows that you wouldn't disclose your source, so he can't pursue that, but your online presence is strong and goes back years. That should be more than enough to convince him you're legit if your phone number checks out too."

"Absolutely." Alejandro reached across his desk and reemerged on camera with a straw fedora. "I'm actually on vacation in Hawaii right now, so I can let any staff know to call me on my alternate number. Use it as long as you need to."

"I'll get Alex to text you the station address," Sam said, her excitement building. "Any way you can drop that in the mail in the next couple of days?"

"Absolutely. The post offices are closed here at the moment, but I'll do it personally first thing in the morning."

"Alejandro." Sam felt the tension across her forehead that had almost taken up residence start to ease. "I can't tell you how much this helps us. Keep the details under your hat for now, and I'll be in touch soon with any other details you may need as it progresses."

"Sounds great. I see too much of this bullshit in the clubs, and it needs to be stopped. I'll do whatever I can to help." He grinned at his cousin and popped the fedora on his head. "I mean, I've got to do something to gain some traction on Dr. Suarez here."

Sara turned around at the stove, and Sam looked at Alex in confusion.

"What?" Alejandro leaned into the computer and looked at Alex as he realized what was happening. "You seriously didn't tell them?"

"Tell us what?" Sara walked back over to the table, wiping her hands on a kitchen towel. "Why do I feel like I missed something?"

"Oh!" Alejandro sat back in his chair and rubbed his hands together with a look of evil delight. "This is just so delicious!"

"Tell us what?" Sam bumped her shoulder to Alex's, who was shaking her head with a look of annoyed resignation.

"I'll put it this way." Alejandro winked at his cousin, clearly enjoying drawing out the suspense. "One of us stayed in college."

"Let me guess," Sara said. "It wasn't you?"

"Much to the annoyance of my mother, no." Alejandro leaned back in his chair and laughed. "And guess what else I didn't do?"

"Wow, look at the time. Got to go, cousin!" When Alex reached for the computer, Sara swiftly intercepted and swatted her hand away.

"Don't even think about it. This is way too much fun." She perched on Sam's lap and leaned into the computer. "Go on, Alejandro. You were saying?"

"Thank you, Sara. You're very kind." Alejandro flashed her a smile. "I was going to say that one of us also went on to get a doctorate in childhood psychology and neuroscience." He paused for effect, rolling his eyes. "Also not me, by the way. Apparently, I throw parties for a living."

"Well, you kept that one under wraps." Sara smiled in Alex's direction and playfully punched her shoulder. "So just one more question." Sara glanced at Alex, who by this time was shaking her head with a look of amused resignation. "Alex seems to be dating one of my best friends. Anything else I need to know?"

Alejandro paused, thought for a moment, then met Sara's eyes. "I'd love to keep giving her shit here, but Alex is one of the most loving people I've ever known. I would, and I have more than once, put my life in her hands without a moment's hesitation, so I'd say your friend's heart is more than safe."

"Thanks, Ale." Alex's face softened with emotion for just a moment, then she snapped back into teasing mode. "Now, let me know when you get back from Hawaii so I can come kick your ass for this."

Sam and Sara waved good-bye and headed back into the kitchen as

Alex wrapped up the conversation with her cousin. It was clear to Sara how close the two were; even though they were speaking in Spanish, the love was palpable as they signed off.

"So..." she said when Alex walked back into the kitchen and started juicing more limes. "Alejandro is my new favorite person." She smacked Alex in the arm again as Alex held up her hand in surrender. "How the hell were you not going to tell us about that big brain?"

"What? And jeopardize my reputation as the prettyboi Latin dance instructor?"

"Oh, damn," Sam said, sliding the bottle of Cachaça over to Alex. "That needs to go on a T-shirt with your picture on the back. I'm willing to bet about half the women at the retreat—"

"Including Charlotte, I hear." Sara arched an eyebrow in Alex's direction.

"...would just *love* to get their hands one of those."

"Jesus Christ." Alex laughed as she took the lid off the Cuban mojo pork roast and breathed in the steam from the savory yellow rice. "I have an idea. Let's eat so that no one else can talk."

The next morning, Sara pulled open the door of the diner and stood in the entryway for a few seconds, just to soak it in. Mara, who was one of the high school students that helped her open the restaurant five years ago, was behind the sky-blue Formica counter holding a coffee carafe, laughing with the group of senior citizens who came to lunch at the diner every day. She'd been promoted to the front-of-house manager as soon as she graduated, and now Sara didn't know what she'd do without her.

The outside deck had grown into the social hub of McCall, and she'd had to hire more waitstaff to handle the buzz of constant activity, even through the winter months. And of course, Family Dinner for the locals still happened every Sunday afternoon. The diner closed after the brunch rush, and all the locals came out of the woodwork right on time and streamed through the glass doors, carrying homemade side dishes to go with Sara's roast. When she'd had to pause it during the pandemic, the locals who could manage it showed up anyway, always with food and Tupperware, and helped deliver hot meals to some of the more vulnerable residents who couldn't leave their houses.

"Thanks, Mara." Sara smiled warmly as Mara handed her a cup of coffee the second she got to the counter. "I got a message to meet Mary here this morning. Has she gotten here yet?"

Mara nodded toward the back of the diner where Mary was sitting on one of the couches. Bright summer light streamed through the window behind her, and she was already halfway through an enormous lemon poppy seed muffin. Sara smiled as she walked over, plunking her bag down beside the couch and sinking back into it with a sigh.

"This was such a good idea, Mary." She signaled one of the servers to come over as she shrugged off her jacket.

Mary finished a bite of the gooey lemon pudding center and leaned over to give Sara a quick hug. "Your lemon muffins are always a good idea. But what did you want to talk about?"

The server arrived just then, and both gave her their orders before they turned back to each other.

"Wait...what do you mean?" Sara said, stirring sugar into her coffee with a look of confusion. "Sam said you wanted to meet me at the diner at noon, so here I am."

"Well, that's ridiculous, because Sam called me at the break of bloody dawn to tell me you needed me to meet you here at noon. She said it was super important but wouldn't tell me what it was. I've been worried sick. It almost put me off my muffin, and that's saying something."

They stared at each other for a moment, equally confused.

"This just makes no sense at all," Sara said, pulling her phone from her pocket. "I always love to see you, but I feel like I must be missing something here."

"Well, give her a call, because if there's no emergency, I'm going to enjoy my pancakes and hashbrowns in a leisurely manner as God intended."

Sara dialed Sam's number and clicked it over to speakerphone when she answered. "Sam, I'm here with Mary, and—"

"Babe," Sam interrupted, the smile in her voice as audible as the words. "Just turn around."

Sara and Mary both turned and looked out the diner window where

Sara's sister Jennifer was standing. Sam and her husband Brian Murphy were a few steps behind her, and she was holding a baby in her arms.

They laughed when Sara and Mary gasped and covered their mouths in shock at the exact same instant. Murphy motioned for them to stay where they were when he saw them jump up, and it was just a few seconds before all three of them came through the door of the diner and headed for the couch where Mary and Sara were still mostly speechless with shock.

"Oh my God," Sara whispered as she carefully touched the cheek of the tiny baby swaddled in the enormously blue blanket she'd bought for Jennifer weeks ago. "What the hell happened? I didn't even know you were in labor!"

"Well, that's the thing," Jennifer said, slowly transferring the baby from her arms to her sister's. "I didn't know either until about twenty minutes before the birth at midnight last night."

"What?" Mary leaned in and stroked the baby's downy head with the softest touch. "You've got to be kidding me. It's your first baby."

"I know, right? I had a backache most of the afternoon but no active cramps. I just thought I'd overdone it painting the nursery." She smiled at her sleeping baby in her sister's arms. "I even took a warm bath, which didn't help, and tried to sleep. When I finally realized I was actually in labor, I knew it was too late to get to the hospital because she was already crowning."

"I was losing my mind." Murphy shook his head and raked a hand through his hair. "I didn't know what the hell to do except call an ambulance and try to catch her like a football."

"A *girl*?" Sara looked up at Jennifer in shock.

"*Her*?" Mary's voice caught as Sara handed her niece over for her to hold. "I thought you guys were having a boy."

"Yeah, that's what the doctor told us, but evidently, sometimes those ultrasounds can be tricky to read when they're turned the wrong way," Jennifer said. "And she's a couple of weeks early, but after they'd checked us out at the hospital and told us everything looked great, we got to take her home."

"I can't believe you didn't call me!" Sara examined the baby's tiny fingers and looked indignantly up at Jennifer.

"There literally wasn't time." Murphy pulled Jennifer closer and kissed her cheek. "Thank God, the ambulance got there in a flash, and about fifteen minutes after that, we were parents."

"Well, it makes sense. I don't know if you remember, but our mom said all her labors with us took under five hours each, including the first."

"What's her name?" Mary said, obviously too entranced with the baby to even look up as she wrapped her tiny fist around Mary's finger.

"Well, Murphy is our last name, of course," Jennifer said, glancing back at her husband. "And her middle name is Elizabeth, after her late grandmother on Brian's side."

Mary and Sara finally looked up from the baby, waiting for her to go on as Jennifer looked at Brian.

"And her first name is Mary," she said, smiling. "We wanted to name her after you. My mother stopped speaking to me when I got divorced and moved to McCall, and you've been my rock ever since, especially after I got pregnant with her."

"Mary Elizabeth Murphy," Mary whispered the words as her namesake continued to clutch her finger with her tiny fist. A tear rolled down her cheek and disappeared as it hit the blanket. "I don't think I've been so honored in all my life."

"I don't know if this is a good time," Murphy offered sheepishly to the circle of heads leaning over the baby. "But would it be okay if me and Sam walked over to the Other Place and had a beer? I've been dying for one since about midnight when my wife was having a baby on our bed."

"Oh, thank God," Sam said, winking at Sara as Jennifer and Sara laughed and told them to get lost, then settled themselves comfortably into the couch.

"So how are you feeling?" Sara helped Jennifer shrug off her jacket and draped it over the back of the couch. "I can't believe you're just hanging out at the diner after you just had a baby."

"I'm really sore, but the doctor said there was no tearing or need for stitches, so I'm honestly okay." The baby stirred, and Mary held her a little closer, still not willing to take her eyes off her. "I think she's more tired than I am. I really didn't get the chance to do much pushing at all."

Sara searched her face. She was holding something back; Sara had always been able to read her like a book. "So what are you worried about? I can tell there's something."

Jennifer laughed as the server brought their food, and Jennifer ordered two of the specials: roast beef and cheddar sandwiches. "I know you think I'm being nice and taking one of those to Brian, but I certainly am not." She smiled at her little one still asleep in Mary's arms and sank back into the couch with a sigh. "I've been ravenous since the moment she was born."

"I think I remember you telling me you wanted to breastfeed, right?" Mary finally looked from the baby to Jennifer. "That'll be why. I went through enough food to feed myself and my husband with all four of my girls."

Jennifer nodded with a look of relief. "Mary, didn't you say your daughter Catherine is a midwife?"

"She's actually the most in demand midwife in Seattle. She even has a waiting list, which I still can't wrap my head around, and also works as a lactation specialist."

"I guess that's the only thing I'm having trouble with," Jennifer said, smoothing the blanket over baby Mary Elizabeth's tummy with gentle fingers. "I don't think she's latching well, and I'm worried she's not getting enough milk."

"Oh, don't worry about that for even a second," Mary said, pulling out her cell phone. "I'll text Catherine and get her to do a video call with you this evening. She'll be able to tell you right away if everything looks the way it should and give you advice on whatever else you're wondering about."

"Thank you so much, Mary. That makes me feel better already." Jenn reached for Mary's hand and squeezed it. "Which brings me to my next question." The server brought both her sandwiches, and Jennifer picked one up before the plate even hit the table, drizzling it with horseradish sauce and taking a huge bite before she continued. "Ordinarily, I'd ask my sister to do something like this, but she has Moxie at home right now and—"

"And I wouldn't be much help anyway since I haven't actually had a baby." Sara laughed, reaching out to touch baby Mary's downy blond hair. "It would just be the two of us calling Mary every five minutes."

Jennifer laughed and leaned into Sara as she looked over to Mary. "Do you think you might be able to come help me for the first few days? I've had the guest room made up for weeks, and I promise not to take up too much of your time. I just already feel overwhelmed and it hasn't been twenty-four hours yet."

"Well, it's nice of you to invite me," Mary sniffed, "But I was coming anyway." Mary smiled at her namesake, who had just opened her beautiful dark blue eyes, blinking up at Mary for just a moment before they fluttered shut again. "I can't think of anywhere else I'd rather be."

CHAPTER ELEVEN

Lily stepped onto the patio of the Other Place to find Alex sitting at one of the tables with two whiskeys already waiting on leather coasters and a brown suede duffel bag at her feet.

"Well, that's a relief." Lily sank into the chair across from Alex and held her whiskey up to the fading evening sun, letting the light shift through it like molten amber. "I was worried when you said to pack for the weekend that it was just a ruse to get me the hell out of your cabin."

Alex laughed and picked her hand to kiss, squeezing it before she let it go. The late June heat was dry and intense but lightened by the first of the evening breezes shifting through the trees, loosening a scatter of pine needles to float through the air and down to the patio. Alex's black T-shirt and faded Levi's made her look like she'd just walked out of a 1950s ad for Cuban tourism. The sleeves clung to the definition in her arms, and the swirling smoke gray tats underscored the mysterious vibe Lily had yet to be able to wrap words around.

"Well." Alex lifted her glass and took a leisurely sip. "As much as I loved coming home with you to find random women in our cabin, I thought it was about time to take you on a real date."

"Ah! My little plan worked." Lily laughed, picking up her glass. "So where are we going?"

She didn't wait for an answer before she closed her eyes, taking the first sip of the intensely peated scotch Alex had chosen. The smoke of it rose through the roof of her mouth as if it weren't there and filled her nose, softening quickly to ash and smoothing the edges of the caramel bite of the scotch itself. She drew in the last of the vapors with the cooling mountain air and opened her eyes to find Alex watching. She was biting her lip.

"This was a dangerous choice." Lily raised her glass and clinked it to Alex's, then sat back in her chair. "You're lucky I love Lagavulin Islay."

"Jesus." Alex shook her head, then raked her hand through the dark layers of her hair. "I chose that because I thought it was the one remote scotch you wouldn't be able to identify. How do you *do* it?"

"Well, the official answer is that I'm not telling." Lily laughed when Alex rolled her eyes. "But the real answer is they use peat to dry the malted barley for the whiskey. Every peat bog has slightly different organic components, but each distillery also throws a few secret herbs into the fires. Not that they'd tell anyone this, especially an American."

"So how do you know?"

"When I spent a month in Scotland last summer, I visited Islay and the Isle of Skye, and everyone loves to tell a writer their secrets."

"Ah…the Queen of Scotch and Secrets." Alex's eyes sparkled over the edge of her glass as she drew in the scent. "Obviously, I concede defeat."

Lily shifted her overnight bag from the back of her chair to the patio at her feet, checking to be sure the zipper was closed.

Alex raised an eyebrow. "Did you leave your laptop in the cabin?"

"Only because you told me to. I usually take it everywhere with me, and I'm already stressed about the—"

"Shh." Alex reached over to touch a fingertip to her lips. "Focusing on it will only make it worse."

Lily looked around at the empty patio, then caught Alex's finger in her mouth. She held her eyes as she swirled her tongue lightly around it, then guided Alex's hand into her shirt to graze her bare nipple. Alex groaned and leaned back in her chair, her eyes still on the white linen shirt buttoned not quite to the center of her chest.

"You're pretty wise for a dance instructor," Lily said, picking up her scotch and leaning back in her chair. "But you're right, actually. Writing when you don't have the words is like trying to spot ghosts in an old house. You're sure you see something, so you turn and walk toward it, only to have it disappear." She traced the rim of her whiskey glass with her fingertip. "The more you chase, the longer they hide."

Alex looked over her head and pointed at a dusky swirl of bats swooping down from the treetops and flying toward the water. "I love bats," she said, her eyes following them long after they'd disappeared like a twisting, pale gray cloud. "I've always loved them. In Cuba, I'd walk home after work at dusk and watch them fly out from under the eaves of the churches and belfries. I always wanted them to land on my hand, but they never did. I just walked around with my hand out like an idiot for years."

Lily leaned in on her elbows. "What do you like so much about them?"

"I don't know." Alex swirled her amber scotch around the sides of her glass, watching as it slid over the cuts and curves of the crystal. "They represent freedom to me, I think. They're so fast that nothing can catch them in the air, and when they finally come back to earth, they disappear until the next nightfall."

Lily finished the rest of her scotch and put the glass back on the leather coaster, watching the golden rivulets slink down the sides. "What makes you feel like you're not free?"

Alex took a long moment to answer, and when she did her voice was lower, more like a scrape than a sound. "I think I'm starting to realize I've felt like that for a while. But I don't know how to fix it without blowing up my life."

"That sounds familiar." Lily met her eyes. "I understand that feeling."

"I know you do." Alex smiled, finished her scotch, and picked up both bags, slinging them over her shoulder. "But I also have a feeling that tonight might help."

Lily stood and rolled the sleeves of her shirt to her elbow. "I'm getting the idea that you have no intention of telling me where we're going."

Alex winked at her and offered her arm as they descended the steps of the patio, then guided Lily away from the parking area and back toward Main Street.

"Don't worry," Alex said, switching the bags to the other side so she could hold Lily's hand. "I spoke to the owner, and she said it was fine for you to leave your Jeep there for a couple of days."

"You know what I just realized?" Lily smiled and leaned into

Alex's arm as they crossed Main Street. "I've actually never been on a date that I didn't have to plan."

"What?" Alex turned to look at her. "You're kidding, right?"

"Nope, but in fairness, I haven't been on many dates since I moved to LA, but the ones I have been on were…"

"Forgettable?"

"That's an excellent way to put it." Lily laughed as Alex led them to the grassy slope that dropped down toward the water. "Just the fact that I literally have no idea what the hell I'm getting into sets this one miles apart."

"Well, I'm banking on you being hungry, but that's the only clue you're getting from me."

Alex steered them down the hill from the center of town to the Mile High Marina, McCall's main marina and community dock space, where the water was unusually calm for a late June afternoon. Boats drifted effortlessly into their slips as the owners returned from a day on the lake, and the gentle lap of the water on the dock became quieter as a passing wake faded into the shore. Lily slipped off her leather flip-flops and carried them as they walked down the dock past the rows of speedboats and local pontoons. The worn, sun-bleached boards were warm and soft under her bare feet, and the breeze coming in off the water loosened the hair tucked behind her ears, brushing it lightly against her cheek.

The slips were taken up by mostly local cruisers and ski boats, each assigned a number and, apparently, a theme; every slip was decorated slightly differently, some with colorful Hawaiian leis looped around the dock pillars, others with potted palms and bright deck chairs on the AstroTurf deck walk, and there were even a few with strings of party lights illuminating the darkening sky. Seagulls swooped close to land on the houseboats at the end of the dock, only to take off suddenly and fly toward the sharp edge of the world where the lake water met the bright orange sky, streaked with violet and pale blue.

They walked to the very end of the dock, where Alex finally stopped at a bright white double-decker houseboat with an expansive rooftop deck and a slick cerulean slide that ended just above the water.

"You can't be serious." Lily shaded her eyes to glance at Alex and then back down the dock. "You rented a houseboat?"

"Well, it's technically a yacht, but I am most certainly serious." Alex tossed their bags onto one of the deck seats and stepped in, offering Lily her hand. "Just because the women you've dated before didn't know how to treat you doesn't mean all of us don't."

Lily took Alex's hand, then stepped onto the lower level of the boat and walked around attempting to hide her shock while Alex took their bags to the cabin downstairs. Everything about it was gorgeous, from the white leather upholstery to the polished brass fittings, and a glance through the windows to the main living area inside made her feel like she'd stepped into the latest issue of *Yachting While Ridiculously Rich Magazine*.

Lily went to the tip of the bow and sank into one of the buttery soft leather seats. There was a small mahogany handle on the wall beside her, and she pulled on it gingerly to reveal a refrigerated minibar with full-size bottles of spirits and mixers, a small bowl of fresh limes, and delicate silver ice tongs.

She released the handle when she saw Alex walk back out to join her, and it clacked shut so abruptly that the sound echoed across the water. Lily covered her face with her hands and looked up at Alex through her fingers. "You literally can't take me anywhere."

"You're adorable." Alex leaned down and took Lily's face in her hands, kissing her softly and pulling away with a gentle bite on her lower lip. "But you can leave those here. I've got drinks for us upstairs."

Lily followed her up the ladder to the upper-level deck, gleaming and luxe with the same white leather seating along the sides, but this space also had a blue Lucite coffee table, several brightly colored beanbag chairs scattered about, and even a woven sun-yellow double hammock to the side of the fully stocked bar. A grill in the center was already prepped with charcoal and a lighter, and a stainless-steel cooler sat ready underneath.

Alex ducked behind the bar and emerged with a bottle of chilled Napa Valley rosé and two glasses. As she opened it, Lily watched the last streaks of fiery sunset sink into the navy blue horizon. The last stragglers on the dock had wandered back toward town, and the calming water made it look as if she were surrounded by rippled glass. Somewhere in the distance, the clang of sailing ropes against a mast reverberated across the lake as Alex handed her a chilled glass of wine.

"I chose a dry rosé based on your taste in whiskey," Alex said. "But even if I didn't know that, I'd have guessed you're not the girl to appreciate a syrupy Riesling."

"Good guess." Lily sank down into one of the beanbags and watched as Alex started the charcoal in the grill. "What are we having for dinner? Now that I'm here, the smell of that grill firing up has me suddenly starving."

Alex clicked the lighter under the perfectly stacked charcoal. "When you were in Havana, did you ever go to La Luna Azul?" It caught, and flames leapt out of the grill, softening into a slow burn as Alex looked over at her. "Like, if you're at the cathedral on the square, it's on the right as you turn onto Quinta Avenida?"

"Oh my God, the Blue Moon?" Lily lay back and looked at the darkening sky, her hand over her heart. "They had the most amazing grilled shrimp tacos that just melted in your mouth. Leaving that restaurant when I left Havana was like leaving a lover." She paused to melt into the memory. "My favorite lover, to be honest."

Alex reached into the cooler and held up a bag of plump, ash-gray shrimp in a bag of herby marinade. "Well, welcome back to Havana. Although I have to admit, I'm worried about the quality of your lovers if you're comparing their skills to the humble shrimp taco."

"Hush it." Lily swooned as she sat up and smelled the marinade when Alex brought it over. "Oh my God. That's exactly what they smelled like! How did you do that?"

Alex laughed, pulling out a cutting board where she sliced an onion and a red pepper into thin strips, then put them aside and tested the charcoal that was just starting to turn a velvet ash gray at the edges. "My aunt owns that restaurant. She has since I was a kid, and this is my favorite dish. I can't do it exactly like they do, but I get pretty damn close."

"You're a dance instructor, and you have these secret mad Cuban cuisine skills? Don't even try to tell me you're not draped with beautiful women at every turn in real life." Lily took a sip of her wine and looked up at Alex. "So, spill it. What kind of women do you usually date?"

"To be honest, I don't date a lot." Alex pulled a stack of thick tortillas with uneven edges out of the cooler and set them to the right of the grill. "I was in school for a long time, and now I feel like I'm working my life away."

"I can relate to that," Lily said, watching the reflection of the sunset through her wineglass as she held it in to the horizon. "And it sounds like that's wearing on you."

"It is, really. But I think being in McCall is giving me some clarity. I've realized it's not the work that's wearing on me, it might be how I'm having to do it."

Lily dropped her shoes to the side, digging her toes into the luxurious AstroTurf. It felt more like lush, deep velvet than faux grass. She looked up and watched as Alex set a foil packet on the grill and closed the lid, then poured herself a glass of the wine and pulled the other beanbag chair over to Lily.

"So," Lily said, spinning the wine in her glass as she spoke. The last of the evening light illuminated the pale blush tint and sparkled against the glass. "Are you going to tell me what you really do for a living, or do I need to get one of the fact-checkers at my publishing company to do a little digging?"

Alex threw her head back and laughed. "You don't miss much, do you? I should have told you by now, but I wanted you to appreciate my merengue skills first, obviously." She paused, then drew in a long breath it seemed she didn't want to let go. "I'm a child psychologist at a major hospital in San Francisco, specializing in neurodivergence. Basically, I work with kids whose brains work differently than the mainstream to help them find solutions for living, and my job is to find unique ways to highlight their brilliance."

It was a moment before Lily spoke, and she shook her head as she clinked her glass to Alex's. "Damn. I did not see that coming."

"Well, I'll take that as a compliment."

"You should." Lily handed her glass to Alex and got up to check the coals. "These aren't ready for the shrimp yet, but they're getting fairly close. Do you want me to vent the rice?"

"Yes, please." The breeze ruffled Alex's hair, and she ran a hand through it, only managing to stand most of it on end. "But how did you know that's what's in the packet?"

"Because those tacos in Havana are served with that gorgeous yellow rice and tostones." She peeked inside the cooler. "Which I see you have the plantains for right here, which means now I'm seriously in heaven."

She lowered the lid on the grill, plopped back into her beanbag, and leaned back until she was almost horizonal, staring at the stars that were just starting to scatter themselves across the deep navy sky. "What was it that made you decide to take a few weeks off?"

"I'm not happy at work, and I don't know why." Alex paused, rubbing the palm of her hand with her thumb. "Or maybe I do, but I don't know what to do about it, which is worse."

Lily nodded and touched her bare toes to Alex's. "Tell me more."

The moon, levitating over the water, glossed everything in a liquid silver cast, including Alex's dark eyes as she looked back at Lily. "I'm in my field to give kids the tools they need to navigate their worlds and to teach them to build their own tools if they have to. But I think I'm frustrated with seeing medication become the default for neurodivergent kids. We're not teaching them to navigate their surroundings using adaptation and intelligence anymore." Frustration crept into Alex's voice, and she shook her head. "When we toss chemicals at every issue, we're just altering a reality we should be teaching them to navigate. Because it's not going to go away."

Lily nodded, finishing the last of her wine. "I completely understand what you're saying. I know that sometimes meds are appropriate, but especially with kids, if they don't learn coping skills early, it's tricky to adapt later."

"And most kids that think differently than the norm, whether it's ADHD or more complex issues like autism, have elevated intelligence. Teaching them to use their differences to their advantage is why I chose to be in the field."

Alex glanced at Lily's wineglass and started to get up to refill it for her, but Lily motioned for her to sit and grabbed the bottle, refilling both their glasses.

"I brought you out here to cook you dinner." Alex smiled, pulling Lily down for a kiss before she walked away. "Not talk your ear off about my job."

Lily leaned down to Alex in the chair, holding her eyes for a moment before she kissed her again. "Alex, I like you." She brushed Alex's lower lip gently with the tip of her tongue as she pulled away. "Like, for real. So I want to know all the things." Lily stood and returned to the grill, sliding out the attached pan for the veggies. "And it's about time, so hit me. Tell me everything."

Alex smiled, balancing the wineglass on two fingers as she watched Lily check the rice and drizzle olive oil onto the grill pan with a scatter of salt. "That might be the most romantic thing a woman has ever said to me."

"Well," Lily said, tossing a wink in Alex's direction, "it sounds like the bar is low, in that case. Excellent. I like those odds."

Lily tossed the sliced onions and peppers onto the sizzling grill pan, inhaling the steam as they started to soften and char. She pulled the shrimp from the marinade with tongs one by one, placing them carefully on the grill, where the heat instantly lifted the lime rich mojo spices to her nose.

"So tell me." Lily placed the last shrimp on the grill, looking over her shoulder at Alex. "You know what you're wanting to shift away from professionally. What are you going toward?"

"That's a good question." Alex got up and reached for the stack of tortillas, wrapped them in a damp cloth and foil, then stuck them on the far corner of the grill to steam. She leaned against the cool edge of the grill, laced her fingers behind her head, and thought for a second before she answered. "I guess I want to get back to the basics of counseling, you know? I want to equip kids in tough situations to navigate the world more successfully through talk therapy and behavioral science."

Lily nodded, flipping the first shrimp to the other side. "You want to get back to teaching them to build their own toolkit."

"Exactly." Alex smiled. "Ideally, in private practice."

Alex waited for Lily to set down the tongs, then slipped her hand around the back of Lily's neck and kissed her. She brushed her tongue lightly down the slope of her neck, stopping just before she reached the center of her chest to graze Lily's nipple through the thin gauze of her shirt with the back of her hand, closing her eyes as it tensed under her touch.

"Goddamn, Lily. I love your mind." Alex circled Lily's hips with her hands and pulled them hard into hers. "But this body drives me crazy."

Lily suddenly noticed the shrimp were burning, and Alex used the tongs to sweep them all off the grill and onto a plate she placed to the side.

"I thought these might be overcooked, but they're actually

perfect," Alex said, biting into a test shrimp, then putting the other half into Lily's mouth. "I don't know how we managed that. I seem to lose track of time when I'm touching you."

Lily laughed as they finished up the other components of the tacos together and fried the plantains for the tostones on the grill pan. The rice was fragrant and fluffy, peppered with raisins and layered with spicy black beans. Alex arranged the shrimp, crisscrossed with grill marks, in the center of the wooden serving board and placed the grilled peppers and onions around them. The tortillas fit perfectly along the side with some spicy mango slaw and sliced avocado to wrap up inside.

Lily pulled a linen blanket she found behind the bar to spread out on the AstroTurf, and they settled with the food between them, along with a few plates and napkins and a fresh bottle of Spanish rosé.

"Oh God, this seriously smells exactly like Havana!" Lily drew in the salty sweet scent of Cuba deep into her lungs and plucked the first tortilla off the top of the stack. "I'd like to be polite and hold back here, but this is just too good not to start on."

Alex laughed and handed her a plate, feeding her a bite of mango slaw as she loaded her taco. "So what kind of women do you date in LA?" She paused, looking as if she were biting back a comment. "And I'm not even going to play like I haven't been dying to ask you this question."

"More importantly," Lily deflected smoothly, pressing two slices of ripe avocado into her taco and layering the grilled veggies over the savory shrimp, "these tortillas look homemade. Did you make them?"

"I might have gotten Sara to let me make them at her house today." Alex leaned over to kiss her cheek as she popped a tostone into her mouth. "It's not like I'm going to make you homemade food from my country and serve it with store-bought tortillas. Like, I think I might go to Cuban jail or something for that."

"As you should." Lily laughed, then paused before she continued. "Okay, about the women I date in LA." She savored the first crispy, decadent bite before she reluctantly returned to Alex's question. "I've been out with a few, but...I don't know how to describe it. They're just too damn pretty for me, I guess."

Alex sputtered, then laughed so hard she had to set down her wineglass.

"I mean," Lily went on, "it's not like they're all supermodels or anything, but there's a *look* they all have, you know? They all look airbrushed, even the masculine of center ones. I call it the Cali Filter."

"Um, no. I have no idea what the hell a Cali Filter is," Alex said, putting the finishing touches on her own taco. "Enlighten me. This is fantastic, by the way, getting the scoop from inside the LA trenches. Totally not what I was expecting."

"I don't know how to put words to it, really. It's just too polished for me. I like some edge to my women, and I'm not usually attracted to femmes. I like a masculine-presenting butch who looks like she can handle me. It totally kills the vibe if she's wearing a skirt shorter than mine."

"Well, you're in luck. I'm fresh out of skirts." Alex laughed, deftly catching a shrimp that escaped her taco. "But I'll keep that in mind." She took a bite and set it back on her plate, reaching for one of the napkins and glancing over at Lily. "You've been here awhile now. What do you miss about LA?"

Lily didn't answer for a moment. She'd expected to miss LA; she'd lived there for five years, and everyone seemed to be dying to move to Southern California. But the only things she came up with were the smell of the sea and her little hidden cottage, and most of what she loved about the cottage she could recreate somewhere else, truthfully. "I guess not much, once I think about it." She finished the last bite of her taco and sat back on her hands, staring at the stars as if the answer were written in code across the night sky. "Most of LA stresses me out."

"And how do you feel here?"

Alex's voice dropped, and Lily followed her gaze. A boat was approaching the end of the dock not far from the yacht, but the top deck was so high, it was unlikely whoever was in the boat could see them. It's common knowledge in a lake town that running lights are required after sundown, but as this one approached, it cut every light, even the illumination for the instrument panel, and glided silently into place at the end of the dock. There were two people on the boat, both tall enough to suggest they'd be men, but it was hard to make out much else in the darkness.

"Not that I'm an expert on boats or anything." Lily softened her voice and glanced at Alex, who was still watching every move they made. "But doesn't something seem off about that?"

Alex nodded, putting a hand on Lily's shoulder when she started to stand to take a closer look. "Let's not make them think someone's watching," Alex whispered, her eyes still locked on the silent boat. "Just in case."

"I'm sure we're making something out of nothing," Lily said, sitting back down and returning to her yellow rice before it cooled off in the evening air. "Nothing ever happens in McCall."

Alex shifted her attention as a truck pulled up to the parking area at the top of the marina, directly next to the path that led to the dock. The truck flashed its lights once as the passenger door opened, and two small figures hurried down the docks, their faces hidden by oversize dark hoodies. The truck pulled back onto the main road as soon as the doors slammed shut, and their hurried footsteps on the empty dock were the only sound. They jumped in off the end of the dock, and the boat accelerated quickly away in the opposite direction, still without a single running light. Lily and Alex watched it until it disappeared around one of the islands. Lily was about to ask whether Alex had recognized the boat from a nearby camp when Alex stood.

"Would you excuse me for a moment?"

Lily nodded and watched through the windows as Alex walked downstairs and pulled her phone out of her pocket. As she started talking, she turned away from the window, looking out over the water. She wasn't gone long, but after she'd dropped her phone back into her pocket, she stayed to stare out the window for a moment before she returned.

Lily finished the last tostone and sat back with her wine. "Everything okay?"

"Totally," Alex said, picking up the food and setting it aside to sit next to Lily. "Except for the fact that you're still dressed." Alex looked over at Lily and flicked open another button on her shirt with one finger.

"Well, that was certainly smooth, Suarez." Lily laughed, melting underneath Alex as she rolled over on top of her.

"That shirt has been driving me crazy since you walked onto the patio. Did you do that on purpose?"

"Alex. Have you met me?" Lily flashed her best angelic smile. "I do everything on purpose."

"Oh, I see how it is." Alex laughed and rolled off her, gathering the last of the food from the blanket. "That's some good information to have."

"I'll help clean up," Lily said, reaching out for the tortillas. "Hand me those, I'll wrap them back up."

"Hell no, Larimar," Alex said, swatting her ass and handing her a wineglass in the same second. "You're lucky I let you get away with cooking. Now, go out there to the other side of the boat and drink that wine while you look at the stars."

"Well, I'd insist on staying and cleaning up, but that sounds way more fun," Lily said, reaching up to kiss her. "But don't get used to telling me what to do, or I'm going to have to put you back in your place."

"Well," Alex teased, clearly watching Lily's ass as she walked away, "a butch can dream."

Lily walked past the velvety AstroTurf to the far end of the deck, which was floored with rich maple hardwood that felt oddly warm under the soles of her feet. She leaned onto the rail and glanced back, but Alex was busy texting, her fingers flying over the screen.

Lily looked up at the drifts of stars scattered across the inky night sky and tried to imagine what it would feel like when she had to go back to LA. She couldn't stay in McCall forever, as dreamy as that sounded. Sooner or later, she'd have to go back to promotional appearances, endless events that had nothing to do with her actual writing, and probably more television cameos like the last one on *The L Word: Generation Q*, which everyone wanted, and she hadn't enjoyed in the least.

But everything looked different from McCall. She was starting to realize that the further away from her writing she drifted, even in the interest of promotion, the more she felt like the world around her was going to swallow her alive. She loved meeting the readers; what she hated was the LA scene, where to stay current, you had to be seen and photographed at events constantly. It was a feeling reminiscent of drowning, constantly flailing to stay above water, to stay visible.

Lily caught sight of something out of the corner of her eye, then walked back to Alex, who had just finished the last of the cleanup. Lily held out her hand. "Come with me."

"Hmm…follow a beautiful woman to the dark side of a deck to gaze at the moon?" Alex pretended to consider it for a moment, then took her hand and kissed it, following Lily back to where she'd been standing. Lily stepped between Alex and the railing, leaning slowly back against the warmth of her chest.

"Do you trust me?"

Alex's hesitated. "Is that a real question?"

"Yes."

"Then the answer is yes," Alex said, the words warm against the top of Lily's head. "I do."

Lily stretched both arms out and turned her palms to the sky. Alex did the same, her arms outside Lily's, palms facing upward on top of hers. "I'm just going to concentrate for a moment." Lily paused, searching for words to wrap around something she'd never been able to explain. "And all I need for you to do is not move, no matter what happens."

She felt Alex nod behind her. "I can do that."

Lily closed her eyes and took a deep breath, letting it out slowly. It took only seconds, as she knew it would; they were waiting. She opened her eyes to see three beautiful brown bats circling above their heads and felt Alex's heart start to race against her back. One of the bats hovered above them for just a moment before it swooped gently to a stop in Alex's open hands. It pulled in its wings and settled contently into her palms, black glittering eyes blinking slowly as she looked from Lily to Alex.

"Breathe," Lily whispered softly. She smiled as she felt Alex draw in a shaky breath.

The other two bats continued to swoop in a crisscross pattern overhead, and one even landed on Lily's shoulder for just a second before flitting off, the sudden wind from its wings stirring her hair.

The bat in Alex's hands stretched her wings slowly and tilted her head before she flew off, hovering for just a second as if to say good-bye. It was a while before she felt Alex let go of the breath she was holding.

"How in the world," Alex whispered as she wrapped her arms around Lily and held her tight to her chest, "did you *do* that?"

"Magic, maybe." Lily turned in Alex's arms and kissed her cheek. "But it's their magic, not mine." She looked at Alex, who still looked a little shocked. "It's hard to explain."

"Just…thank you for that," Alex said, looking up into the sky where the three bats were still circling. "It was all I wanted when I was little—I was obsessed with it—but they never even came close. I think I just needed a little magic in my life back then." Alex kissed her, cradling her face, and pulling her as close as possible. "I don't have anything nearly that magical to offer you, but did you happen to notice that the floor was warm under your feet when you walked out here?"

"I did!" Lily said, leaning down to touch it with her fingers. "How is that possible, by the way?"

Alex stepped back and pulled up a wooden handle that fit flush against the floor. She folded back a wooden panel twice, then did the same on the other side.

"No way!" Lily clapped her hands together when she saw the steamy blue swirling water of a hideaway hot tub emerge. "That's amazing. I walked right over it and had no idea."

"The best part," Alex said, tugging her shirt and sports bra over her shoulders and dropping them to the floor, "is that because it's sunken into the floor, no one can see us once we're in it."

"So..." Lily slowly unbuttoned her shirt, letting it fall from her shoulders. "When I get completely naked and get into that water with you, no one will be able to see what we get up to?"

"Exactly," Alex said, her eyes drinking in every inch of Lily's skin. "If you don't give me a heart attack before you actually get in the water."

Lily threw her head back and laughed, slipping off her shorts and underwear and lowering herself into the steamy, bubbling water beside Alex. She brought her fingers to her lips. "Is this salt water?"

"It is. It reduces the amount of chemicals you need to use in it, apparently."

Lily leaned her head back and looked at the stars, her entire body relaxing into the motion of the water. "How did you find this?"

"The same way I found McCall, actually. I knew I needed to get away for a few weeks, and my cousin Alejandro, who has a house on the other side of the lake, said it was finally time I saw McCall. He's had his place for a few years, but I was always too busy to come." Alex ran a wet hand through her hair and pulled Lily closer. "So I was searching for lesbian friendly places to stay because Alejandro's flashy lake house is just too damn big for me, and the posting for a Latin dance instructor at Lake Haven popped up."

"Oh, wow. And that was way too perfect to pass up?"

"Exactly," Alex said. "We have family in Idaho, which is why Alejandro found McCall years ago, but he mainly comes for the ski season. He says it offsets the blazing Miami sun he has to live in for the rest of the year."

"So Alejandro is your cousin," Lily said, taking a sip of her wine and setting it back down on the edge of the hot tub. "Do you have brothers and sisters?"

"I think I would've had several, but my father was killed when I was three, so they never really got the chance to have more, and my mom never remarried. My mom and my aunt are super close, so I grew up with my cousins all around me. It was great at the time, but as an adult, I can see how tough it was just to survive as a single mom."

"And that's why you were walking home from a job just before nightfall as a kid? And why you maybe needed to see a little magic sometimes?"

Alex scraped her hair back with wet hands and moved closer to Lily, both of them leaning their heads back to look at the stars through the rising steam. "I think it made me want to help kids in tough situations, you know?" Alex's voice seemed as far away as the stars. "The more tools you have, the more chances you have of improving your life and getting where you want to go, no matter what's happening around you."

Lily nodded, running her fingertips lightly over Alex's hand. "Have you ever wanted your own kids?"

"You know what?" Alex said thoughtfully. "I knew a long time ago that I needed to be able to focus on my career, and I guess I've just never seen myself as a parent. As much as I love and relate well to kids, it never felt like my path." She ran her hand up Lily's thigh slowly. "What about you? I mean, I'm almost forty, but you're just twenty-eight, right? That's totally a possibility for you if you wanted it."

Lily nodded, tucking a damp lock of hair behind her ear. "I don't know why, but I've never wanted children. I like them much more than most adults but just never wanted any of my own."

"Do you get tired of people asking you that question?"

"Truthfully, yes," Lily said. "You and I are involved, so you have every reason to ask me that. But I feel like for most people, whether a woman has children or when she's getting married is the constant default question. Even for someone they barely know."

"Every damn time." Alex waved off a bug threatening to dive-bomb the water. "But when they're talking to men, people tend to ask about their career or their goals for the future."

"That's exactly it." Lily stretched her toes out to the opposite edge of the tub. "I decided a long time ago I wasn't going to feel obligated to explain when people asked me that question. I'm a woman, so they're going to judge me no matter how I answer. Why hand them ammunition?"

She looked over through the hazy, rising steam. Alex's shoulders looked even more sculpted wet, and the blue glow coming up from the underwater lights highlighted the strong angles of her jaw. Lily had tried not to think about it, but the truth was, Alex reminded her a lot of Sam. Especially how she looked in the water.

Lily pulled her hair back with an elastic. "Remember the night we met at the bar in McCall, and I told you that you could ask me one question—"

"But to make it good because I was lucky to get even that?"

"Exactly." Lily laughed and reached for her wine, finishing the last of the delicate chilled rosé. "Well, I think you've earned one more."

"Oh, now I'm drunk with the power," Alex teased, pulling Lily over onto her lap to face her. "So anything I want to know is up for grabs?"

"Yes, sir." Lily's voice was low and hot like the water as her mouth moved down Alex's neck. "But I'd make this one count. You never know if you'll get another."

❖

"Sam."

Sam sat up slowly, turning to Sara and raking her hand through her hair. "What's going on?

"I don't know," Sara said, her voice low and tense. "But I keep hearing noises from outside."

Sam got up and looked down at the front of the house from their bedroom window. "What did it sound like?"

"I don't know. Like pounding?"

"Seriously?" Sam switched on the closet light and reached for a pair of jeans. "Like on the door?"

"No, fainter than that, but I thought I heard the front door open when I woke up a few minutes ago. But that's silly. I saw you lock it when we went to bed, and Moxie is in for the night. When I checked on her, she was reading Lily's latest book."

Sam dropped her phone in her back pocket, then walked to Sara's side of the bed and took her phone off the charger, making sure it was on with the volume turned up. "Baby, I'm sure it's nothing, but I want you to stay here and let me know if you hear anything else, okay?" Sam handed her the phone and pulled on her shoes and a hoodie. "It's probably just bears."

"Okay. But be careful, okay?" Sara pulled Sam's face to hers and kissed her. "Are you sure you don't need me to go with you?"

Sam tried not to laugh, pulling the covers back up around Sara and zipping up her hoodie. "Not that you're not my tiny blond hurricane, who is certainly a force to be reckoned with, but I got it this time, love." Sam stopped again at the closet and removed her service weapon from the safe, checking it for ammunition before she strapped it on. "Just hang out up here for me, okay?" Sam said as she cut the light and headed for the door. "And stay away from the windows."

Sam pulled the door shut behind her checked the time. It was after two a.m., and she doubted bears would make that much racket. She'd installed a concrete fence years ago, as well as scent-blocking trash bins. Bears were smart; they'd figured out the trash situation at her house quickly and left it alone since then.

She climbed the stairs quietly and turned the handle on Moxie's door without opening it. "Moxie?" She kept her voice low. There was no answer. "I'm just checking on you. Let me know if you're in there." She waited another few seconds and quietly opened the door. Moxie wasn't there. Her bed had been slept in, but her lamp had been left on, and the black Converse she wore every day were missing. Sam let herself out and went back downstairs, slipping out the front door and standing on the step until she heard the sound she was waiting for.

She turned and started down the path to the barn, and sure enough, the second she rounded the corner, she saw Moxie retrieving the ball from the edge of the concrete and putting it up again. It made a satisfying swoosh as it slid through the net, and Sam watched as she grabbed it with one hand and shot again.

Sam pulled her phone out of her pocket. *Hey babe, I'm down here at the court with Moxie. Everything's fine, she's just shooting some hoops, and I'll probably join her.*

Moxie saw Sam out of the corner of her eye and stopped in her tracks. "I'm sorry if I woke you up." She looked down, turning the basketball in her hands. "I just couldn't sleep, and I got sick of lying there awake."

Sam held up her hands for the ball and shot, smiling as it sank through the hoop and bounced back in Moxie's direction. "I used to do the same thing when I was in high school." Sam watched as Moxie spun the ball on the heel of her hand. "Dad hung a backboard and net on this huge oak tree in the yard, and I'd go out there whenever I couldn't sleep."

"Really?" Moxie said before she did a perfect short layup. It hit the rim, and she retrieved it just before it bounced off the concrete, tossing it in Sam's direction. "Did it help?"

"Nah. Not really." Sam turned the ball in her hands, then tossed it back to Moxie. "I've been seeing your light on most nights, though." She paused. "Something on your mind?"

Moxie sank to sit where she was on the court, and Sam joined her, stretching out her legs and leaning back on her hands. It took a few minutes for Moxie to find her words, so Sam just watched the stars till she had them.

"I don't know what to say because it doesn't make any sense." Moxie shoved her sleeves up to her elbows, catching the string from her sweatshirt hood and twisting it in her fingers. "Everything's so great. You and Sara have been amazing." She paused. "I didn't even know foster parents like you existed. There's always enough food, like really good food, and I'm even making friends in town that go to McCall High School."

Sam stayed quiet and held the space for Moxie to unfold her thoughts.

"But every time something good happens, it makes me more nervous, you know?" Moxie hesitated, biting her lip. "Like, I want to get used to it, but I know it's all going to disappear."

Sam nodded. "And you almost don't want all the good things because you know you'll miss it when everything changes?"

"Yeah. And everything always changes," Moxie said, jerking a knot into the string. "And I feel like that would be worse than not knowing how this feels in the first place."

"Yeah, that's scary. And it makes perfect sense to me." Sam lifted her hoodie so Moxie could see her gun. "Since there doesn't seem to be a serial killer down here, I'm going to take this off while we talk, okay?"

Sam felt Moxie watching as she unbuckled the harness and laid it carefully on the edge of the concrete. She returned and stretched back out back on the court, and Moxie followed suit.

"So what made you want to be a cop?"

Sam considered the question for a moment. Truth was, she couldn't remember ever wanting to do anything else; she'd just always wanted to be just like her dad, Gus. "Well, my dad was the chief of police here in McCall the entire time I was growing up, so that had something to do with it." Sam smiled over at Moxie, then looked back up to the stars. "But I guess beyond that, it just fit me. I loved being a captain on Lake Patrol—"

"The cops out there on boats?"

"That's them," Sam said, smiling at the memory of Sara describing them the same way when she'd first come to McCall. "To tell you the truth, I like that a lot more than being on the administrative end of things as the chief."

"Yeah. I get that." A gust of breeze swept through the trees and across the court, lifting two leaves beside them into a silent dance on the concrete. "It has to be a lot less exciting behind a desk. Fewer teenagers holding up coffee shops and stuff." Moxie turned toward Sam, leaning up on her elbow. "You should tell them that. Tell them you're not as happy."

Sam opened her mouth to tell Moxie that it wasn't that simple. That she couldn't just say she wasn't happy and go off in search of something different, but she caught herself just in time and turned Moxie's words over and over in her mind.

"You know what?" Sam tossed a rock she found beside her down the court and listened to it skip over the concrete and come to a stop before she continued. "I don't know at what point I stopped making my happiness a priority, but you're right. Maybe it just really is that simple." Sam looked over and smiled. "Thanks for that. I'm going to think about the best way to get that done."

Moxie grinned and flopped back over on her back. "Sara said she wants to take me shopping in Boise for school clothes."

"Yeah, don't worry. I told her I'm coming with."

Moxie laughed, a spontaneous deep giggle that Sam had never heard before. It sounded a lot like happiness. "Good, because I was secretly afraid we'd have to go to all the girly stores, and they always take one look at me in there and roll their eyes."

"Not on my watch they won't," Sam said. "I told Sara that since my style is more similar to yours, I get to take you to my favorite stores first. Like Title Nine and Patagonia."

Moxie nodded and seemed lost in thought for a moment. "I had a Patagonia jacket that I loved last fall. I got lucky and bought it at a thrift store next to my school, but I couldn't find it when I left that last foster placement."

"I don't want to brag, but I'm kinda the jacket guru." Sam made a point of brushing her shoulder off and shot Moxie a serious look. "What did it look like?"

"It was just a black puffer ski jacket. Man, that thing was warm, though." Moxie pulled her sleeves down over her hands. "The year before that, someone stole my coat at a football game in September, and there was no money for another one." She hesitated. "Well, that and Mom was usually too high to drive me anywhere to get one."

"So what did you do for the rest of the year?"

"I played a lot of basketball because the gym was warm." Moxie's smile didn't reach her eyes. "And I just pretended like I had one but didn't want to wear it."

Sam put her finger to her lips and pointed across the court as an opossum waddled out from the trees and onto the concrete, three babies attached like Velcro to her back. Moxie didn't make a sound as she rooted through the leftovers of the sandwich that Moxie must have brought down from the house. The bandit snarfed down every crumb with a series of satisfied grunts, and when she disappeared back into the woods, Moxie finally giggled at the babies holding on for dear life.

"I'm going to tell you something right now that's going to sound impossible." Sam glanced over at Moxie, her deep brown eyes luminous under the lights. The moon was low and nearly full over the treetops, and the air seemed to soften and still around them as if it too, was listening. "And that's okay. Just tuck it in the back of your mind, and someday, you'll remember and realize it's true."

"Okay." Moxie nodded. "I'll remember."

"Here it is." Sam zipped up her hoodie and paused, choosing her words carefully. "I'm not going to let your world fall apart again. And it doesn't matter what that takes." She paused, glancing over at Moxie. "Wherever you choose to be, when life goes sideways, you have backup. You have me."

Moxie nodded, and it was a long time before she spoke again. "You know why I haven't been able to sleep?"

Sam looked over at her and shook her head.

"I'm so afraid of doing something wrong." Raw emotion crept into Moxie's voice, and she dug her fingernails into the palm of her other hand. "I've never been this happy, and I'm afraid to make a mistake and make it all disappear. It just makes me feel frozen sometimes."

"That makes total sense to me. It's really scary when things seem too good to be true. I think that's why I slept in the hall so long and drove my parents crazy." Sam reached for the basketball beside them and rolled it to Moxie to distract her from unknowingly scratching her hand. "But I think what you don't realize yet is that we *expect* you to mess up. You're a kid, and that's your job—to make mistakes and do the wrong thing, then learn and try again." She looked over at Moxie and held her eyes. "You're safe now. You don't have to be perfect or keep everything together. You can just be a kid."

"You were right." Moxie swiped at a tear with the cuff of her hoodie. "That does sound impossible."

"I'm not going anywhere. But it's not your job to believe me," Sam said. "I'll just prove it to you."

Later, after Moxie had beaten Sam in two consecutive rounds of Horse and finally seemed tired enough to sleep, they walked back into the house and semi-quietly raided the cookie jar together. After Moxie climbed the stairs, cookie bag in hand, Sam slipped into bed with Sara, who turned over and sleepily reached back for Sam to scoot closer and spoon her. "How is she?"

"Baby," Sam whispered, reaching for the lamp on the nightstand. "We need to talk about Moxie."

CHAPTER TWELVE

The next afternoon, Alex reluctantly pulled herself away from Lily and left her at the marina to sunbathe with Sara on the yacht while she went to Sam's to place a planned initial cold call to Travis, the suspected trafficker.

The call itself took under three minutes, and as soon as she hung up the phone, Sam clicked off the recorders and leaned back in her chair, raking both hands through her hair.

"Dude, I'm not sure what I just witnessed there, but that was pure gold. I know FBI agents that aren't that smooth undercover. How did you even know how to talk to him like that?"

"Are you kidding?" Alex said, pulling some lip balm out of her pocket and smoothing it on. "I've spent way too much of my life listening to Alejandro buttering up filthy rich clients to not know a few things."

Sam got up and grabbed two cold Sam Adams bottles out of the fridge and came back to the table. "I can't believe he didn't insist on knowing who your contact was."

"Well, he thinks I'm Alejandro, so when I started dropping hints, I heard the keys of his computer clacking right away, so he was definitely checking me out. He must have run my phone number first, which of course came back to Alejandro, then googled me. And when he saw Alejandro's clubs and restaurants—"

"And the beautiful women of Miami draped all over him," Sam cut in, flipping the top off Alex's beer.

"Exactly." Alex took a long swig before she went on. "When all that matched up, I guess he started to think I was legit. I didn't expect him to ask, actually."

"Actually," Sam said. "I knew we had it at one point right after you used an acronym. What was the meaning there?" Sam slid a piece of notepaper toward her, where she'd written *MSOG* while Alex was still on the phone. "Because after that, I could tell he didn't have any doubts about you."

"Actually, we can thank my cousin for that too." Alex swiped at a moisture ring from the beer with the side of her hand and reached for the coasters on the table. "Miami is a hot spot for sex trafficking, and so countless Cuban girls are targeted. Alejandro makes sure he stays in communication with the trafficking task forces so when he sees something that doesn't look right in the club, or someone enquires about 'backroom services,' he knows exactly who to call."

"Does he see a lot of it?"

Alex nodded. "He's learned a lot of their code words and phrases, and he emailed me a list last night." Alex took a deep swig of her beer. "And MSOG stands for Multiple Shots On Goal."

"What?" Sam's face was blank until the meaning dawned on her. "More than one girl?"

"Exactly." Alex brought up the list in her phone and slid it over. "I chose that one to drop into the conversation because it showed I might be a bigger client who wanted multiple girls, which of course is more valuable to him."

"Before I forget about it," Sam said, pulling her wallet out of her back pocket and handing Alex a card. "When your cousin sent the SIM card from his phone, he also sent his driver's license in case you need it in there. This is going down in two days, so after the Tuesday evening meet we planned at his place, I'll overnight Alejandro his stuff back to Hawaii Wednesday morning."

"I spoke to him the night after we did the video call, and he's doing nothing but lying on the beach with his new Colombian girlfriend. His clubs have multiple contact numbers for him, so I don't think he's too worried about it."

"Rough life." Sam checked the recording of the phone call and sent a copy to her phone. "I'm stressed as hell about this."

"Yeah, not only do you have to work with a newbie, but there's a lot riding on what happens." Alex took a deep swig of beer. "But if we do it right, we get to help bust one of these losers for good and get those girls out of there."

Sam sighed, tapping her thumb on the raw wood table. "It's not just the girls inside, although that's huge. It's all the girls that will pass through there in the future if we can't take him down."

"So I just need to keep him talking, right? We just need enough to take to a judge and ask him to sign a search warrant?"

Sam nodded and jotted down two points on a notepad, then slid it over to Alex. "Yep. Specifically, we need him to acknowledge that they're underage, if they are, and that they are available to you in exchange for money. That's what's going to get us in there on a search warrant for sex trafficking."

"And I'll be wired for sound?"

"Sound and video, actually, and we'll test it several times before we go. Boise is sending up a handful of people from their SWAT team in case something goes down, and we're going to position ourselves both outside the mansion and in boats on the lake side. I checked it out, and we can gain entry quickly both ways if necessary." Sam got up and grabbed two more beers, popped the tops, and handed one to Alex.

"I was doing some work at the resort this morning, and Charlotte told me that she rescheduled all your lessons as well, so you'll have the day free." Sam grabbed a coaster and tapped her bottle to Alex's. "She also asked me if I knew where you were this weekend."

"And what did you say?"

"I told her nicely that I did know, but that it wasn't my business to talk about."

"Damn. She's a hard one to shake." Alex took her time finishing the beer and took the bottle to the trash. "Thanks so much for helping me arrange that slip for the yacht. Lily's loving it so far."

"Damn, dude." Sam rolled her eyes and smiled. "I might have messed myself up there. Sara texted me some insanely gorgeous pictures when she got there, and I think she might be in love with that thing. I'm in trouble."

"Speaking of which, I'd better get back." Alex folded the notepaper into her pocket and stood. "But after we nail this loser, we can have dinner or something so I can clue Lily in. I hate not being able to tell her."

"Yeah, good luck with that. She's beyond perceptive. That girl watches everything." Sam walked Alex to the door and handed her a small canvas sack she'd hung on the doorknob.

"Is this what I think it is?" Alex peered inside and instantly laughed. "Oh, damn. You're not kidding about this undercover thing. You've got all my bases covered."

"Yes, sir. It's a soft pack to wear in your boxer briefs on Tuesday." Sam took it out of the pack and held it up. "If Travis has any inkling that you're not a dude at some point, the first thing he's going to do is look at your crotch, and this might get us back on track."

"Jesus Christ. I live with Lily. What am I supposed to say if she sees this somehow?"

"I'd say to leave it here, but trust me, this thing takes a little getting used to. You need to at least wear it around for a while to get used to how it...lies."

"Fantastic." Alex rolled her eyes and opened the door. "That'll be easy to explain."

Alex drove to her cabin at Lake Haven and dropped off Sam's bag of equipment before she headed back to town to pick up a few things for dinner. When she finally had everything she needed, she parked at the marina and walked down the dock, smiling at the sound of Lily and Sara's mingled laughter drifting down from the upper deck of the boat. The breeze held the warmth of the late afternoon sun and riffled through Alex's hair as she took off her shoes and climbed aboard.

"Are you two decent up there?"

They both told her to "come on up" in giggling, singsong unison. Alex climbed the ladder and reached for the camera on her phone when she saw the scene she'd walked into. Sara had definitely brought the party; there were nineties pop ballads on a beach speaker in the corner, colorful beach towels laid out in a giant square on the AstroTurf, as well as a mostly empty pitcher of margaritas and several lidless cans of spray cheese with every cracker known to man strewn across a party platter.

"Alex!" Lily said, holding up one of the cans. "How have I lived this long without spray cheese?"

"Oh, I love that stuff. Especially the bacon flavor." Alex plunked down on the towel blanket, grabbed a handful of crackers, and reached out for the spray cheese. "Gimme it."

"See, I told you everyone secretly adores spray cheese." Sara piled a Ritz cracker dangerously high with aerosol cheese and gazed at it adoringly. "I have no idea why Sam is the exception to the rule. I've been trying to get her to see the light for five years now."

"How did your visit with Sam go?" Lily said, licking her thumb and reaching for another cracker.

Alex wasn't prepared for that question and stumbled over her words. "It was good. I think we got everything…"

Her voice trailed off, and Sara jumped in with a pointed glance in her direction. "Done?"

Alex nodded and shoved a cracker in her mouth. "Yeah. Exactly." She hated not being able to talk to Lily about what was going on, but she was ever more uncomfortable with lying. Lily was someone she could see building a future with, which was a dizzying first for her. She'd had a few girlfriends through the years, but they were usually in a rush to get married, and Alex wanted to focus on getting through grad school and building her career, so eventually, they'd fizzled out.

Something about Lily was different, though. Alex knew she didn't want to mess this one up. From the first night at the whiskey bar—in fact, the second she'd seen Lily open those ice-blue eyes when she'd finished her whiskey—she was hooked. And now she had no choice but to lie to the girl who noticed everything. Fantastic.

"Well," Sara said, dusting herself off, crumbs flying everywhere as she gathered the pitcher and speaker. "I'll leave you two to clean all this up and head home. Sam doesn't know it yet, but she's taking me and Moxie to the diner for cheeseburgers tonight."

Alex looked up, shading her eyes from the glare of the sun reflecting over the smooth lake water. "Because you need more cheese?"

"Alex." Sara sniffed, bag looped over her arm as she slipped her flip-flops back on. "I'm offended that's even a question. It's like you don't know me at all." She winked as she waved good-bye and disappeared down the stairs.

Alex hooked a finger under one thin bikini strap and pulled Lily to her. "Two things." She smiled, tracing Lily's bottom lip with her thumb before she kissed her. "First of all, I missed the hell out of you."

Lily opened her eyes and smiled. "What's the second thing?"

"I hope you know how to drive a boat because I thought we'd find a cove out there somewhere and sleep under the stars."

"You're kidding me." Lily narrowed her eyes, clearly trying to figure out whether Alex was kidding or not. "You don't know how to drive this thing? Because there's no way I'm even—"

Alex kissed her again, this time pulling Lily's body underneath hers. "I know a few more things than you think, Ms. Larimar."

After they'd cleaned up and started the boat, they coasted out to the far side of Payette Lake, where the sun was just starting to sink into a deep, hovering gold over the million-dollar lake homes.

Alex pulled Lily over in front of her to hold the captain's wheel and whispered into her ear as she steered. "I'm trying to pay attention to where this thing is going, but I refuse to be responsible if you insist on wearing just this tiny blue bikini." Alex dropped one strap from her shoulder and traced the line of Lily's ear lightly with her tongue.

Lily reached back and held the back of Alex's neck, fingertips light and warm on her skin. Alex kissed down her shoulder as she slid one hand under the strap and into her bikini top, brushing Lily's nipple lightly with her fingertips.

Lily turned to look at Alex and ran her tongue slowly over her bottom lip. "God, I'm instantly wet when you do that."

"Brace yourself, gorgeous." Alex's words were a warm whisper down her neck. "I haven't even started with you."

Lily smiled and put her hands back on the wheel, leaning back against Alex's chest as Alex guided them toward Gold Dust Cove, a secluded lagoon surrounded on three sides by thick groves of swaying pine and ash-leaf maple trees. The boat cut silently through the glassy water, sending mirrored ripples in both directions as Alex pulled into the middle of the cove. She cut the engine and listened to Lily's breath slow and deepen as she barely brushed her nipples with her open palms, then slicked her fingers into Lily's mouth and rolled her nipples between her wet fingertips. Lily's head fell back against Alex's shoulder as Alex untied the string to the bikini at Lily's hip. The sky-blue scrap of fabric dropped to Lily's ankles, and Alex placed one knee between her thighs to nudge them open as she slid her fingers over Lily's clit.

"Jesus." Alex breathed the words into the warmth of her neck and dipped lower, stroking with the flat of two fingers, rhythmically dipping inside then sliding up and over her clit. "You're so fucking wet." She felt Lily's clit stiffen, and she deepened her touch. "Turn around, baby."

Lily turned, and Alex sank slowly to her knees in front of her. Alex looked up and held Lily's eyes as she lifted one thigh and draped it over her shoulder. Lily leaned back against the captain's wheel, her hands tangled in Alex's hair as she closed her eyes and melted into the slow slick of Alex's tongue over her clit. Alex gave her the intensity her body was begging for, stroking her inner thighs as her tongue moved in deep circles around her clit. Lily's breath caught when Alex slid two fingers inside, stoking her achingly slowly, then draped her tongue directly over Lily's clit, shifting the rhythm to intense, focused strokes.

"Jesus Christ." Lily's thigh tensed across Alex's shoulder, her hands moving to her own breasts, stroking her nipples. Alex lowered her tongue to meet her fingers inside, then dragged it back up to Lily's clit, teasing it with the tip until she moaned, then covering it with intense, relentless strokes.

She was listening intently to everything Lily's body was telling her, every breath, every moan, every detail from her thighs starting to shake to the deep pink flush moving across her chest as she leaned back over the captain's wheel and circled her hips against Alex's hand.

Alex curved her fingers slightly inside until she found the tense spot she was looking for, then intensified the rhythm of her tongue over Lily's clit, working her until Lily started to tremble, her fingers tightening around the back of Alex's head. Lily's orgasm flowed into her hand and down her wrist as she came, her body tight and rhythmic around Alex's fingers, clit still throbbing against Alex's tongue until the last wave of her orgasm faded like expanding ripples on still water.

Alex gently lowered Lily's thigh off her shoulder as she stood, pulling Lily against her chest to hold her until her thighs stopped shaking.

"I forgot to warn you that I'll get you wet," Lily whispered against her chest, her breath slowly returning to normal.

"That," Alex said in a raspy whisper against the top of her head, "is the sexiest fucking thing I've ever seen."

Lily laughed, pulling back slowly and looking out the window to see they were drifting closer to the shore. "Did we drop the anchor?"

"Oh, shit." Alex laughed as she reached past her to hit the anchor button on the control panel. "It's clearly your fault for distracting me."

Lily pulled her bikini bottoms back up and tied them again at her hips with shaking fingers. "I'm suddenly starving. Tell me you brought stuff for dinner?"

"Of course I did," Alex said, hitting a couple of switches on the control panel and turning back to Lily. "You even have time for a shower if you want one, while I get the grill going."

"You're going to have me completely spoiled in a single weekend, Suarez." Lily stood on tiptoe to kiss Alex, pulling away reluctantly. "This has been amazing."

Alex swatted her ass and told her to get to the shower before she had to take her again, and not one word of it was a lie. No one had ever turned her on like Lily. She just needed to get through this week without fucking it up.

CHAPTER THIRTEEN

The doorbell rang, and Sara ran to the front door from her kitchen, swinging it wide open to reveal Jennifer and baby Mary Elizabeth. "Oh my God, how is she still sleeping?" Sara lowered her voice as she stroked her niece's cheek with a gentle finger. "Didn't you just now get her out of the car seat?"

"I have no idea, but this is the sleepiest baby in the history of babies." Jennifer laughed. "Thank God."

Jennifer handed her carefully to Sara and followed them into the kitchen. Bright sunlight filled the main living area and kitchen, then fell across the raw wood kitchen table in a wide beam of translucent gold. Jennifer pulled out a chair and eased into it, shrugging off her jacket and dropping it over the back.

Sara watched her from in front of the open fridge. "You're moving kind of slow. Is everything okay?"

Sara poured a virgin mimosa and set it in front of her sister, then transferred the tray of scones from the oven to the marble countertop.

"Yeah, kind of." Jennifer winced as she settled a sleeping Mary Elizabeth back into her carrier and put her on the chair beside her at the table. She squished up her face and protested, then relaxed back to dreaming before Jennifer had even tucked the blanket around her. "I'm fine, really, just having some trouble adjusting to breastfeeding. It's a lot more painful than I expected, and my nipples are starting to crack."

Sara clinked her own mimosa to Jennifer's glass and went back to placing the hazelnut scones into a breadbasket, covering them loosely with a yellow-checked linen tea towel. She handed them to Jennifer to place on the table and took the antique rose teacups filled with fresh butter, chocolate hazelnut spread, and Devon cream out of the fridge.

"This is the stuff no one tells you about until it happens, isn't it? I can't imagine how painful that is." Sara said, dropping a silver butter knife into each cup and placing them on the table beside the scones. "Is there anything that makes it better?"

"Thankfully, yes. Mary whipped up some creamy herbal remedy with some shea butter right in my kitchen, and it's started to help already."

Sara handed her a floral saucer with a still steaming scone on top. "So how is it having her around the first few days?"

"Are you kidding?" Jennifer went straight for the chocolate hazelnut spread and slathered it over her scone, licking the knife before she put it back. Sara rolled her eyes. "She's a godsend. Brian has some big case he's working with Sam on, although he hasn't said what it's about, and it's clearly intense. He gets home late and cuddles Mary Elizabeth as long as he can stay awake, but with Mary being there to help me, at least he's not so stressed about supporting me."

"I won't be seeing much of Sam for the next couple of days either. But from what I know about it, it should be winding down to a manageable level after this week." Sara split her own scone, paused to breathe in the fragrant steam, then spread a generous amount of fresh butter across it, then followed that with a squeeze of fresh lemon.

Jennifer scrunched up her face as she watched, then took a bite of her chocolate-laden creation. "I've never seen anyone else do that, you weirdo. What's your thought process there?"

"Listen, a fresh scone, creamy butter, and bright lemon goodness. How could that be wrong?"

"A few different ways, but seriously, thank you for this." Jennifer took a deep breath and relaxed into her chair. "It's great to get out and about with the little one while Mary's at the drugstore, although I swear I couldn't do this without her. She's just so unshakable. No matter what happens, she's seen it before and knows what to do." Jennifer paused, then downed the last of her virgin mimosa. "But back to why you invited me over. I know you. You have a reason."

"Shut up," Sara retorted playfully. "You don't know me."

"I certainly do," Jennifer said with a sniff. "Now spill it."

Sara poured Jennifer's mimosa and gave her own a top-off, then paused before she answered. "I don't know whether to bring it up, but I've done some research online, and I know that pregnancy and the postpartum stages can sometimes stir up past issues with eating disorders, so I'm just..." Sara's voice trailed off.

"Checking on me?" Jennifer smiled and leaned forward to hug her, then held her for an extra second. "I love you for that, but I think instead of answering, I'll just refer you to Exhibit A." Jennifer held up her scone, dripping with chocolate spread and toasted hazelnuts, and took a big enough bite to underscore her point.

"Thank fuck. And you look gorgeous, by the way. I've never seen you look so happy." Sara laughed, nudging the basket of scones toward her. "Just remember, I'm here if you want to talk about anything."

"Honestly," Jennifer said, turning to tuck the blanket around her daughter. "I barely remember what that's like anymore, being scared of food. Brian just makes me feel so beautiful, and the whole time I was pregnant, he couldn't keep his hands off me."

"Ugh." Sara held up a hand with an exaggerated eye roll. "Straight people. I mean, that's fine if that's the lifestyle you've chosen, but I don't need to hear the details."

"Hush it." Jennifer laughed and tossed a linen napkin at her. "You know I'm going to tell you whether you want to hear it or not."

"Kidding." Sara laid a hand over hers for just a moment, her eyes soft. "You know I love to know everything about you and your little family."

"By the way, you mentioned something the other day on the phone about you and Sam coming to a decision." Jennifer turned to Mary Elizabeth, who was suddenly awake and making a little face, and pulled her up to rest on her shoulder, patting her back gently as she spoke "Tell me everything."

"I think it wasn't so much a decision as an epiphany, you know?" The oven timer went off, and Sara got up and pulled on an oven mitt. "Having Moxie around has just proved to us that we still want a family. Even if we can't conceive."

"I knew it!" Jennifer's excitement stirred little Mary Elizabeth until she put her head back down on Jennifer's shoulder with a soft sigh. "I had a feeling that would happen."

Sara turned to pull out a muffin tray of tiny quiches that instantly filled the kitchen with the rich aroma of crispy bacon and sultry French gruyere cheese. Sara carefully placed a few of them on a plate and garnished them with a sprinkle of julienned scallions. "Anyway, so in that direction..." She transferred one to her sister's plate and kissed Mary Elizabeth on the cheek. "We're thinking about adoption."

"Really?" Jennifer laid Mary Elizabeth gently down in her carrier again and smiled when she tried valiantly to bite her own wrist but nodded off too soon to succeed. "How soon?"

"Like, right away." Sara cut into her quiche and the rich, buttery crust fell away to reveal a buttery melted gruyere center. "Sam has already started on the paperwork. She tripped over herself trying to get a head start when we realized we were both thinking the same thing."

"Sara, I'm so happy for you. You're going to make an amazing mother, and I know how long you've wanted this." Jennifer tried a bite of the quiche and her eyes fluttered closed in bliss. "When do you guys go back to work?"

"In just a few days. I'm dying to get back to the diner, as you might imagine. The retreat season flew by this time because we barely had to do anything with the actual programming. Charlotte has been wonderful with that, and she kept the rest of the staff on schedule, so it's been pretty uneventful this year, at least for us."

Jennifer made a face as she sipped her mimosa. "And at what point did she stop hitting on Sam?"

Sara laughed and leaned back in her chair with her next bite of quiche on her fork. "Well, that pretty much stopped when Alex took over as the Latin dance instructor. But Sam's patience was wearing thin by then, so it was good timing. She'd actually starting hitting record on her phone whenever Charlotte was lurking around."

"Oh yeah, I remember Alex. I met her in the drugstore one day, and I swear Mary was flirting with her."

"Oh, most definitely." Sara popped the quiche into her mouth and smiled. "Not that I blame her. Alex looks just like Sam, and that Cuban accent doesn't hurt a damn thing."

Jennifer's mouth dropped open. "Sara!"

"What?" Sara flashed her best innocent smile. "I'm just stating the obvious."

"Fair enough," Jennifer said, spearing the last piece of crust with her fork. "I'm straighter than straight, but I'm not going to lie, Mary and I both watched her walk all the way out of that drugstore."

❖

By the time the charcoal in the deck grill had turned to ash-coated coals, the sun had set, and the first of the stars had started to sparkle over the treetops. Alex turned just as Lily stepped onto the top deck looking like old-world Hollywood.

Her hair was dark and wild, with just a smudge of smoky eyeliner and pinky nude lips. An ivory, crushed silk slip clung to her body, falling around her hips like water as she walked barefoot across the deck. The neckline of the slip was wide across her collarbone, barely covering her nipples with the thinnest scraps of silk, then came together in a deep vee at her waist, as if the entire dress was just a bolt of slinky fabric draped across her naked body. A renaissance painting coming to life under the dusky starry sky.

"Lily." Alex reached for Lily, and she melted into her arms. "You look…" She paused, smiling down at the smattering of honey-colored freckles just beginning to appear on her cheeks. "Stunning."

"I packed something a little fancier just in case we happened to end up on a private houseboat in a beautiful cove at sunset."

"Well." Alex pulled her closer, drawing in the sultry, dark vanilla scent of her skin. "That was a damn good guess." She slid her hands around Lily's waist, then down the dip of her lower back to her ass with a tortured moan into her neck. "You're not wearing anything under this, are you?"

"Not a damn thing." Lily nodded at the grill that had started to smoke in earnest. "Now, eyes on that grill."

"I had a feeling grilling was going to be a bad idea." Alex ran her hands over Lily's body as if trying to memorize it, then kissed her and reluctantly turned back to the coals. "You're going to have to stand over there, then. I'm only human."

Lily dragged one of the beanbag chairs closer and sank down in it, smiling as Alex's eyes followed the silk draping itself across her thighs.

"Didn't we just establish you have a grill to watch, Alex?"

Alex turned back with a wink in her direction. "How am I supposed to watch anything with you looking like that?" She leaned down to the stainless-steel cooler and brought out a muslin-wrapped package and container of fresh green salad.

"Ooh…Now you've got my attention," Lily said, leaning forward for a better look. "What are you making?"

"It's just a simple Cuban mojo grilled steak," Alex said, unfolding the cloth around the two sirloin steaks inside. "The mojo spice is similar to what we had on the shrimp, but you'll find the flavor is much more complex with the steak recipe."

"Did you marinate it beforehand?"

"I did. It's been in an orange juice, olive oil, and spiced salt marinade. I made it yesterday and stored it in Sara's fridge. Then I rubbed it a few minutes ago with a chili, garlic, and lime zest dry rub."

"So did you learn to cook from your aunt that owns the restaurant?"

Alex looked up as a crane took off across the water from the sandbar, stirring the air as it passed. The air settled back into stillness, mirroring the glassy surface of the still water below. "That's right, Alejandro's mom." Alex shook a few drops of water onto the metal grates of the grill to test the temperature. They crackled and steamed instantly, disappearing into the ash-covered charcoal below. "My mother was a terrible cook, but she adored her sister's cooking, so we all spent a lot of dinners together." She stirred the coals and picked up the olive oil with a glance in Lily's direction. "I just paid attention, I guess."

Alex rubbed the same spices into the grain of the steak with her fingers and a little olive oil, then laid the steaks carefully on the grill. They instantly sizzled and filled the air with the rich, smoky scent of grilling meat as she arranged the salad on two plates, topped it with a pineapple vinaigrette, and handed them to Lily. She settled the plates on the table on the far end of the deck and came back for the silverware and napkins Alex held out to her.

Alex checked her watch again, peered carefully at the steaks, and used the tongs to take them both off the heat and onto the cutting board. "These have to rest for a few minutes, so that gives us just enough time for…" Alex's voice trailed off as she got out her phone and chose a song. The Bluetooth speakers on the boat picked up and filled the air with Luis Fonsi's "Despacito."

Alex turned and held out her hand for Lily. "Dance with me?"

Lily smiled and took it, her eyes locked on Alex. "You seem to forget that I don't dance, Suarez."

"I'll have to stop you there, Miss Larimar." Alex held her gaze as one hand slid low around Lily's waist and the other held Lily's hand at shoulder height. "There's a difference between don't dance and can't dance. You most certainly can dance, and just as a reminder, lying is a sin."

Lily melted into the step Alex taught her in the cabin, then spun in her arms when Alex tapped her waist.

"Gotcha," Alex said, her smile turning to laughter when Lily realized what she'd just done. "That was just a dead giveaway." She tapped her waist twice with one finger, and Lily turned the other direction, falling back into perfect step with Alex afterward.

"Whatever," Lily said, her dress swirling around her hips as Alex moved their bodies. "I might have wandered into a few underground Latin dance clubs in Havana."

"And why didn't you tell me this?" Alex said, turning her halfway around so Lily's back was to her, their steps perfectly together. "That's very useful information for someone trying to seduce you."

Lily turned back around, following Alex as she shifted them into a parallel step. "You really want to ask me why I didn't tell you something, Dr. Suarez?"

"Touché." Alex pulled her close as the song ended, her hand sliding from Lily's waist slowly up her back to hold the base of her neck as she kissed her. "That is an excellent point."

Alex reluctantly let her go and returned to the steak, which she cut into slices on the cutting board and topped with a drizzle of garlic oil, a sprinkle of chili flakes, and a few fragrant cilantro leaves. She brought the entire board over to the table and set it carefully between them where Lily was opening a bottle of Sauvignon Blanc.

"Thank you for that," she said. "I completely forgot the wine."

Lily looked up and held her eyes for a long second, then touched Alex's bottom lip with a gentle fingertip before she leaned in and followed it with a kiss. "No one has ever made me feel like this."

Alex held Lily's face in her hands, her breath warm on Lily's lips. "I've been thinking that same thing since the night we met."

❖

By the time they were finished with dinner, the stars were dusted across the night sky like incense wafting through an abandoned temple. The cool evening air smelled of faint campfire and clean water, smoothing out the tart undercurrent coming from the thickets of ripe raspberries in full bloom on the islands. Lily breathed it in and picked up the last slice of steak from Alex's plate with her fingers.

"What?" She flashed her best innocent smile. "You've clearly tapped out, and I'm not about to let something that delicious go to waste."

Alex laughed and took the dishes down to the kitchen, then reappeared to lead her to the deck railing to look out over the water. The evening breeze sifted through the trees on the island surrounding the cove, shifting the treetops just enough to sweep the sky, and the pewter moon hung low on the horizon, the reflection carving a wide swath of glittering light across the water.

Lily leaned on the railing and looked down into the dark water. "I've only been here a couple of weeks, but I already can't imagine going back to LA." Her stomach tightened at the thought, and the memory of LA felt like watching a movie of someone else's life.

"So what about LA has come into focus for you since you've been here?" Alex turned toward Lily, her elbow on the railing. "What is it that you don't want to go back to?"

Lily sighed, trying to find an analogy to describe the weirdness of a town where only image mattered and success was never achieved. It was only rented, and the rent was due every day. Keeping up was exhausting.

"I used to think what bothered me the most was that everyone knew me. I couldn't go anywhere without someone asking me about my books or where they'd seen me on TV." Lily tucked her hair behind her ear, the wind picking up the ends and brushing them across the nape of her neck. "But I'm starting to realize that what was making me feel so alone was that I was alone—no one really knew me. Not the real me, anyway. LA requires a perfect image, and who you really are has nothing to do with it."

"That must have felt lonely."

"It was." Lily's chest started to tighten as if to remind her. "I felt so alone, and there is all this pressure to produce, to become more famous than yesterday, to come up with the next thing to go viral on social media." Lily laced her fingers together, squeezing so hard, her knuckles slowly turned white. "And all I ever wanted to do was to write books that people loved, and now I'm having panic attacks and hating my life."

"Is there anything about the scene that you do want to go back to?"

Lily paused, sifting through the memories of endless parties and awards and "being seen." She knew the answer; it was only one word, but it was the one word she'd been seeking for years. "No."

Alex smiled. "Then, maybe it's time to make room in your thoughts for how to hold that boundary for yourself."

"What do you mean?"

Alex paused. "If you know you don't want to go back—and even if I hadn't heard your words, I would be able to tell from your body language that just the thought of it stresses you the hell out— then maybe it's time to put your mental health first and honor that truth you've uncovered."

Lily turned to face Alex. The light from the deck painted her face with sheer liquid gold. "Like, just tell my agent that things have to change for me to be healthy?"

"Yes. Exactly that." Alex slid her hand around the back of Lily's neck, pulling her gently into the warmth of her body. "Maybe it's time for your work to become part of your life instead of the reverse. If your body is clearly telling you things aren't right, then think about holding your ground until you find a compromise, a space between where you're finally comfortable." Lily smiled, and Alex leaned down to kiss her before she went on. "Everything else will fall into place."

Lily rested her head on Alex's chest for a moment while she let the words sink in. The heaviness of dread she'd been carrying started to lift like dense fog rising over water. Maybe it really was that simple. Maybe it was just time to get back to writing, the only part she ever cared about anyway.

Lily rolled her eyes playfully as she looked up. "God. It's like you're a therapist or something."

"Not right now." Alex cupped Lily's face in her hands, her eyes soft, her voice husky with emotion. "I'm just the one over here falling in love with you."

Lily slipped her hands under Alex's shirt as Alex kissed her, the softness of her body melting into every angle of Alex's. Alex tilted her head to the side gently and kissed her neck, her tongue tracing a path to her ear.

"I know I talked about sleeping under the stars, but I think we may want to go downstairs to the cabin for what I want to do to you."

Right on cue, a ski boat idled past the corner of the island with its floodlights on. It didn't turn into the cove, but it was enough for Lily to volunteer to grab the whiskey from the bar and head to the downstairs cabin.

"Perfect," Alex said into her neck, both hands slipping around her hips and over the curves of her ass. "I'm going to make sure everything is put away in the kitchen, and I'll join you with some glasses."

Lily hesitated. "Do you remember if Sara left any spray cheese?"

Alex shook her head and laughed, which seemed to startle a heron wading at the edge of the water. "I can literally lift you with one arm. Where does someone so small put all the spray cheese?"

"And crackers," Lily added without a hint of a smile. "I'll need crackers."

"Yes, ma'am." Alex was still laughing as she headed to the kitchen. Lily grabbed the crystal decanter of whiskey she'd seen at the bar and headed down to the interior cabin they'd slept in the night before.

The sleeping cabin was trimmed in dark wood, which highlighted the smooth white marble floors, cold and solid under her bare feet. A fresh white marble bathroom with a freestanding tub was just off to the side, but the raised bed was the central focus of the room, expertly layered with a dove gray duvet, crisp white sheets, and a cozy charcoal knit blanket at the foot. A lush, padded suede headboard set off the polished teak cabinets on either side, and an antique mercury mirror cast a hazy reflection as Lily set the decanter on the nightstand and switched on the lamp.

Alex came through the door just as she was reaching for her nightgown, but Alex walked around the bed and picked her up, wrapping Lily's legs around her waist.

"Don't you dare. I've been waiting to take that dress off you all night." She smiled, her hands warm and strong around Lily's hips.

Lily brushed Alex's nipple with her fingertips and leaned in to kiss her. Alex groaned and lowered her to the bed, then tugged her own shirt over her head, unbuttoning her chinos to reveal black boy shorts and sculpted abs. Lily trailed her fingers over the angles of Alex's body, pulling her down on top of her.

"So," she said, the words she needed just out of her grasp. "Do you ever…" Lily was distracted as Alex pushed the silk slip up Lily's thigh to her waist. Alex kissed her as she wrapped her hand around Lily's thigh, her touch light as it strayed to the inside.

"Weren't you going to ask me something?" Alex's words were a whisper, light as thought against the delicate skin between her breasts. Lily's nipples tensed; suddenly all she could think about was the warm swirl of Alex's tongue.

Lily's eyes fluttered shut and her fingers sifted through Alex's hair, melting under the warmth of her words. "I don't remember."

Alex held her eyes as she slid down to kiss the sensitive curve of Lily's belly and slid her hands over her inner thighs. Alex closed her eyes as her fingertips barely brushed Lily's swollen clit, then dipped lower.

"You get so wet for me." Alex's words dripped with sex, and the breathless scrape of her voice was intense. "I fucking love it."

"Oh my God." Lily arched her back, her cheeks flushed, her words a desperate whisper. "I might die unless I feel your tongue on me."

Alex slid her forearms underneath Lily's hips and lifted her body to her mouth. Her breath hovered still and warm above Lily's clit before she slicked her tongue across it, then dipped lower and licked her way back up before pulling Lily's clit gently into her mouth. She held it for just a moment before she started really working it, giving Lily the firm, swirling strokes she was aching for.

Lily felt as if she were melting into the bed, every part of her searching for Alex's touch at the same time. "Please." Lily stretched her arms above her head and pushed against the leather headboard. "I need you inside me."

"Not yet." Alex moved up to kiss her, then dipped two fingers into Lily's mouth as she sank back down between her thighs. "But soon."

Lily groaned as Alex took her fingers out of Lily's mouth and worked her nipples in a slow rhythm, then lowered her mouth again and started to strum Lily's clit with her tongue until she arched, every muscle in her body taut.

"Are you ready to come for me, baby?"

"Yes, now." Lily's words were rushed and breathless. "Please."

Alex worked her tongue deep inside until Lily was right on the edge, then slicked her tongue up and surrounded her clit, stroking it until it started to throb and Lily's whole body tensed. A fine mist of sweat shimmered across Lily's chest, and her thighs started to tremble around Alex's face. Her fingers tangled into Alex's hair and Lily held on tight, her only anchor in a swirling sea of intensity as the orgasm rolled through her body.

She felt Alex move up to sit between her thighs before she'd even caught her breath. Alex put a finger to her lips, and Lily lay back, disappearing into the downy pillows as she closed her eyes again. She felt Alex move over her, nudging her thighs farther apart. The last faint wave of Lily's orgasm faded as Alex kissed her, whispering into her ear as she slid two fingers inside and stroked Lily slowly, leaning into her and guiding the motion of her hand only with her hips.

"You're going to come for me again, Lily." Alex's gaze was intense as she moved with Lily in a deep rhythm. She pressed Lily's knee to her shoulder with her left hand, still stroking inside her with the other, and held her eyes. "And I'm going to be right here, watching you take everything I'm going to give you."

Lily arched and laid her arm over her eyes, trying not to fall over the edge before Alex even finished speaking. Alex's deep scrape of a voice, the intentional way she moved her body, and her dense, smoky haze of sexual confidence was like a drug. Alex's breath was warm against her neck, and Lily wrapped her legs around her waist as she moved inside her. The heel of her hand just grazed her clit with every stroke, and Alex seemed to know when she was close, slowing her rhythm until Lily groaned, arching into the bed.

"Don't stop, Alex," she whispered. "Just don't stop."

Alex leaned into her, her breath rhythmic as she fucked Lily until she came underneath her, Lily's wetness filling her hand, her body contracting around her fingers until her breathing finally slowed, and every muscle in her body relaxed into the bed in the same breath.

After a moment Alex smoothed the damp hair around her face and bit her lower lip lightly, pulling it until Lily opened her eyes. "How do you feel?"

"Thirsty."

Lily laughed as Alex reached into one of the built-in cabinets and pulled out a frosty bottle of FIJI spring water. Alex unscrewed the lid and handed it to Lily, who sat up to see where it had come from.

"Exactly how many minibars are there on this yacht?"

The neon-blue glow disappeared as Alex pulled out a water for herself and closed the door. "If you'd ever met my cousin Alejandro, every one of them would make perfect sense."

"So." Lily took a deep swig of the water and looked at it admiringly before she nearly finished it. "What's he like?"

"He's one of the most intelligent, generous, and ethical people I know," Alex said. "We give each other shit, but he's probably the closest person to me."

Lily nodded and lay back against the pillows for a moment, her eyes fluttering closed. "I think there's a wake rocking the boat, and it's making me sleepy."

"Don't even think about falling asleep, Miss Larimar." Alex laughed, "And that rocking you're feeling was our handiwork." Alex traced the line of her cheek with the tip of her finger, kissing her forehead as she got up and headed for the bathroom. "I'll be back in one minute."

"Maybe just a little nap, then." Lily's words were muffled by the duvet as she curled into the center of the bed and nearly disappeared under the pile of satiny soft, white pillows. She was teasing Alex, actually; orgasms like that usually put her right to sleep, but she didn't want to miss a minute of this night with Alex. She listened to the bathroom door shut and sat up, running a hand through her tangle of hair and looking out the double glass doors to the black, shimmering expanse of water.

She got up and looked around for something to wrap herself in, but the only thing she found was the charcoal knit blanket at the foot of the bed. She wrapped that around her and opened the sliding glass doors that led to a teakwood balcony with a polished brass railing. The dense trees on the island were lit up with fireflies sparking the darkness with random points of light, and night birds swooped low over the calm surface of the lake, their wings rippling the surface of the water as they glided over it with silent intention.

Lily had never been in love. The closest she'd come was…well, never. In LA, there was so much noise, so much jostling and distraction that it was like trying to canoe across a lake in a tornado. The harder you paddled, the more the wind and water pushed back until you found yourself spinning slowly in dark, choppy water with no memory of where you were trying to go.

With Alex, everything was different. The water was calm, smooth, and quiet; every stroke of the paddle, every kiss, every intensely intimate moment moved them smoothly across the water to the deepest part of the lake. And the silent ripples rolling outward from her paddle as it cut into the slick surface of the water were changing every part of her.

Lily smiled as Alex stepped behind her and wrapped her up in her arms. She leaned back into Alex's chest and took the crystal tumbler of whiskey she held out for her, a single square cube of ice clinking into the silence.

"Ice?"

"Hey, not all of us are little whiskey badasses," Alex said, kissing her neck and pulling Lily closer. "Some of us need an ice cube."

Lily drew in a long breath of the whiskey, the vapors lingering in a sweet, slow burn at the top of her palate. She sipped, then handed it back to Alex. "No shame in the ice game, Suarez. You like what you like."

The ice clinked and settled in the glass as Alex drank and set it on the railing beside them, her hands sinking to Lily's hips and pulling them back into hers. Lily turned to face her, her eyes sparkling as she met Alex's gaze. "Is that for me?"

"Yes, ma'am."

Alex's fingertips grazed Lily's clit, then dipped deep into the wet heat of her before Alex raised them to her mouth, her eyes closed, as if memorizing the taste of her. Lily traced the outline of the leather harness across Alex's hips with her fingertips. The harness had replaced clothes, the strong, beveled edges of the black leather mirroring the defined cuts and angles of her body.

Lily turned to face the railing again, letting the blanket slip down her body and puddle around their ankles on the deck. She heard Alex groan behind her, her hands on Lily's hips and then felt the words, warm against the delicate skin of her neck.

"Are you sure?"

Lily nodded, guiding Alex's hand to the back of her neck as she leaned forward over the railing and arched her back into a deep curve as Alex pressed her thighs apart with one of her own. Alex stroked Lily's clit lightly with the cock, then pressed it inside her, achingly slowly, shifting her hand from the back of Lily's neck to her shoulder, pulling her back onto it until their hips met.

Lily's breath caught, and Alex stilled, her words soft behind her. "Is it too much, baby?"

"God, no...I need you deeper." Her voice was a rough whisper, and she reached back to pull Alex's hips closer. "I need you to fuck me. Really fuck me."

Alex groaned and moved all the way inside, her breath deepening as Lily slid her hand underneath them, sliding her slick fingertips over Alex's swollen clit with every stroke. Alex held Lily's shoulder with one hand and her waist with the other as she fell into a gentle rhythm.

"Oh, Jesus Christ," Alex whispered, her voice a deep scrape of desire. "You're so fucking beautiful. I love watching your ass move."

Her hand sank from Lily's shoulder all the way down her back to grasp her hips pulling them back against her cock with every rhythmic stroke.

"Baby." Alex slowed her pace slowly and leaned down to whisper in Lily's ear. "Come to bed with me. I need you to watch me come."

Alex turned her and picked her up, wrapping Lily's legs around her waist as she carried her to bed. Fireflies followed them inside, caught up in cool breeze coming off the water, and Alex left the doors open as she lay down on the bed, Lily still sitting across her hips. Lily's hair was wild, her chest flushed pink, her thighs glossed with sex as she sat back on Alex's cock, Alex's hands warm around her hips. She reached behind her to steady herself on Alex's thighs as she began to move inside her. Lily moved her hips with the same rhythm, her clit slicking across the smooth leather harness every time Alex stroked deep inside.

"Lily." Alex bit her lip, drinking in the sight of Lily's naked body riding her, meeting every thrust. "I'm…"

Lily smiled, leaning down to kiss her, her fingertips lingering over Alex's tense nipples as she sat back up. "Come for me, Alex." She held Alex's eyes as she reached down, slicking her soaked, swollen clit. "I want to watch you come inside me while I ride you."

Alex wrapped her hands around Lily's hips and took over, thrusting into her as Lily leaned closer, whispering into her ear as Alex shuddered to an orgasm underneath her. After a few minutes, when her breath finally slowed, Alex kissed her long and deep, then pulled Lily down onto the bed. She tossed the harness onto the bench at the foot of the bed and settled in behind her, pulling the cool, fluffy duvet over both their bodies. The sound of the water lapping gently against the boat and Alex's warm body behind her lulled Lily to the edge of sleep within just a few breaths.

"Lily." Alex's voice was a mix of softness and strength Lily had never heard. "Since the day we met, I haven't been able to close my eyes at night without seeing a future with you."

Lily held her breath as Alex pulled her closer, then turned over to meet her eyes, her words soft as thought against Alex's lips. "I love you too."

Alex wrapped Lily tight in her arms and they drifted into sleep together, the fireflies still pricking the darkness around them with golden light.

CHAPTER FOURTEEN

A lex switched the music off and chatted with the last of the dancers in her Monday afternoon class as they filed out of the activity hall on the way to the lodge for dinner. Nerves were starting to get to her about the undercover operation scheduled for tomorrow. Sam had been in touch via text all day with updates, and she was expected at Sam and Sara's this evening to go over the logistics and where backup would be if things went unexpectedly south.

It was too late to stop it now, not that she wanted to anyway, but the gravity of the mission was coming into sharp focus now that it was careening closer. According to Sam and Murphy, the SWAT backup and assigned officers from McCall and Boise were already in town and ready to go, and she was scheduled to be at the station tomorrow morning, a few hours before her meeting with Travis, to wire up and test the system.

Alex changed out of her dance shoes and into her leather flip-flops, pulling the wooden double doors shut behind her as she made her way back to the cabin. The air was warmer than usual for a late mountain afternoon, and the chatter of retreat-goers buzzed in the background as she veered onto the lake path. The waterfront staff had long since secured the boats to the docks and put away the Jet Skis for the night, but the lazy sound of the lapping water and subtle thud of the ski boats against the bumpers made her glance down the docks.

Charlotte sat alone at the very end of the dock, her blond ponytail shimmering in the sunlight. Alex stopped in her tracks, thumbing through every excuse not to stop when she saw Charlotte drop her face into her hands.

This is a terrible idea. Alex turned slowly and walked down the path to the docks, willing Charlotte not to turn around so she still had the option to abandon ship as long as possible. Alex shook her head, glancing back up toward the lodge. *This is exactly like the moment in every horror movie where a stupid white girl decides to wander outside at midnight to "look at the moon."*

There was something different about Charlotte this time, though, obvious even from the slope of her shoulders. The dock boards creaked under Alex's feet as she walked and the cast-iron clang of the dinner bell from the lodge rang out over the water. Alex looked at her watch. She had exactly twenty minutes before she was in danger of missing Monday Night Manicotti, and that just wasn't going to happen. It was on her calendar every week for a reason.

"Hey, there."

Alex sat on the edge of the dock by Charlotte, who barely looked at her, then wiped her smudged mascara with both thumbs before she looked over the water in the opposite direction.

"I just came to see if you're all right," Alex said, softening when she saw Charlotte was genuinely upset. "But I can leave if you'd rather be alone."

Charlotte didn't say anything, just grabbed the sweatshirt beside her and dabbed at her face. Her white denim cutoffs had a smudge of dust along the thigh, and she was barefoot, her ankles disappearing into the deep green water lapping against the dock. Her tan was a perfect amber gold against her bright yellow triangle bikini top, and as usual, she looked like she'd walked right out of the glossy pages of *Southern Living* magazine, except for the dark mascara smudges still shadowing her eyes.

Alex took the continuing silence as a hint, but when she got up to go, Charlotte reached up and tugged on her shirt in a silent request for her to stay.

"Sorry," she said. "I guess I'm just having a bad day." She stopped, watching a passing Jet Ski as it sped by the dock. The wake had almost reached the shore by the time she spoke again. "Or a bad life. I can't tell anymore."

Alex nodded, confused. This was not energy she'd ever seen from Charlotte. So," she said. "Tell me."

It was only three words, but from the look on Charlotte's face, it was the last thing she expected to hear. She looked back out over the water and her shoulders sank.

"Do you remember the other day when I came to one of your dance classes and stayed to dance with the woman whose wife had a sprained ankle?"

Alex nodded. "The retired cop with two left feet?"

Charlotte cracked a smile, but it faded quickly. "Well, when I was leaving, I heard the woman I was dancing with ask her wife if she was upset."

Alex arched an eyebrow. "Because you were flirting your ass off?"

Charlotte rolled her eyes. "I may have flirted a little bit, but what are you supposed to do in that situation?"

Alex looked over and smiled. "Dance?"

"Damn, Alex." Charlotte seemed to try and fail to quell the annoyance in her voice. "Can you at least try to focus here?"

"You're right. Sorry." Alex bumped Charlotte's knee with her own as she stirred the water with her feet. A wide swath of sunlight caught the downy blond hair on Charlotte's thighs, and Alex reminded herself to not be an idiot. "Seriously, go on. I'm listening."

"Well, I pretended not to be listening as I walked past, but I heard her wife's answer: 'She needs the attention. It's okay.' "

"Ouch." Alex shook her head. "I get why you're upset."

"No," Charlotte shot back, meeting Alex's gaze with red-rimmed eyes. "You don't. If she was just being rude, I could handle it. I'm used to jealous little potshots from partners. What bothers me is that she was..." She paused, rubbing the center of her palm with her thumb. "That she didn't even sound mad. She sounded like she pitied me or something."

Alex turned toward Charlotte, shading her eyes from the sun. "And how did that make you feel?"

"God. You sound like a shrink."

"Yeah. I've heard that a time or two." Alex smiled but kept the question out there between them. "How did it make you feel when you heard her say that?"

Charlotte shook her head. "At the time, I just shrugged it off, but it's still bothering me, and it's been days." She caught a tear on the back of her hand. "I mean, am I really that pathetic? Does everyone see me that way?"

Alex stayed silent until it was clear it wasn't a rhetorical question. "First of all, you're not pathetic. You're struggling with something right now, but that doesn't make you pathetic." She paused. "It makes you human."

"Yeah, well, for someone who's spent a lifetime perfecting her stage presence, you find out pretty quick you're being judged a little more harshly than everyone else. I should be used to it."

"I can see where that would be true. You have an acting background?"

Charlotte smiled, then raised her feet out of the water and watched until the ripples faded away. "You could say that. I've been competing in pageants since I was two. I turned thirty this year, and I just couldn't go for Miss Georgia again this year and not get it." She turned back to rubbing the center of her palm, her thumb white from the pressure. "Not that I would've placed in the big one anyway."

"What's the big one?"

"Good God." Charlotte shot her a look that was only half teasing. "The Miss America Pageant in Vegas every year. It's the holy grail for my mother, or at least, it was until she gave up on me."

Alex nodded, watching as Charlotte gripped the edge of the dock, her arms locked and stiff. "I'm guessing that you competing was pretty important to your mom?"

Charlotte laughed, but it didn't reach her eyes. "We're going to need a much bigger word than important. I was an only child, and I think my mom decided pretty early on we were going to win everything in the world of pageants. And we did for a while. And then I grew up, went to college, and wanted to quit."

"Let me guess." Alex watched an iridescent blue-green dragonfly land delicately on Charlotte's shoulder. "And she didn't?"

"It was worse than that." Hurt flashed across Charlotte's face for a split second until she pulled it back into neutral. "When I decided I wanted to really concentrate on college instead of always pulling out to do competitions, she just deflated, so I stayed in them, and somehow, I managed school at the same time. But this year, I was just done. I can't even explain why. I didn't tell her until it was too late to enter." Charlotte's shoulders slumped, and she let her feet sink deeper into the water. "I didn't want her to be able to talk me back into it."

"Actually, that makes sense. You were protecting yourself and your autonomy as best you could at the time." The dock lifted gently and floated back down with each wave of a passing wake. "What do you mean she deflated?"

"She said it was the biggest disappointment of her life." Charlotte's voice cracked, and she focused her gaze on the island across from the docks. "That she'd sacrificed so much her whole life to give me this opportunity to win Miss America, and I shit on it."

"Damn," Alex said. "She didn't mince words."

"Southern women do not take pageants lightly." Charlotte paused, her voice flat. "She doesn't even know I'm gay, so even without the pageant thing, the fact that I'm not married to a man with multiple kids by now is the ultimate failure."

The sun shimmered over the water, and the silence settled beyond the dock as the last of the retreat-goers finally made it into the main lodge for dinner.

"I get that." Alex pulled up a picture on her phone of her mother, dressed perfectly for Sunday Mass, and showed it to Charlotte. "Clearly, I'm not praying the rosary every day and turning out an endless supply of Catholic grandchildren, so there's always been an understanding that things could be more to her liking. But to her credit, she was great about the gay thing. I think she figured out early on that I wasn't going to be needing a closet full of pageant clothes."

"You're from Cuba, right?"

"Yep. That's where I get my fabulous fashion sense, or so I'm told." Alex paused. "How did you know that? We've never talked about it."

Charlotte cracked a smile and answered in perfect Spanish. "Well, no offense, but either you were the hottest Florida retiree to ever play shuffleboard, or you grew up in Cuba. The accent just wrapped it up for me."

Alex leaned back on her hands and laughed, then continued in Spanish. "That's scarily accurate. I'm not sure I've ever heard it put like that." She paused. "Also, you speak literally perfect Spanish. I have to admit, I didn't see that coming."

"No one ever does," Charlotte said, watching the dragonfly as it hovered in front of them and flitted off across the water. "I have a degree in Romance Languages from Tulane University, and a master's in Third World Development Studies."

"Damn, girl." Alex nodded slowly. "Want me to be honest with you?"

"Sure. Why the hell not?" Charlotte shook her head. "Can't get any worse."

Alex chose her next words because they were the truth and left the softer, easier ones on the pile. "You're smart as hell, but somehow, every bit of your self-worth is still wrapped up in your looks." She paused. "I get it, though. That pageant shit is notoriously hard to shake."

Charlotte shot Alex an annoyed look but stayed silent for a long moment before she looked back over her shoulder. "Go on."

"And you're feeling unfulfilled because you're still stuck in that place of needing approval at any cost instead of telling people to go fuck themselves and doing what you want to do."

"Damn, Alex," Charlotte said, not quite suppressing a smile. "Don't hold back. Tell me what you really think."

"Look, you're clearly underestimating yourself and that big, beautiful brain, which is a damn shame, so I'm not about to mince words with you. Besides, I know I'm not telling you anything you don't already know." Alex paused, waiting until Charlotte met her gaze, then held it as she spoke. "No one is coming to save you here. You have to save your damn self."

Charlotte took out her phone and asked Alex to hang on for a moment while she pulled something up from her email. Alex knew the words she'd chosen were rock-bottom blunt, which wasn't the route she'd take with a client, but this was a different situation, and sometimes, when people were ready to hear the truth, only the truth would do.

Charlotte handed Alex her phone. It was an acceptance letter from Tulane School of Law dated May 15, 2022. Alex looked at the reply icon at the top and saw it wasn't highlighted. "That's from this year, and you haven't replied. There's probably still time. What's holding you back?"

"I've wanted to utilize my language skills in immigration law for *years*, but it's a risky, cutthroat field for a woman. I guess I just don't want to fail." Charlotte's jaw tensed, and as she kicked at the water, the water splashed up onto her calf. "What if I fail?"

Alex shaded her eyes as the glare of the sun intensified over the water and glinted like daggers in their direction. "What if you stop caring about who thinks what and show up for yourself for once?" She softened her voice and slowed her words so each one landed. "What if it all works out?"

"That's it?" Charlotte smiled and shook her head. "Just reinvent myself?"

"You're allowed to evolve," Alex said, giving her shoulder a nudge. "You're allowed to reinvent yourself as many times as it takes. And in my experience, if you're not failing once in a while, you're not trying hard enough."

Charlotte was silent for a long time, as if letting each word sink into her memory, then she got up and offered Alex her hand. Alex took it and stood, slipping her sandals back on to shield her feet from the sunbaked dock. Charlotte fell into step beside her as they walked back up the dock toward the lodge. "You're headed for the manicotti, aren't you?"

"Listen, I don't know what to tell you except my priorities are in order." Alex shot her a wink and paused at the end of the dock. "Care to join me?"

"Tempting," Charlotte said, glancing down the trail leading to the staff cabins. "But I think I'm late for a call with a law school in New Orleans." She paused, her voice soft. "But seriously, thank you for this I won't forget it."

Alex hugged her warmly and watched her walk down the trail until she turned at the halfway point and smiled back at Alex, who headed back up the trail to the main lodge just in time to catch a glimpse of Lily on the porch before she turned and walked away.

❖

Later that evening, Sam bit her lip in concentration as she rearranged the AV equipment on the kitchen table for the fifth time in five minutes. Sara glanced up at her as she spooned steaming beef jus over the thinly sliced steak in her cast-iron skillet and replaced the lid. She dropped her oven mitt onto the counter and walked up behind her, running her hands up Sam's abs and resting her head on her shoulder.

"What's up with you tonight, baby?" Sara's voice was gentle. "I've seen you work with this equipment before. It can't be that stressing you out."

Sam raked a hand through her hair and sank into one of the kitchen chairs, pulling Sara to sit on her lap. She started to speak, then lost the words and closed her eyes, rubbing them with the heels of her hands. When she finally looked back at Sara, her eyes were red, and the lines in her forehead more deeply etched than Sara had ever seen them.

"I don't know how to describe it." Sam leaned her head back, staring at the soaring Aspen ceiling dappled by the falling evening light. "It's not a bad thing. It's good, in fact. Gathering evidence on this loser could start the ball rolling and allow the FBI to get a warrant and nail this guy."

Sara put one hand on Sam's chest and one hand on her own, then took a deep breath, smiling as Sam followed. After a few more breaths, the worry on Sam's face started to ease, and she slid her hand around Sara's neck to pull her in for a kiss.

"How do you know how to do that, my love?" Sam paused. "How do you know a thousand different ways to calm me?"

Sara touched their foreheads together and closed her eyes for a moment before she answered. "Because your heart is mine. I can feel what you need."

Sam brushed a stray blond wave away from Sara's eyes and held her gaze. "What would I do without you?"

Sara's face brightened as she held up her left hand, admiring the sparkling, canary diamond ring Sam had proposed with five years earlier, now accented by a slim yellow gold wedding band. "Well, you were smart and locked that down early, so you don't even have to think about it."

"Thank God." Sam pulled her in for another kiss, her hand warm around Sara's waist. "I would have proposed the second you came in for that damn boat license and threw a little fit, but I had to find the perfect ring. Takes some time, as it turns out."

Sara's mouth dropped open in protest. "I didn't throw a—"

"I think we've established you most certainly did." Sam pulled her closer. "And it was adorable."

Sara winked and slid her hands into Sam's hair, ruffling it just enough to remind her of what Sam used to look like when she came home from Lake Patrol. "So what's got you so stressed?"

"I do feel stressed." Sam paused. "But it's not the bad kind of stress. It's the kind that reminds me what I'm doing is important and could change someone's life. I just don't want to get this wrong and fuck it up."

Sara smiled, then got up and gave the beef strips another stir, lifting the lid on a pan of sautéed onions and peppers in cast-iron skillet behind it. "By the way, didn't you tell me last night that you had something big you wanted to talk to me about?"

The doorbell rang, and Sam promised to tell her after dinner as she hurried to open the front door. Alex was there, holding a bottle of Sauvignon Blanc, condensation already dripping down the label in the late summer heat.

"Dude," Sam teased, holding the door open for Alex and playfully rolling her eyes. "Where's the beer? This might as well be wrapped in flowers or some shit. It's like you don't know me at all."

"Whatever." Alex gave Sam a playful punch and walked through to the kitchen, handing the bottle to Sara with a warm hug. "I know where the amazing food comes from in this house, so I choose hostess gifts accordingly." Sara gave the label a look of approval then handed her the bottle opener. "Besides, I'm committed to expanding your palate when it comes to wine."

"Good luck with that." Sam popped the top off a Sam Adams and caught the cap. "I married a chef, so that ship has sailed. If she can't do it, no one can."

"She's not wrong," Sara said, spreading a floury baguette with liberal lashings of sweet cream butter. "I tried the same thing on that first trip we took together and gave up in about five minutes."

Alex poured Sara a glass of the golden wine and then one for herself, sitting with Sam at the table and looking over the equipment spread out from end to end. "Is this the audiovisual equipment for tomorrow?"

"Most of this will be at work behind the scenes, but yes." Sam handed Alex a pair of dark Ray-Bans. "What you're holding now contains the main visual component, and you'll have a backup for audio only. Both transmit wirelessly to a phone we'll give you, which will upload in real time to the cloud."

"Wireless?" Alex took a sip of wine and reached for a coaster before she set it back on the table. "So I'm not going to have a hundred wires crisscrossing my chest under my shirt like in the movies? Way to take the thrill out of it."

"God, no," Sam said. "I'm expecting this guy to be cautious, so there won't be any wires. In fact, it's possible he'll have someone pat you down before he starts talking."

"Once you have this stuff on me..." Alex popped the Ray-Bans onto her face. "All I have to do is make sure my phone is on?"

"Basically, yes, but take a look at the sunglasses." Sam pointed out the tiny pinhead camera where the screw should be near the temple. "You don't want to wear these on your face. They are designed to work when you have them hooked over the neckline of your shirt." Sam cleared away the rest of the equipment and took the plates Sara handed her, followed by the silverware. "Just make sure your phone stays powered on. The AV equipment will transfer the recording even if it's dropped into a pocket or bag."

"That sounds a lot less stressful than what I was imagining."

"Well, yes and no," Sam said, taking a long swig of beer. "It's a lot more discreet than what we used to use, but the important thing to remember is that your phone is the vital component here. The actual recording devices are beyond tiny, so they aren't equipped to record and store, only to transfer the data to the cloud."

"So let's imagine the worst-case scenario." Alex rubbed her temples as she picked up the sunglasses and examined them. "What if something goes wrong, and we don't get the recording?"

Sam raised an eyebrow. "Honestly?"

"Yeah," Alex said. "Hit me with the facts. I'd rather know the stakes up front."

"It's possible that something will go wrong, and we won't get anything. And if he's tech savvy, he'll take precautions to make sure nothing can be recorded."

Sara turned around as she pulled the two toasted baguette halves out of the oven. The warm scent of buttery roasted garlic rose like steam into the air as she placed them on the counter to cool. "So if that happens and we don't get the actual recording, we can still use the information Alex gets from him, right?"

Sam shook her head, her thumb tapping the table in a nervous rhythm. "No. At that point, everything she hears is hearsay and inadmissible in court. We can still use the information to plan another undercover mission, but I can't see this guy letting just anyone into that mansion. We got hella lucky with the Alejandro angle, but we can't use it twice."

"Great. It's a one-shot deal." Alex and Sam made uneasy eye contact, and both finished their drinks in one long swig before they went on. "No pressure."

All three looked up as Moxie's bedroom door opened, and she hurried down the stairs, her Converse dangling from one hand and a duffel bag from the other. She flashed them a smile as she sat on the last stair and laced up her sneakers.

Sara turned to wash her hands, talking to Moxie over her shoulder. "You're going into town for a pickup game with the basketball team, huh?"

"Yeah, which is weird since I'm not on the team, but one of the girls invited me yesterday. The coach's daughter, I think." Moxie zipped up her duffel and stood, slinging it over her shoulder. "I was actually coming down to tell you. How did you know?"

Sam looked up from the equipment on the table. "I told her. The coach mentioned it to me today in the diner when we were both there for lunch. He used to be an officer back in the day, but he just does coaching now."

Sara smiled and pulled a paper bag out of the fridge. "Welcome to small-town life, where everyone knows your business." She handed the bag to Moxie, who looked into it, then up at Sara.

"Are these snacks?"

"Yep. I'll save some dinner for you too, of course. Just text me on your way home. I just thought you might get hungry beforehand."

Moxie shook her head, silent for a minute before she looked up at Sara. "I'm never going to get used to the food." She paused. "There's just always food."

Sam glanced at Alex for a long second, then back to Moxie. "I know you like to run to and from town, but will you call me if it gets dark so I can come get you?"

Moxie said she would and waved as she ran out the door, pulling her hair into a ponytail as she went.

Sara watched the door for a long moment after she disappeared. "I hate letting her go anywhere by herself with this guy so close." She twisted the dish towel around her hand and turned to Sam and Alex.

"The thought of him seeing her keeps me up at night, but we can't keep her locked in the house, and every other teenager in McCall walks everywhere, so she's only being normal."

"I know." Sam leaned back in her chair, fingers white around her beer bottle. "I want her to have a normal life, but I worry every second she's not in the house."

"Welcome to parenthood." Alex raised her glass and clinked it to Sam's bottle and Sara's wineglass. "Prepare to be sleep deprived for the rest of your life."

"Sign me up." Sara stood behind Sam and leaned down to kiss her cheek. "I wouldn't have it any other way."

❖

Later, after savory Philly cheesesteak sandwiches loaded with creamy pepper jack cheese and tender strips of marinated steak, Alex volunteered to load the dishwasher while Sam put the leftovers away. She looked up just in time to see Sara jump into the couch and settle in.

"Your Sara dashed off to the den pretty quickly. What's she doing?"

"Yeah." Sam recorked the wine and made a space in the fridge for it, glancing over at Sara settling into the leather couch with the remote in her hand. "Just wait for it."

The familiar strains of the *Days of Our Lives* theme song filled the room, and Sara opened her computer on the end table beside her.

"I guess the baby was fussy today when it aired, and Mary missed the episode, so all three of them waited until the baby was asleep to watch it together."

"God. That's adorable." Alex smiled over her shoulder at Sara laughing with Mary and Jennifer on a split screen. "I never thought about settling down until this summer, but seeing you two together and being out of the city has had a weird effect on me."

"Ah, another confirmed bachelor hits the dust." Sam laughed and snapped Alex with the dish towel. "You're really into Lily, aren't you?"

"I am." Alex paused as she shut the door to the dishwasher and turned around, leaning against the counter. "She's amazing. I just don't want to fuck it up."

"What makes you worried you're going to fuck it up?"

Alex shook her head, lowering her voice with a glance in Sara's direction. "It's just the Charlotte thing."

Sam rolled her eyes as she whispered back. "Tell me you didn't..."

"Oh God, no." Alex shook her head, watching Sara on the sofa giggling with Mary and Jennifer, watching *Days of Our Lives* and eating a dish of peppermint ice cream all at the same time. "But I had a decent conversation with Charlotte this afternoon. I think I get now why she pursued me so hard."

"But you can't tell me, right?" Sam pulled the ice cream out of the freezer and held it up. "On a side note, do you feel like some ice cream or a glass of whiskey?"

"God. Whiskey." Alex smiled, sinking back into one of the kitchen chairs. "And, no, I can't tell anyone."

"Thought so. Don't worry, I get it." Sam pulled out the decanter of Gentleman Jack and two rocks glasses, dropping a cube of ice into each. "I have a feeling we're going to need a lot more than whiskey to get us through tomorrow."

CHAPTER FIFTEEN

Alex tossed her keys on the record player table as she stepped into the cabin. The whiskey had done nothing to get rid of the dread lying heavy in the pit of her stomach, which she hoped was more nerves than premonition. A glance around the cabin told her that Lily hadn't been back since that morning, when they'd woken up together in Alex's bunk. Lily had seen Alex talking to Charlotte that afternoon, and although there was no reason to assume she was upset, Alex wished she'd had a chance to explain.

She was just pulling her shirt off on the way to the shower when she remembered a book she'd promised to lend Charlotte during their conversation on the dock. As she reached for it, she also caught sight of the canvas bag Sam had given her the day before.

No time like the present. Alex emptied the contents of the bag onto her bed. She'd never packed before, but the thought didn't bother her: she had more than enough masculine energy to pull it off, and it made sense that it gave her visual credibility if Travis doubted her gender. She placed the soft pack in the front of her boxer briefs and zipped her khaki pants back up, untucking her button-up to help hide it. It felt surprisingly heavy and strange, and the slight motion of it when she walked was difficult and unexpectedly distracting. *Damn,* Alex thought as she picked up the book and tucked it under her arm. *I'm glad I took Sam's advice and practiced with this thing.*

It was a short walk past the main lodge to Charlotte's staff cabin, and as Alex approached, she saw Charlotte sitting at her desk, taking notes as she listened to someone on speakerphone. There were no chairs outside her cabin, so Alex opened the door quietly, holding up the book for Charlotte to see before she placed it quietly on the table beside the door. Charlotte mouthed a thank-you as Alex pulled the door shut, stepping back out on the trail just as a trio of chipmunks chased each other across the path in front of her.

The water beside her was eerily silent, shimmering in the darkness under a thumbnail moon as blown ash clouds drifted across the sky. Alex felt the air shift as an owl took off from a pine tree just back from the trail, but there was no sound, and for the first time, she felt every eye in the forest as she walked slowly back to the cabin. The air was still and heavy, as if a thunderstorm was hovering in the distance, but the surface of the lake was motionless—a serene slab of endless black glass.

Everything was just a little too calm.

An hour later, Lily peeked into the windows of her cabin to see if Alex was home, and sure enough, she was on her bunk, focused on a sheet of paper lying across her lap. Lily paused, her hand on the doorknob. Truthfully, she'd gone into town for dinner just to avoid running into Alex after she'd watched her walk up the docks that afternoon and give Charlotte that long hug. She trusted Alex. Well, as much as she trusted anyone. Charlotte was the one she didn't trust, although now, that it was obvious to everyone that she and Alex were a couple, she'd half expected Charlotte to make one last desperate play for her.

It was more than that, though. Their weekend on the yacht had been amazing, but Alex had seemed preoccupied with her phone or maybe just preoccupied in general. There was just something in the air, almost as if there were someone else in the room with them, someone Alex saw, but she didn't.

Lily forced herself to turn the knob and go in, smiling as Alex stood to hug her. Lily melted into her arms, drawing in the warm scent of her and letting herself melt against the familiar angles of Alex's body.

"I was waiting for you to get home," Alex said, her lips moving gently from Lily's mouth to her forehead. "I missed you at dinner."

"I just went into the diner for one of Sara's Reuben sandwiches." Lily relaxed as she studied Alex's warm eyes, and the thought crossed her mind she d spent all that time worrying for nothing. "There should be an addiction warning label on those things."

Alex pulled her closer and whispered in her ear. "I think what I'm hearing you say is that you want me to take your clothes off and ravish you in my bed?"

Lily laughed, her hand dropping to Alex's abs and over the taut curve of one hip. Then her hand stilled as she felt it under her fingertips, the unmistakable shape of it burning into her skin. She stepped back, her breath gone. Alex looked confused and started to reach for her, then followed Lily's gaze to the front of her pants.

"Lily, let me explain." Alex's words fell from her mouth in a rushed scatter, every one of them louder than they needed to be. "I mean, I can't actually, but it's not what you think."

"What do you mean you can't explain?" Lily's eyes filled with tears. "You're clearly not thinking of me with that, or you would have just told me, so what other explanation can there be?"

"Shit." Alex raked a hand through her hair and paced toward the bathroom. "Lily, you're going to have to trust me here. I can't tell you why I'm packing, and I know that sounds laughable, but it's the truth." She paused, reaching out for Lily's hand. "But I'm not cheating on you. I wouldn't do that."

"Really?" Lily said, betrayal quickly honing her words to a razor's edge. "If it's not for me, then who is it for?"

Alex paled, and she shoved her hands deep into the pockets of her khaki trousers. "I can't tell you. Not yet." She looked up, her jaw tense. "And I know that just sounds like an excuse, but it's not."

Lily took another step back, her arms crossed tightly across her chest. The tears burning the backs of her eyes blurred her vision with liquid anger as she tried to think of a reason Alex wouldn't be able to tell her why she was packing. The clear truth was that the reason didn't even matter. She wasn't wearing it for her, and that was all she needed to know.

"Just tell me one thing truthfully, Alex." Her voice was a wounded scrape, and she blurted out the rest of the sentence as if she couldn't wait to push the words as far away from her as possible. "Where were you just now? Before you came back to the cabin?"

Alex's shoulders dropped, and she stepped back to lean against the bunk bed frame.

"Just…" Lily's words dropped at the speed of her heart. "Tell me." Alex looked into her eyes and spoke, her words strangely flat. "I was at Charlotte's cabin."

Lily's tears blinded her with their sudden heat, and she swiped at them with her forearm as she picked her bag back up and put it on her shoulder, the world turning under the ball of her foot as she headed for the door.

"Lily, wait."

Alex put her hand on her shoulder to stop her, and Lily shook it off. She turned to tell Alex she'd known it was going to happen anyway, that she'd known all along, but the words disappeared. She backed out of the cabin, willing Alex to meet her eyes, until she realized there was a reason she couldn't look at her. Lily watched Alex crumple to the floor before she made herself turn and walk away.

"Hey, there!" Sara gave Lily a quick hug at the door, almost tipping over a nearly empty bowl of ice cream in one hand. "I didn't know you were coming over."

It didn't take long for Sara to notice Lily's tearstained face and motion her in, guiding her to the living room with her arm around her shoulders. A phone rang in the background, and Sam glanced their way with a worried look as she went to grab it off the kitchen counter.

"Lily, what's wrong?" Sara led Lily over to the leather couch and handed her a glass of water. "What happened?"

"I just can't…" Lily just shook her head and wiped her face with the sleeve of her faded jean jacket. "Talk about it." She paused, glancing back at Sam, who was still on the phone. "Not yet anyway…" She stopped abruptly and took a deep breath to steady herself. "I just came to ask if maybe I could stay the night in your old cabin next door?"

Sara nodded, taking the box of tissues from the table and handing it to her. "Of course you can. It might be a bit dusty, but the sheets are clean, and there might even be a bag of Hershey's Kisses in the fridge if Sam hasn't found them." She paused as Lily took a handful of tissues and twisted them in her lap. "But what's going on? Are you sure you don't want to talk about it?"

Lily shook her head slowly and met Sara's eyes for the first time. "I'll just come over tomorrow, and we'll talk, okay?"

Sam walked toward the couch from the kitchen, clicking her cell phone off and dropping it in her pocket. Lily looked up, her eyes red and swollen. "What did she say?"

"What did who say?" Sara shook her head, looking back at Sam as well. "What am I missing?"

"I told Alex we'd take care of you." Sam put a warm hand on Lily's shoulder and squeezed it gently. "She just wanted to know if you were here and safe, but she didn't tell me anything else, and I didn't ask."

Lily nodded and buried her face in her hands, her narrow shoulders shaking with the quiet sobs. When she gathered herself and looked up again, Sam had returned with a shot of whiskey in a rocks glass with no rocks, then whispered to Sara that she was going to go catch the last of the pickup game in town with Moxie and drive her home. She leaned down to give Sara a quick kiss and let herself out, scooping her keys off the hall table as she went.

Sara offered Lily the whiskey, but she waved it off as she reached for more tissues.

"So," Sara said, downing a long sip of the whiskey as she looked out the windows to the expanse of night sky. "Tell me what happened. It might all be a mistake."

"Well, I saw Alex and Charlotte hugging today on the docks." Lily rubbed her eyes with her fingertips and looked up, taking the glass out of Sara's hand. "But I brushed it off and went into town to eat dinner at the diner. But when I came home to the cabin after, I guess I surprised her."

"And?" Sara sat cross-legged on the leather couch, clutching the fuzzy throw from the back. "Please don't tell me Charlotte was in your cabin with Alex?"

"Nope." Lily took a long swig of the whiskey. "Worse."

"What could be worse than that?"

Lily sank back into the cushions and stared up at the antler chandelier dangling from the ceiling. "She was packing."

"Packing what?"

Lily let those two words sink in for a few seconds and nodded when Sara's hand flew to her mouth, and she sucked in a shocked breath. "You've got to be *kidding* me," Sara said as she grabbed the glass from Lily. "What did she say?"

"That's just it. She didn't really say anything." Lily sniffed as she plucked a fresh tissue out of the box, dropping a twisted handful of damp rejects on the growing pile at the end of the coffee table. "Except that she would never cheat on me, but let's just say that it was clear that whatever she was wearing, it wasn't for me. All she said is that she 'couldn't explain yet.'"

Sara finished the whiskey and put the glass back on the table, her eyebrows narrowing as she listened to the scenario. "And?"

"That I needed to 'trust' her."

"I swear to God," Sara said, glancing down the hall to her bedroom. "If I came home and Sam was strapped on for someone else, it would be her staying in my old cabin until she came up with a believable excuse."

"So…" Lily finally broke into a smile. "Permanently?"

"Exactly." Sara shook her head. "I actually like Alex, so I want to give her the benefit of the doubt." She paused, shaking her head as she pulled the sleeves of her bright blue fleece down over her hands. "But I know from experience that Charlotte is an elite-level flirt and laser focused on what she wants." She paused, drawing in a long breath. "No matter who else gets hurt."

Lily nodded. "I asked her where she'd been." Lily's voice cracked, and she covered her eyes to block out the movie reel playing in her mind. "And she said she'd just come back from Charlotte's cabin."

"So that's why you're sure it wasn't…" Sara paused. "For you?"

"Yeah." Lily shook her head, her fingers tense and white around the tissues. "I was the last thing on her mind if she forgot to take it off."

"Lily." Sara's eyes welled up with tears. "I'm so sorry. I wish there was something else this could be."

"At least I know now, I guess." Lily dried her eyes and picked up her pile of tissues, dropping them in the trash under the kitchen sink. "How do you feel about walking me over to your cabin?" She paused, looking at her bag by the door. "Shit. I just have my purse with me. Should I go back for my toothbrush and stuff?"

Sara got up and picked up Lily's bag, holding her hand out. "Don't worry about anything. There are new toothbrushes in the bathroom drawer, and I even still have a stack of clean pajamas upstairs in the loft chest of drawers."

"Thanks, Sara." Lily gave her friend a long hug before they walked out into the cool night air. "I'm always alone in LA, but somehow here, I knew I could just come over and we'd figure it out."

"Always." Sara opened the door and put her arm around Lily as she stepped outside. "LA is overrated. If you're going to get your heart broken, it might as well be in McCall, where your best friend knows to drop a flask in your bag for the night."

Sam's security lights glinted off the stainless steel flask that had appeared in Lily's bag. She pulled her in for a hug, and they started the short, dark walk to the lakeside cabin.

Alex watched the sunrise the next morning from the chairs outside the cabin, the sheer wash of gold light moving slowly across her body as she stared out over the water, still listening for the sound of Lily's footsteps on the path. She hadn't been to sleep since Lily left, and it was everything she could do to not run to Sam and Sara's house and tell Lily everything. But what could she really say to her? She'd given Sam her word she wouldn't tell anyone until it was over, and the case was so involved at this point that it would take telling Lily every detail to have even a shot at her actually understanding. There just wasn't time.

Alex stared at the diving watch on her arm; she had exactly an hour to get her act together. She'd been sitting outside in jeans and a sports bra since dawn, her eyes on fire from tears and lack of sleep. She had to find a way to shake it off before she fucked up the entire operation. There was a lot more at stake today than her relationship, and everything was riding on her ability to get herself together and act like the only thing on her mind was access to underage girls.

Shake it off. Time to draw a line under this and get into the mindset of a sex trafficker. A fish flipped out of the water just past the shore and swam away, the ripples expanding until they met the sand just beyond Alex's feet. *All I have to do is forget that the future I never knew I wanted just disappeared into thin air.*

An hour later, Alex walked into the McCall police station three minutes before she was supposed to be there. The receptionist, a portly woman in pleated corduroy pants and an "I Love Cats" lapel pin, escorted her to a conference room in the back where Sam and a dozen other officers were sitting around a long table. The air was initially tense and silent, at least until Murphy whistled through his teeth and started a slow clap.

"Damn, man." Murphy shook his head as a ripple of laughter started around the table. "You look so fly, I'm starting to think *I* might be gay." The room filled with laughter, and the tension faded as Murphy looked Alex up and down.

Alex smiled and straightened the placket on her G-Star button-up denim shirt. She'd used nipple tape underneath to give the shirt a distinctly masculine line and rolled the sleeves casually to her elbows. Slim linen trousers and Italian leather loafers completed the laid-back Miami vibe.

"What can I say?" Alex took a seat at the table and winked at Sam and Murphy. "I'm Cuban. We know how to dress."

Alex pulled a notepad placed at her seat closer and uncapped a pen, looking to Sam.

"Gentlemen." Sam stood and pushed a tray of the audiovisual equipment down to Alex. "This is Alex Suarez. She's our undercover for today's operation, posing as Alejandro Suarez, a successful Miami nightclub owner. Alejandro is actually her cousin, so we have a rock-solid backstory via social media and online presence, but clearly, she's going in posing as a man, so this has some innate challenges."

Sam paused and picked up her coffee cup, tense lines deepening around her eyes. Alex pictured how Lily must have been crying at her house the previous night and tried again to focus.

"As you know, this is an undercover sting, but we aren't here to bust anyone. Our mission is to gather evidence that will hold up in court. All we're looking for here is audio or video evidence of the sex trafficking of underage girls so we can hand it over to the FBI."

Sam paused and introduced Art Levy, an agent on loan from the Boise FBI headquarters. Levy had wavy silver hair and a polished brass belt buckle that made the Glock semiautomatic weapon on his hip look tiny. He stood and cracked his knuckles, his booming voice reminiscent of an Alabama auctioneer, swift and Southern.

"Good morning. Chief Draper is in charge here, obviously, but I'm here to make sure that the evidence we gather is done in the cleanest way possible. The whole thing is a wash if we can't use what we get or it won't hold water in court." He cleared his throat and glanced at Alex. "I have to admit, this is the first time I've sent in a woman undercover posing as a man, but I guess what's important here is that the job gets done."

He nodded awkwardly and handed Alex a Rolex watch. It was solid white gold, with a deep blue face surrounded by diamonds and yellow gold accents.

"Good Lord." Murphy leaned over to Alex as she slipped it on her wrist and fastened it. "Is that thing real?"

"Yes, sir," Agent Levy relied. "It's borrowed from the evidence locker at headquarters, but if this guy Travis has the money we think he does, he'll know it's the real thing, and it will be a subconscious clue that Alejandro here is legit." He smiled for the first time. "But don't lose it. It's worth more than my house and yours put together."

"Yeah, it feels like it." Alex smiled and extended her wrist to Murphy so he could get a closer look. "Great. No pressure."

The next hour was spent going over the plan of action once she was inside and mechanics of the audiovisual equipment, which turned out to be easier than Alex thought it would be; all she had to do was make sure the sunglasses stayed hooked over the button on her shirt so Travis stayed in the frame. She also recorded a new outgoing voice mail message for the phone in case Travis called it.

"Make sure this phone is powered on and stays on silent." Agent Levy slid the iPhone containing Alejandro's SIM card over to Alex. "Your personal phone will stay with Chief Draper until we're done." Alex pulled her phone from her pocket as he spoke and handed it to Sam. "Remember, the AV setup does not store info internally. It uploads to the cloud via your phone in real time, so the phone is by far the most vital part of actually getting what he says on record."

"Got it." Alex felt her heart pounding and tried to slow her breathing. The enormity of what was riding on today settled over her like a weighted blanket, and she wished again she'd gotten more sleep. "Let's do this."

"We'll have backup teams on boats behind the house, disguised of course, and in unmarked cars out of sight just down the road from the house with SWAT already in place. If you feel like you're in danger, leave if you can, or use the trigger phrase we talked about and we'll move in as a last resort. Your safety and the safety of the girls in there is paramount. If we don't get the evidence, we don't get it. It's not worth dying for." Agent Levy smiled at Alex for the first time. "But I've seen the same pictures Travis has, and you look exactly like your cousin, so barring anything unforeseen, I think we have an outside chance of this going off without a hitch."

Sam wrapped up the meeting, directing the backup teams to take their positions on the lake and join the SWAT officers down the street from the mansion.

"Alex, you're going to be driving a Mercedes that Agent Levy brought up, and I'll ride with you and let you drop me off at the SWAT van before you get to the mansion." Sam handed Alex the keys, and they walked out together to the parking lot, where Levy got into the car headed for the mansion. The sun was bright and unyielding, and Sam shaded her eyes as Alex clicked the locks on the Mercedes. "How are you doing?" Sam said, her arm balanced on the top of the open door.

Alex motioned for her to get in, where the scent of new leather and money unfolded around them. She leaned her head back against the headrest and rubbed her temples. "Honestly?" Alex's voice was rough. "I feel like shit."

"I've never seen Lily so torn up." Sam looked at her watch. "I don't want to upset you going into this, but I care about her, and I've got to know why. Sara said she was sworn to secrecy, so she didn't tell me a damn thing last night after I left them alone to talk."

"Sam." Alex turned toward Sam with tears in her eyes. "Lily thinks I'm cheating on her with Charlotte, but I'm not. I don't have time to explain it right now, so you're going to have to trust me. I would never do that."

"Why does she think that?"

Alex looked up at the ceiling and wrapped the steering wheel in her fist. "Some really shitty timing, and"—she grabbed the packer underneath the fly of her pants—"this."

"Oh shit." Sam went was quiet as Alex's meaning sank in. "She thought you were strapped for Charlotte, right? So you really didn't step out on her."

"No." Alex strummed the steering wheel with her thumb. "And I never would. I'm in love with Lily. I couldn't tell her what was really going on or why the hell I was wearing it, so of course, she jumped to that conclusion given what was in front of her. I would have done the same."

Alex revved the engine and backed out of the lot, heading for the winding road that led around to the north shore of the lake. "And I can't tell her the truth until this gets done, so let's get this wrapped the fuck up."

CHAPTER SIXTEEN

At exactly noon, Alex pushed the intercom button at the gated entrance to the mansion and waited.

"Hello?" The voice coming out of the stainless steel box was scratchy but distinctly feminine. "State your name, please."

"Alejandro Suarez." Alex channeled the laid-back presence of her cousin and tried to focus. "I have an appointment with Travis at noon."

The enormous iron gates opened with a reluctant click, and Alex drove slowly through them to the circle drive in front of the residence. The glittering lake in the background was the only thing that looked like it belonged there; the four-story mansion in front was built in Spanish Colonial style, complete with imported palm trees, a soft yellow wash of color, and white stucco arches. Expansive windows framed white iron balconies, and the front door was Gothic curved teak with hammered metal hinges.

Alex put the car in park and pocketed the keys, slipping Alejandro's license into the card slot on the back of the phone case before she dropped it into her pocket. White shell gravel wound into a path that crunched underfoot as she approached the door, and Alex's heart pounded in the cage of her chest as she reached for the doorbell.

The door swung open before she touched it to reveal a tall woman in a pinstripe suit standing in the doorway who looked Alex up and down slowly without meeting her eyes. She was beautiful in a nondescript way, like someone everyone met but no one remembered. "Are you Alejandro?"

"Yes, ma'am." Alex smiled.

The woman did not smile back. "Travis is waiting for you." She stepped back from the door to allow Alex in, flipped the five deadbolts back into place, and walked toward the marble staircase in the foyer where she turned at the first step. "Do you have any weapons on you?"

"No, ma'am."

She looked at her for a moment before she finally spoke. "Hold your arms out straight."

Alex raised her arms to shoulder height and held them out while the woman ran her hands down her sides and up the insides of her legs to her groin. She grazed the packer, and Alex was happy she hadn't thrown it into the lake like she'd wanted to after what had happened with Lily.

The woman didn't say anything, just turned around and led Alex up two flights of stairs to a marble landing, then down a short hall with sparkling crystal chandeliers and a Turkish carpet runner in shades of garnet and royal blue. She knocked on the last door on the left, then held it open for Alex and closed it behind her as she left.

"Hey, Alejandro, right?" A man older than Alex was expecting stood and came around the front of the desk, hand extended. "I'm Travis. We spoke on the phone."

Alex shook his hand, then followed his invitation to sit in one of the black velvet chairs across from the desk. The office was opulent but tasteless, and a black semiautomatic handgun was clearly visible in a leather tray on the bookcase behind him.

Alex forced herself to look away from the gun and dragged her eyes back to Travis. "It's great to meet you. Thanks for seeing me while I'm in town."

"You're from Miami, right?" Travis's gaze dropped to the Rolex on Alex's wrist, then directly to her shoes. "I took a look at your clubs online. I think you may have the life I've always wanted."

"If you love being surrounded by beautiful people and obscene amounts of money, that's probably true." Alex laughed and forced herself to make eye contact like a man with nothing to hide. "But I come to McCall a few times a year, mostly in the winter to ski and get away from the city. That's why I was referred to you. It's more discreet than using local girls who might know people."

"Understood." Travis leaned back in his tufted leather office chair. "I used to own a modeling agency in California, but obviously with my current focus, I needed a home base that was a bit more discreet as well." He offered Alex a drink from the bar before pouring himself a double vodka on the rocks and returning to his desk. "Let's get the basics out of the way before we start talking about what you're looking for. I assume Miranda patted you down when you arrived?"

"She did. Although I've had more enjoyable pat downs, I've got to say."

Travis smiled. "Miranda is all business." He gestured toward a framed photo in the bookcase of a much younger Miranda, arms around Travis, in front of the Eiffel Tower in Paris. Her hair was blowing around her face, and her cheeks were flushed the same shade as the rose-colored sunset behind them. "Or at least, she is now. She started as a model in the late nineties, then became a talent scout with my agency when she aged out." He leaned toward the phone on his desk and pushed a button. "Miranda, would you come up here please?"

It was only a few seconds before she knocked lightly on the door and slipped into the office again. Travis nodded in Alex's direction. "If you could do a wire check for Mr. Suarez, I'd appreciate it."

The silence in the room was heavy, and Alex was very aware of her breath as she stood, stepped away from her chair, and faced Miranda. This time, Miranda made eye contact as she swiftly unsnapped the front of Alex's denim shirt, exposing Alex's abs and the center portion of her chest. Alex transferred the sunglasses to the front pocket and looked at the ceiling. There was fuck-all she could do about it now. If Miranda hadn't figured out Alex was a woman yet, the nipple tape barely hidden by the front panels of her shirt would be a dead giveaway.

"She's just checking you for any type of listening or recording devices," Travis said, downing the vodka without a flinch. The ice settled with a hollow clink in the bottom of his glass as he pushed it to the edge of his desk. "I'm sure you understand the need for discretion in these situations. Unfortunately, not everyone has the same tastes that we do."

Miranda checked both of Alex's ears for listening devices, then slid her hands around from her abs to the small of Alex's back, checking just under her belt with her fingers, then sliding them around to the front. She looked again at Alex's chest, then met her eyes once again. When she stepped back, Alex looked down to button her shirt back up, and her heart stopped. The tape over Alex's right nipple had been clearly visible, although her shirt must have hidden it from Travis's view.

Travis, ice tongs in his hand, peered at Miranda as if silently reminding her of something she already knew.

Miranda held out her hand. "I'll need your phone."

Alex's heart sank to her stomach as she pulled it out of her back pocket. She felt the room close up in the span of one second, and a fine mist of sweat broke out across her face.

Travis got up and headed for the row of liquor decanters behind him in the bookcase bar. "She'll give it back, don't worry. She just needs to make sure it's off while you're here."

Miranda turned the phone over in her hand and found the button to power off the device, holding it up for Travis to see as it powered down. He pulled his own phone out and clicked a button on the screen. He held it to his face for a few seconds before clicking the speaker. The outgoing message that Alex had recorded in Spanish and English filled the room for a few seconds before Travis ended the call.

"Just checking that it's off, and it is." He laid his own phone on the desk. "You can give it back to him."

Miranda started to give the phone back, but it slipped out of her hand and tumbled to the ground. She picked it up and handed it back before she looked back at Travis. "She's clear." She paused, a flash of something moving across her eyes that Alex didn't recognize. "I mean, *he's* clear."

The room fell silent, and Alex stopped breathing for the split second it took Travis to laugh. His smile didn't reach eyes, and his gaze dropped to Alex's crotch as she finished buttoning her shirt and tucked it in. "Sorry about that," Travis said with a nod toward the door, clearly meant for Miranda. "She seldom cracks a joke, but I guess today's the day."

Miranda slipped out the door, and Travis turned back to pouring the vodka. Alex sank back into the velvet chair, her voice calm, deep, and even. "Strange sense of humor," Alex said, forcing herself to meet Travis's eyes. "But I've been called worse."

"I apologize." Travis sat back in his chair and pushed a double vodka Alex didn't ask for across the table. "She's actually just returned to the company after spending the last five years in LA trying to make it as an actress. I was happy to give her a job again, but my requirements for an assistant have now expanded past model scouting, and she's just...settling in."

"No worries," Alex said, her mind racing. She intentionally slowed her breath and kept eye contact. "It takes more than that to offend me."

Travis clinked his glass to Alex's, then leaned back. "Now that we've gotten security out of the way, let's get a little bit more specific about what you're looking for."

Alex took a slow sip of her drink. Travis believed she was Alejandro, that was clear, but she'd also just watched her phone power off, so anything Travis said from this point on wouldn't be recorded. Alex cleared her throat and looked down as if she was thinking about the question, but she was really fighting off a sudden, maddening urge to cry. Her only chance to help these girls was gone. In a single split second.

"Well, I'm looking for something a little different than what I've gone for in the past," Alex said, steeling herself and pushing emotion aside. The only choice she had was to play it out. "I've gotten to a point in my career where I've accumulated a fair amount of success. I have plenty of choices when it comes to women, but let's just say my tastes have...shifted in the last few years."

Travis nodded, ice clinking in his glass. "Go on."

"I'm looking for someone younger to put on my payroll. I'm tired of having to be in a relationship in order to get my needs met, and several of my friends feel the same way."

"I can understand that," Travis said. "It's not worth the hassle, so to speak. I came to that conclusion myself a few years back."

"Exactly." Alex paused, running her hand through her hair. "I hired a personal massage therapist last year, but she was in her early twenties and didn't quite grasp what the job entailed. I'd like to go with someone younger so that's not an issue."

"You know my girls are not actual massage therapists, right?"

"I don't give a shit whether they can even spell massage." Alex's words started to show an edge like torn metal. "I want someone I can train to do the job properly. And the job has nothing to do with massage therapy."

"I like a man who knows what he wants." Travis smiled as he swilled the remaining vodka. "And you've come to the right place."

"I hope so." Alex let the anger simmering just under the surface seep into her voice. "I'm sick of dealing with girls who don't understand the assignment."

Travis pulled a pad of paper out of his desk. "Tell me a little about what you're looking for in terms of appearance and age."

Alex's mind spun. She was bluffing; she had no idea what to say. "I'm looking for a girl between thirteen and fifteen, and I'm assuming that all your girls are attractive, so her looks matter less than her motivation to please her new boss."

"That narrows it down a bit. I think I have a couple of girls you might like." He pressed the intercom button again. "Miranda, will you please send Kylie and Katie to my office?" He leaned in and lowered his voice. "If you like what you see, we'll talk money and delivery to Miami within the week. I can have Miranda escort her directly to your residence."

Alex cleared her throat. "I'm sure you know that discretion is of the utmost importance here. But if this goes well, I have a very wealthy circle of friends in Miami who will be interested in the same services." She paused. "May I ask how you source your inventory?"

"Trust me on this," Travis said, tapping his pen on the pad of paper, each word slow and deliberate. "No one will miss these girls."

There was a soft knock at the door, and Miranda stuck her head in and waited for a nod from Travis before she opened it wider and ushered in two girls wearing bikinis. Alex felt physically sick as Travis introduced them.

"Katie and Kylie, this is Alejandro. He's a very important client."

Both looked to be about fourteen, and neither knew where to look except the floor. Alex's heart broke when Katie, a slight, quiet girl with freckles, started to unhook her bikini top. Kylie, a taller blond, looked instantly frightened and crossed her arms over her chest.

"That won't be necessary." The words came out in a rush, and Alex consciously slowed her speech. "I've seen what I need to see. I prefer that the rest is left for a more private setting." Alex forced herself to look Travis in the eye. "I don't like to stop the ball once it gets rolling, if you know what I mean."

Travis's face reflected understanding and a hint of admiration as he held Alex's gaze. He nodded slowly, then said, "I do indeed."

Both girls looked to Travis, who ignored them, then to Miranda as she motioned for them to follow her out.

A deep wave of nausea roiled in Alex's gut, threatening to explode, but she stalled by fiddling with the Rolex while she regained control. It was only a few seconds before she looked up at Travis. "I like the smaller one. Katie. How old is she?"

"They are both fourteen, but Katie is an excellent choice. More compliant. Kylie has just joined us, so this is her first foray into our world. She may need some initial training."

"Perfect." Alex shifted in her chair and crossed her legs. "Not to put a rush on things, but I leave tomorrow to go back to Miami, and I'd like to get the details tied up before I go. I'll need to know the finder's fee, which I assume you do by wire transfer?"

"Wire is always more discreet, and the fee will be in the forty-thousand-dollar range." A tinge of excitement pinged in Travis's voice. "I'll text you the exact price, including delivery, within just a few hours, along with the bank information you'll need to do the transfer. Once it's complete, I'll be in touch with details of her arrival."

"This was far easier than I imagined." Alex stood and offered Travis her hand. "I appreciate your professionalism."

Travis smiled, his excitement flooding the air in the room. "And I can count on your recommendation to your inner circle in Miami?"

Alex nodded. "Absolutely. Good help is hard to find, and I just found the guy with the golden ticket."

Travis laughed, then walked Alex to the door and said good-bye, handing her over to Miranda, who was already waiting in the hall. His office door closed, and the air was suddenly different, heavy, their footsteps loud and foreboding as they walked down the hallway and winding staircase to the front door.

"Thank you for your kindness, Miranda," Alex said softly as she opened the door. Miranda stopped, the door in her hand. Their eyes met for what seemed like an instant and forever until Miranda looked down, stepping back to let Alex exit. She heard it shut behind her and looked over her shoulder to where Miranda stood looking through the window. And then she was gone.

As Alex pulled out of the driveway, she forced herself to drive slowly, fighting back the frustration that flooded in with the memory of

Miranda switching off her phone. They'd been so close. Alex's hands tightened around the steering wheel until her knuckles were strained and white. Somehow, it was even worse to know what was going on in that mansion and not be able to do a goddamn thing about it.

Alex knew she should have driven directly to the station to debrief and return the equipment, but she kept driving. There was no way she was ready to talk about what had happened in there. She followed the winding road that circled the entire lake, then spent a few minutes just looking out over the water before she felt steady enough to return to the station.

When she finally turned onto the road that led into downtown McCall, Alex locked the Mercedes, pocketing the keys as she walked through the front door. The same receptionist looked up from her coffee cup, thumb poised over the button that would open the door to the hall.

"I'm looking for Captain Draper?"

"They're expecting you," she said, peering over her pink-framed reading glasses. "Go on through, and I'll let them know you're here."

She buzzed Alex through with a nod to the same conference room at the end of the hall. Alex's steps slowed, and she glanced to the right just in time to see the sign for the women's restroom as another wave of nausea overwhelmed her. She ran through the door and just made it to the trash can, where her empty stomach refused to cooperate as her body went through the silent motions of vomiting.

When it was over, she stayed where she was, her hands balanced on the edge of the trash can. She heard the door open, and if she could have moved, she would have, but that just wasn't an option.

"Hey, buddy."

Alex lifted her head when she heard Sam's voice, wiping the tears from her cheeks with the heel of her hand and accepting the damp paper towel Sam held out.

"I'm sorry, I—"

"Don't you dare apologize," Sam said, pulling Alex into a strong hug. "That shit is emotional, and I've felt like this myself more than once. You did an outstanding job in there."

Alex stood straighter and wiped her face with the damp cloth. It took a minute to steady herself, but when she was ready, she followed Sam down the hall to the conference room where everyone was sitting around the table. Sam sat down and pushed Alex's real phone across the table to her.

"Look," Alex said, pulling out a chair and accepting a bottle of water that Murphy handed to her. "I'm sorry, guys. If I could have stopped her turning off the phone, I would have, but he even called it with his mobile when I was standing there to make sure it was off." She took a deep swig of water and leaned back in her chair. "But you were right. Moxie was right. We can't fucking prove it, but it's sex trafficking, exactly what we thought it was."

No one answered. In fact, no one said anything until Murphy raised his hand. "Call me Captain Obvious, but is anyone else confused?" Murphey stopped, looking around the room. "What the hell are you talking about, Suarez?"

Agent Levy turned his computer around and pressed a button. The video on the screen jerked to a start around the time Travis called Miranda up to the office to do a wire check. Alex watched the process carefully, leaning forward slightly when she thought Miranda had caught sight of the tape she was wearing on her chest. Miranda's eyes only flicked down for a fraction of a second, and her expression was stoic, but watching it back, something in her eyes told Alex she'd seen it.

The tape jerked to a stop and went to black the second Miranda hit the power button. Alex leaned back in her chair. "He didn't say anything we can use, did he?"

Agent Levy shook his head. "We didn't get jack squat from that. We were all pretty bummed until Murphy here decided to check the cloud a few minutes afterward, and we realized you had turned it back on." He clicked another key on the computer and another recording started playing, picking up right as Travis was turning around with the two vodkas on ice.

Everyone looked at Alex, who let her head sink into her hands for a second before she looked up and pounded her fist on the table three times, one for each word. "Hell. Fucking. Yes."

Murphy laughed and fist-bumped Alex across the table. "You must have been pretty nervous if you forgot you turned it back on."

"I didn't turn it on." Alex took a deep breath. "That's why I was so bummed. I thought everything that came after was lost."

"I don't get it." Sam paused, staring at the screen. "How did it power back up?"

Alex took the phone out of her pocket and pushed it to the center of the table with the car keys. "I couldn't have turned it back on if I wanted to. Travis was staring right at me."

Sudden understanding flashed across Sam's face. "Miranda."

"Exactly. She dropped it on the floor as she was handing it back. She must have done that on purpose because she wanted to hit the power button." Alex paused, remembering the way Miranda had looked at her when she left, like she'd wanted to say something but couldn't. "And I know she saw the tape on my chest when she was checking me for wires, so she definitely knew I was a woman. She probably put it together from there."

Agent Levy hit pause on the recording. "What tape?"

"I put tape over my nipples so I'd pass for a man easier."

"Sweet baby Jesus." Levy winked in Alex's direction and leaned back in his chair. "Well, I don't care if you wrapped yourself in chicken wire, you got the job done like a pro. I have FBI agents that aren't that cool under pressure."

"Do you think we got enough to hold up in court?"

Levy nodded. "We have a team pushing the arrest warrants through as we speak, and we're moving on assembling a care team with psychologists and social workers to make the transition as easy as possible for the girls. We'll move in as soon as—"

The phone with Alejandro's SIM card pinged from the center of the table, and Levy picked it up, a slow smile spreading across his face. "Travis just texted you the final price and his bank details. We've got the bastard."

After they'd wrapped up the details, Sam checked her phone and offered to walk Alex out to her car.

"You look exhausted, man." Sam handed Alex another bottle of water and held the conference door open for her. "I bet you had a sleepless night between this and the Lily situation."

"You have no idea." Alex rubbed her temples as they walked. "I'm going to try to find her and explain, but she could be halfway back to

LA by now." She paused, steadying her voice. "I finally found the love of my life, and I fucked it up in five minutes."

Sam led her down the main hall to the front desk, checking her phone as she opened the front door. "I'll let you take it from here, buddy. I think there's someone out there that wants to talk to you."

Alex stopped in the doorway and looked at Sam. "You're kidding, right?" She paused, rubbing her temples, her eyes strained and red. "Well, it had better be quick. I seriously can't take much more today."

Sam stepped back in and motioned toward the parking lot as she headed back to her office.

Alex rounded the corner of the station and stopped dead in her tracks when she saw a pissed-off Lily sitting on the hood of her car.

CHAPTER SEVENTEEN

Lily hopped off Alex's car and walked toward her, slowing as they met in the middle of the parking lot. The heat shimmered just above the concrete, and faint country music drifted in from a ski boat pulling into the community docks. It was all Alex could do not to reach for her, but Lily's arms were crossed tightly across her chest, her face pale and drawn.

"I'm so glad you're here." Alex looked across the lot to Lily's Jeep. Her bags were packed and sitting in the back seat. "I was afraid I was going to be too late to catch you before you hopped the next flight to LA."

Lily's voice was tight, as if being pulled from opposite directions. "*How* could you not tell me about the undercover thing last night?" Her voice finally cracked, and she looked out to the lake to regain her composure, her eyes following a crane as it dipped closer to the surface of the water, then disappeared in the grove of trees along the shoreline. Lily finally turned and looked back to Alex. "You let me go last night thinking that you'd just slept with Charlotte."

"Lily. I couldn't tell anyone." Alex folded her hands behind her head and looked to the sky. "I promised Sam I wouldn't. Everything was riding on it. We could've lost our chance to stop him and rescue those girls." Alex stopped suddenly and looked at Lily, shading her eyes with her hand as the sun reemerged from behind a cloud. "Wait, how do you even know about this? I literally just left the debriefing and was on my way to find you."

"Well, I got my first clue when I went back to Lake Haven and confronted Charlotte." Lily paused, drawing an imaginary line between two rocks on the pavement with the toe of her white sneaker. "I found her on the docks wrapping up the planning for the last night of camp." She paused. "And...I might have accidentally pushed her in the lake when she denied it."

"Oh, sweet Jesus." Alex tried not to laugh. "What happened after that?"

"She was actually great about it, considering." Lily met her eyes for the first time and smiled. "She said she probably had it coming."

"Well, she's not wrong there." Alex led Lily over to her car, and this time, they both took a seat on the shiny turquoise hood, still warm from the sunshine. "So what did she tell you?"

"The truth, I think. She told me you were talking to her about going back to school when you two were on the dock, and she even showed me the book you lent her last night." Lily hesitated. "And I recognized it right away from our bookshelf."

"That's the only reason I was at her cabin. She was on the phone when I got there, and I literally set the book inside the door and left." Alex bumped her shoulder gently into Lily's and drew in the sweet jasmine scent of her hair. "But that still doesn't explain how you know about the undercover thing."

"Well, after my conversation with Charlotte I drove straight back to Sara's. I was so confused. I felt like Charlotte was telling me the truth, but it still didn't explain why you were wearing...what you were wearing."

"And by that time me and Sam were already at the location so Sara could tell you?"

"Exactly. Although it took us a while to figure out that you were packing and not actually strapped on. Sara mentioned you were impersonating your cousin Alejandro, and it finally dawned on us why you'd be wearing it." Lily turned to face Alex. "But I still don't get how you could let me go all night thinking you'd cheated on me." Lily bit her lip. "How could you do that?"

"Lily." Alex took Lily's tense, cold hands in hers and tried to wrap words around the moment that had been replaying in her mind since it happened. "I'm a therapist. I keep secrets for a living. It's just completely ingrained in me. If I'd had time to think about it, I probably would have told you, but everything was over so fast, and by the time I got myself together, you were already with Sam and Sara."

"So then, you couldn't have told me even if you wanted to." Lily's hands began to warm in Alex's, and her voice softened as she looked into her eyes "You must have been so upset too."

"I was." Alex turned and took Lily's face in her hands. Tears burned behind her eyes, and she stroked Lily's cheek softly with her thumb. "I stayed up all night worrying that the woman I loved was somewhere thinking I'd cheated on her."

Lily smiled and leaned into Alex's shoulder. "The woman you love?"

"Lily, I've been in love with you since the first night I met you." Alex pulled Lily over to sit across her lap, facing her, hands around her hips. "In fact, it's the reason I talked to my cousin a couple of days ago about renting his yacht."

"What?" Lily wrapped her legs around Alex and leaned back against her hands. "Why would you do that?"

"Because I'm going into private practice." Alex held her eyes. "Here. In McCall. But first, I was planning to take a little time off to convince the most beautiful woman in the world to move to McCall and live with me on the water."

"What?" Lily arched an eyebrow. "I thought you said you weren't interested in Charlotte."

Alex laughed and pulled Lily closer, biting her bottom lip lightly before she pressed every inch of Lily's body into hers. She kissed her like love, like fire, like she couldn't draw a breath without her, and Lily melted under her touch, whispering that she was in love with her too. Alex reluctantly let her go when they heard someone behind them. They both turned to see Sam leaning out the door, smiling.

"We have rules about loitering around the parking lot of the police station, you know."

Lily turned around and winked at Sam. "Then I guess you'd better get your ass back to your office, Draper."

❖

Sam loosened her tie and dropped her keys on the entry table as she walked into the house, sweeping Sara into a long hug as she came out of the kitchen.

"Tell me about dinner, gorgeous." Sam kissed her neck, breathing in her scent before she let her go. "I'm starving."

Sara looked pale, and when Sam glanced into the kitchen, there wasn't a trace of dinner. Sam knew her well enough to know that if Sara wasn't cooking by this point in the afternoon, there was something seriously wrong.

"I'm so worried about Moxie." Sara shook her head, looking up the stairs to Moxie's room and dropping her voice to a whisper. "She's been up there all afternoon, and she won't tell me what's wrong."

"Is she upset about something?"

"She has to be. She hasn't eaten since this morning, and she won't open the door." Sara's voice cracked, and she leaned into Sam. "What if it's something really serious?"

Sam took off her tie and draped it over the chair, then gave her a long, tight hug, whispering in her ear as she pulled away. "Let me take a shot at it, baby." She smiled and kissed Sara's forehead. "Maybe it's something we can solve together."

She pulled two Cokes in glass bottles out of the fridge and climbed the stairs. When she got to the top, she looked down the hall past Moxie's door and saw two black trash bags sitting in the hall. She sat next to the door and leaned against the frame, twisting the tops off the bottles.

"Hey, Moxie." Sam tapped lightly on the door and smiled when she caught sight of the lace of Moxie's Converse in the space under the door. She must have been sitting just on the other side. "You don't have to talk if you don't want to, but do me a favor and open your door just enough to take this Coke."

Sam listened as Moxie reached up and turned the doorknob, putting one small hand through the crack and wiggling her fingers. Sam put the bottle in her hand, and Moxie shut the door again. Sam leaned against the door frame and waited. Sometimes being on the other side of the door is all you can give, and Sam knew exactly how that felt.

"I know it's stupid." Moxie's voice was thin and sad.

Sam sat up straight and put her hand on the door as if to touch her. "What do you mean?" Sam watched Moxie's fingers under the door, tugging on a thread from the sisal carpet in her room.

"Having my bags out there." She sighed, and Sam heard her head come to rest on the other side of the door. "It's not like I have anywhere to go."

"Well, I don't want you to go anywhere, so I'm pretending they're not there." Sam paused, her mind heavy with the awareness that every word was important. "What happened to make you want to leave?"

Moxie didn't answer. Sam watched the space under the door, and it was all she could do not to open it when she saw a tear drop on the other side. "I just don't want to hold you guys back."

Sam looked down the stairs and saw Sara climbing them quietly in her bare feet. When she got to the top, she handed Sam a paper bag stuffed with Moxie's favorite cookie, mocha chip with extra chips.

Sara tiptoed back downstairs, and Sam took a cookie out of the bag. "What would make you think that?"

"I don't know." Moxie's fingers pressed hard into the carpet, her fingertips white and tense. "I heard something the other day when Sara's sister was here with her baby. It's just been living in my head, and it started really bothering me today."

"I get that." Sam bit into a cookie and thought back. "I walked in on them talking about my hair one day, and I almost shaved it off. Those two don't hold back."

Sam smiled at the little laugh that came from the other side of the door. "No, it's nothing like that. They weren't even talking about me."

Sam took the rest of the cookies out of the bag, tore the bag in half to create a makeshift plate, then used it to slide a fresh cookie under the door. "I'm not sure I want to know, but I'll ask anyway. What were they talking about?"

"It wasn't anything terrible. I'd rather know the truth anyway." Moxie's words were muffled from the cookie now in her mouth. "Sara was just saying that having me here had made you guys realize that you wanted a family."

Sam saw Sara standing at the bottom of the stairs and waved her up as she responded. "And that we were thinking about adoption?"

"Yeah." Moxie's voice dropped until it had almost faded away. "It makes sense. She's, like, an amazing mom. And everyone wants a baby."

Sara covered her mouth with her hand and went even paler than she had been before when she saw the garbage bags in the hall. She reached for the doorknob, and Sam laid a hand on her wrist to gently hold her back.

"Anyway, I just don't want to be in the way, you know?" Moxie sniffled quietly. "She said you had already started on the paperwork and everything."

Sam pointed down the hall, and Sara got up and tiptoed down to it, letting herself in quietly and returning in under a minute. "Moxie, do you remember our first conversation in Moxie Java?"

"When I was holding a gun on you?" Moxie sniffled again and slid the torn paper back under the door with just a chocolate chip on it. "Yeah. I think I'll remember every bit of that till I'm ninety."

"Well, I told you that day I don't lie. And if you want me to tell you the truth now, I will."

Moxie was silent for a long moment, then said in a voice that sounded much younger than it ever had, "Yeah. I'd rather just know."

"Well, we're definitely looking at adoption." Sam took the papers that Sara brought from her office, placed a fresh cookie on them, and slid them slowly underneath the door.

She watched as Moxie's fingers plucked up the cookie and smiled as a flurry of crumbs dropped onto the papers. She and Sara watched the strip of daylight underneath the door as Moxie picked up the papers and stood, the scuffed white edge of her Converse pressed against the door.

"Oh my God." Moxie's words were a whisper, as quiet as the door as it opened. She stood in front of them, her adoption papers in her hand. "It's me. You want to adopt *me*."

Sara wiped a tear from her cheek with her fingertips and leaned into Sam's shoulder. "I was talking about you that day, Moxie. Just you."

Sam smiled and winked at Moxie. "I've known for a while, and when I brought it up to Sara, she asked me what took me so damn long."

"So." Moxie pushed her glasses up on her nose. "You really aren't waiting for a baby?"

"Nope." Sara shook her head. "We want you. To be our daughter, share our last name, and let us drive you crazy worrying when you start to date in high school."

Moxie flashed them a smile. "Does it help that I'll be dating girls?"

"Oh, thank God." Sam leaned dramatically on the door frame and high-fived Sara. "I mean, straight would have been fine, I guess, but I was hoping for a gay daughter."

Sara pulled Moxie into a hug and Sam wrapped her arms around both of them. "So," Sam said, holding Moxie and Sara tight. "Is that a yes?"

EPILOGUE

One month later

Sara pushed open the door to the diner and double-checked for the third time that the Closed sign was visible. Mary was putting the finishing touches on the party decorations, and Jennifer and Murphy were supposed to be tacking up the bunting on the back wall, but only half of it was hung. What they were actually doing was standing under it kissing, a babbling Mary Elizabeth dangling between them in the carrier Murphy had strapped onto his chest.

Sara had just opened her mouth when Mary stole the words right out of it. "Hey, you two!" Mary shot them her best stern look from across the diner. "Canoodle on your own time. We've got less than thirty minutes to go."

Jennifer and Murphy laughed and got back to tacking up the green-and-white bunting along the wall, McCall High's school colors. Sara caught sight of Mara behind the Formica countertop and made a beeline for her. "How's the food? Is the kitchen caught up, because if not…" Sara peered through the windows on the double doors behind the counter. "I mean, if they need help, I can get back there and—"

Mara reached under the counter and handed Sara a frosted pink champagne glass full of fizz. "Your wife has already been here and banned you from the kitchen. And they're under strict orders to chuck you out if you set foot back there."

"Thanks, Mara." Sara took a long swig of the sparkling rosé and a deep breath. "And you're sure everyone got their shirt out of the boxes by the door?"

"I handed them out personally, and everyone on the guest list is here." She took a breath and smiled at Sara, who felt as relaxed as a meerkat eating caffeine cookies. "We just lowered the main table." Mara pointed to the wooden community table that Sara had made for the diner when she'd opened the restaurant. She'd designed it to fit snugly against the ceiling when not in use, but it lowered easily with a pulley system for the locals' potluck on Sunday or special events. "And the kitchen is going to start loading it with party food in about three minutes." She put her arm around her and squeezed her shoulders. "I know how important tonight is, and I just want you to enjoy it. I've got this handled."

Sam walked in from the back patio wearing slim white jeans, her arms looking even more sculpted in a snug black crewneck T-shirt. Sara could see the patio behind her was already packed with Moxie's friends, family, and locals milling around while Mara and the diner staff finished with the final touches.

"Hey, gorgeous." Sam walked up with a clipboard and showed it to Sara. "The list you gave me is done, and everyone has a drink—"

"Strawberry limeade? That's Moxie's favorite."

"Everyone has a strawberry limeade slush, plus one of those useless striped paper straws that Mary brought." Sam winked as she set the clipboard on the counter and circled Sara's waist with her hands. "Also, don't look now, but your kitchen staff is coming out with the party food platters."

Sara whipped around to see platers of mini pulled pork sliders, newspaper-wrapped portions of savory garlic fries, and piles of fresh tamales pass them on the way to the main table, followed by homemade chicken empanadas and stuffed poblano peppers on a stick.

"Oh God, the menu is so random. Do you think everyone will find something they like? I just did a mix of all of Moxie's favorite foods and tried not to get fancy with it." Sara's voice trailed off, and she bit her lip. "But not fancy is not my forte."

"Baby, it's amazing." Sam leaned in and kissed her. "And I texted Moxie to meet us here at five for dinner, so everything is right on schedule."

Sam led her into the main dining area. Mason jars full of sparkling firefly lights glowed in the center of every table, the bunting was bright and colorful, and Jennifer was just finishing placing tall glass jars of daisies and sunflowers around the room. The community table in the center of the room was piled high with food and slushes in ice buckets, complete with a make-your-own ice cream cookie sandwich station at the very end, with toppings to roll them in and a big stack of napkins.

Sara leaned into Sam's shoulder and looked up at her. "You know what those mason jars remind me of?"

Sam smiled, tipping her face up to kiss her. "The jars full of flowers that Mary lent you for that pancake breakfast in the park the summer we met?"

"How did you know?"

Sam looked over to Mary, who was fussing with one of the same jars. "Because I asked Mary weeks ago if she still had them. It just felt right to use them today too."

"You're the most romantic butch I've ever met." Sara stood on her tiptoes and whispered in her ear. "But don't worry. I won't tell anyone."

"Of course you won't." Sam laughed, holding Sara tighter. "Because you've told everyone already."

Mara turned on the background music, and Sara took a deep breath, relaxing just a bit into the tangible hum of joy in the air. Sam checked her watch and quickly signaled the people milling around on the patio into the main dining room, and as the patio door closed behind them, the chatter slowed to a hushed buzz as they watched Moxie walk past the plate glass windows and slowly push the front door open. She hesitated when she saw the Closed sign on the door, then stepped in.

Everyone shouted "Surprise" at the same time, and Moxie's face unfolded into a wary smile until she spotted Sam and Sara in the crowd. "But it's not my birthday."

A tall man with a white mustache emerged from the back of the crowd carrying a leather briefcase, which he plunked down on the only empty table in the front of the diner. Moxie recognized him and smiled, her eyes darting between him and Sam and Sara, who were making their way to the front, holding hands.

Moxie pulled the sleeves of her hoodie down over her hands for the first time in months and smiled. "Hi, Judge Hanson."

"Well, hello there, Miss Moxie." He squeezed her shoulder with genuine affection and motioned her, Sam, and Sara over to the table. Everyone moved closer, jockeying for the best view. "And you're wrong. It actually is your birthday in a roundabout way."

He unclasped his suitcase and pulled out a handful of papers.

"First of all, let's get this out of the way." He handed Moxie one of the pens and a sheet of paper. "When you sign at the bottom of this page, your name change from Maria to Moxie becomes permanent."

"I didn't think you'd remember." Moxie looked at him in shock, the pen still in the air. "You actually did that for me?"

"Moxie, when we ironed out the details a few weeks ago, you told me how much it meant to you to change it. Yours is a special circumstance, so I had to make a few calls to get it done, but of course I remembered." He smiled as she signed the paper and handed it back to him. "I'll give this to the clerk to file, and it'll be official."

Applause rippled around the room, and Moxie took the copy he handed back to her. She studied it carefully, then looked over at Sam and Sara. The judge smiled, and the crowd hushed and jostled in the background.

Moxie showed him the paper. "This says Moxie Draper."

"Because that's your name." He reached into the briefcase and brought out a manila folder. "Your adoption is final today too."

He turned toward the crowd as Sam and Sara went to stand with Moxie. "Ladies and gentlemen, I'd like to introduce you to Moxie Draper." He glanced over at Moxie, who reached for Sara's hand, then Sam's. "From this day forward, the daughter of Sam and Sara Draper."

The crowd erupted in cheers, and Sam and Sara enveloped their daughter in a hug, whispering in her ear before they all turned back around.

"Now." The judge turned back to the room, filled with the tangible warmth of love, friends, and family. "And all of you made it clear that you want Moxie to know that she didn't just gain parents today. So I'll let you take it from here."

Sam and Sara watched with Moxie as Jennifer and Murphy peeled off their hoodies to reveal T-shirts beneath that said *Moxie's Aunt* and *Moxie's Uncle*. Even baby Mary Elizabeth had a onesie with *Moxie's Cousin* lettered across the front. Mary went next, but put her own stamp on it when she handed Moxie a T-shirt with *Mary's Granddaughter* written across it, pulling her in for a long, sweet hug before she let her go.

Sam then pointed across the room to Moxie's friends lined up in the back, who all opened their jackets at the same time to reveal shirts emblazoned with *Moxie's Posse* on them. Moxie laughed, then ran to hug them as Sara rang a bell and officially welcomed everyone to the party.

As everyone started for the food, laughing and taking pictures, Sam and Sara met an emotional Moxie in the center of the crowd.

Tears she didn't even try to hide dampened her flushed cheeks as she smiled at her parents. "So this is real? I'm adopted?"

They nodded and pointed to the wall behind her. Near the end of the row of old photos Sara had rescued and restored when she'd first bought the diner was a picture of the three of them taken the first time they'd brought Moxie to see the diner. Sam and Sara stood in front of the counter, each looking down at Moxie as she smiled into the camera. It hung between their wedding photo and Sam's favorite photo of her and her father behind the counter when she was little.

"We put this one up as a placeholder," Sara said, "But Mary said she'd take an official family photo for us tonight to frame for the wall." Sam whistled over the crowd and signaled Mary. She took her sweet time walking over, of course, a jacket draped over her arm.

Mary winked and handed the jacket to Moxie. "Remember a few days ago when you went to play that pickup game of basketball in the park?"

"Yeah, the one where someone's dad was there keeping score?"

"Kind of." Mary smiled at Sam. "That was Ronald, my brother. He was also Sam's dad's lifelong best friend and McCall High's current basketball coach."

Moxie shook her head, confused.

"He was there because I asked him to check out your basketball skills." Mary paused, her eyebrows narrowing. "And before you think I got you on the team, I didn't tell him a damn thing about who you are."

"Does that mean…"

"It means it took him less than ten minutes to call me and tell me that he wanted you for the McCall Wildcats varsity team this year."

Moxie looked up at Sam, shocked, and it occurred to her then to look at the jacket Mary had handed her.

"Your moms had that altered for you," Mary said. "I just agreed to keep it safe until tonight."

Moxie held up the jacket, now in pristine condition with *Draper* emblazoned across the back in gold felt letters. She stared at it for a long minute, then looked up at Sam. "Is this your varsity jacket?"

Sam took the jacket and turned it around to show her the front. The embroidered patch with *Sam* across the front panel had been replaced with a new one in bright gold thread. *Moxie.*

"It was mine," Sam said, holding it out for her to slip over her shoulders. "Now it belongs to my daughter."

❖

Hours later, when the last of the guests had left the diner and Moxie had gone to the park with her friends, Sam and Sara pushed open the door to the back patio where Lily had just switched on the gas fireplace and the golden strings of bistro lights crisscrossing the wooden deck. Violet dusk was just starting to smudge over the last streaks of the fiery watercolor sunset on the horizon, and the familiar sounds of laughter from the ski boats returning to the community docks drifted in from just down the hill.

Sara set out chilled champagne flutes while Sam uncorked a bottle of Veuve Clicquot, its vibrant yellow label slicked with condensation. The cork arched over their heads with a sharp pop, and delicate foam spilled out over the sides of the bottle as Sam poured.

"I've been saving this bottle for a special occasion." Sam pulled Sara close and looked into her eyes. "And I can't think of anything more special than starting a family with you."

"So," Alex said as Sam handed her a glass. "How does it feel to be parents?"

Sam and Sara looked at each other and laughed. "Exactly the same as it's felt since Moxie first came to live with us," Sara said. "Amazing and nerve-racking all wrapped up in one."

"Well, you're both naturals at it." Lily took the glass Sara handed her and sipped the foam that was threatening to spill over the top. "And something tells me Moxie's not going to be an only child."

Sam smiled at Sara as she handed her a glass and poured one for herself. "Lily, how's the new book coming?"

"The book is amazing, and my agent is finally getting over the shock of me moving to McCall. I think we're past the stage where I'm worried he's actually going to have a heart attack." Lily waved away a bee gunning for her champagne and continued. "And we've finally hammered out an agreement on how often I come back to LA, which amounts to just a couple of weeks a year, basically just a press tour when I have a new book come out."

Alex leaned back in her chair and raked a hand through her hair as the last of the sun sank into the horizon, making way for the stars. Sam opened her phone and slid it across the table to her and smiled as Alex started reading.

"Are you kidding me with this?" Alex looked at the email again and then back at Sam. "They approved the grant we applied for?"

"Yep," Sam said, tangling her fingers into Sara's. "As soon as we get it we can start renovating and hiring staff for next summer, and then Lake Haven Retreat Center will officially turn into a summer camp for foster kids from across the country."

"Best news ever." Alex clinked her glass to Sam's. "I'm excited to be working together again."

"I think the main reason our grant application was approved is because there'll be a child psychologist on staff. Evidently, they checked you out pretty thoroughly and were impressed, to say the least."

Sara sipped her champagne and looked over at Alex. "And with you being in private practice now, you can adjust your schedule for the summer season. It worked out perfectly."

"So how does that work with the police force, Sam?" Lily zipped up her jacket and settled back in her chair. "Are you going to be doing both? That sounds exhausting."

"Well, for our first summer season, they've agreed to hire an interim chief to come in and take over, and after that, depending on how it goes, I'm actually considering retiring from the force to run the camp full-time." Sam looked at Sara and smiled. "We've talked about it, and we'd both like to make the camp a year-round thing so that more foster kids have the opportunity to come to the mountains."

Lily pointed up to the sky as a pair of bats started to weave an invisible pattern just above the bistro lights, and Alex pulled her closer.

"I'm surprised they aren't landing on your shoulder." Sam leaned back to watch as one of them dipped below the lights. "You've always been McCall's version of Snow White."

"I don't know." Lily smiled, squeezing Alex's hand. "I think when I was still having panic attacks and really struggling after LA, they stuck around to comfort me somehow. But the happier and more relaxed I am, the fewer of them I see."

"Well, I hit the jackpot when you decided to stay in McCall," Sara said, finishing the last of her champagne and reaching for the bottle to top up her glass. "And the girls' nights on the sundeck of the yacht don't exactly suck."

Lily and Sara giggled as Sam rolled her eyes and pretended to be annoyed. "Well, the next time you decide to throw one of those, drop anchor somewhere out in the middle of the lake. The last time you two did it at the docks, we had a noise complaint at the station."

"I'm not worried. We have connections." Sara gave her wife an angelic look. "But since Jennifer isn't here at the moment, let's just blame it on her."

"Actually," Lily said, glancing over at Alex. "Alex and I are thinking about buying a house here in McCall, so maybe we'll have to crank up the volume and really make the next few count."

Sam smiled, watching Sara laugh with Lily and Alex. She leaned back in her chair for a moment and looked up at the black velvet sky, then raised her glass.

"So." Alex pulled Lily closer and looked to Sam as they all raised their glasses. "What are we toasting to?"

"It occurred to me tonight at the party that all of us have found love in McCall in some way. You and Lily, me and Sara, Jennifer and Murphy…" Sam paused to put her arm around her and pull her closer. "Even Moxie found her family here."

"It doesn't surprise me." Lily laughed as one of the bats swooped over their heads, dipping so close it ruffled Alex's hair. "McCall has always been magic."

"Excellent point." Sam smiled. "So here's to love and magic in McCall."

Sam's champagne flute met the others in the center of the table, and the musical clink of the glasses rose like sudden sunlight into the black velvet sky.

About the Author

Patricia Evans is currently writing your new favorite novel in her hand-built tiny house, nestled deep in the forest, where she's surrounded by a bevy of raccoons and a sleepy brown bear named Waddles.

She travels to Ireland and Scotland several times a year in search of the perfect whiskey and cigar combination and spends most of her time trying to ignore the characters from her books that boss her around as she writes by the fire.

Follow her adventures:
www.tomboyinkslinger.com
@tomboyinkslinger on Instagram
patricia@tomboyinkslinger.com

Books Available From Bold Strokes Books

Lucky in Lace by Melissa Brayden. Straitlaced stationery store owner Juliette Jennings's predictable life unravels when a sexy lingerie shop and its alluring owner move in next door. (978-1-63679-434-1)

Made for Her by Carsen Taite. Neal Walsh is a newly made member of the Mancuso crime family, but will her undeniable attraction to Anastasia Petrov, the wife of her boss's sworn enemy, be the ultimate test of her loyalty? (978-1-63679-265-1)

Off the Menu by Alaina Erdell. Reality TV sensation Restaurant Redo and its gorgeous host Erin Rasmussen will arrive to film in chef Taylor Mobley's kitchen. As the cameras roll, will they make the jump from enemies to lovers? (978-1-63679-295-8)

Pack of Her Own by Elena Abbott. When things heat up in a small town, steamy secrets are revealed between Alpha werewolf Wren Carne and her human mate, Natalie Donovan. (978-1-63679-370-2)

Return to McCall by Patricia Evans. Lily isn't looking for romance— not until she meets Alex, the gorgeous Cuban dance instructor at La Haven, a newly opened lesbian retreat. (978-1-63679-386-3)

So It Went Like This by C. Spencer. A candid and deeply personal exploration of fate, chosen family, and the vulnerability intrinsic in life's uncertainties. (978-1-63555-971-2)

Stolen Kiss by Spencer Greene. Anna and Louise share a stolen kiss, only to discover that Louise is dating Anna's brother. Surely, one kiss can't change everything...Can it? (978-1-63679-364-1)

The Fall Line by Kelly Wacker. When Jordan Burroughs arrives in the Deep South to paint a local endangered aquatic flower, she doesn't expect to become friends with a mischievous gin-drinking ghost who complicates her budding romance and leads her to an awful discovery and danger. (978-1-63679-205-7)

To Meet Again by Kadyan. When the stark reality of WW II separates cabaret singer Evelyn and Australian doctor Joan in Singapore, they must overcome all odds to find one another again. (978-1-63679-398-6)

Before She Was Mine by Emma L McGeown. When Dani and Lucy are thrust together to sort out their children's playground squabble, sparks fly, leaving both of them willing to risk it all for each other. (978-1-63679-315-3)

Chasing Cypress by Ana Hartnett Reichardt. Maggie Hyde wants to find a partner to settle down with and help her run the family farm, but instead she ends up chasing Cypress. Olivia Cypress. (978-1-63679-323-8)

Dark Truths by Sandra Barret. When Jade's ex-girlfriend and vampire maker barges back into her life, can Jade satisfy her ex's demands, keep Beth safe, and keep everyone's secrets…secret? (978-1-63679-369-6)

Desires Unleashed by Renee Roman. Kell Murphy and Taylor Simpson didn't go looking for love, but as they explore their desires unleashed, their hearts lead them on an unexpected journey. (978-1-63679-327-6)

Here For You by D. Jackson Leigh. A horse trainer must make a difficult business decision that could save her father's ranch from foreclosure but destroy her chance to win the heart of a feisty barrel racer vying for a spot in the National Rodeo Finals. (978-1-63679-299-6)

Maybe, Probably by Amanda Radley. Set against the backdrop of a viral pandemic, Gina and Eleanor are about to discover that loving another person is complicated when you're desperately searching for yourself. (978-1-63679-284-2)

The One by C.A. Popovich. Jody Acosta doesn't know what makes her more furious, that the wealthy Bergeron family refuses to be held accountable for her father's wrongful death, or that she can't ignore her knee-weakening attraction to Nicole Bergeron. (978-1-63679-318-4)

Tides of Love by Kimberly Cooper Griffin. Falling in love is the last thing on either of their minds, but when Mikayla and Gem meet, sparks of possibility begin to shine, revealing a future neither expected. (978-1-63679-319-1)